THE TAMING OF THE DREW

THE TAMING OF THE DREW

STEPHANIE KATE STROHM

Sky Pony Press
NEW YORK

Sky Pony Press books may be purchased in bulk at special discounts for sales promotion, corporate gifts, fund-raising, or educational purposes. Special editions can also be created to specifications. For details, contact the Special Sales Department, Sky Pony Press, 307 West 36th Street, 11th Floor, New York, NY 10018 or info@skyhorsepublishing.com.

Sky Pony® is a registered trademark of Skyhorse Publishing, Inc.®, a Delaware corporation.

Visit our website at www.skyponypress.com.

10 9 8 7 6 5 4 3 2

Library of Congress Cataloging-in-Publication Data is available on file.

Cover design by Sarah Brody
Cover photo credit Nina Masic/Trevillion Images

Print ISBN: 978-1-5107-0215-8
Ebook ISBN: 978-1-5107-0216-5

Printed in the United States of America

For the Valley Girls: here's to bonfires, bold moves, and a summer we'll never forget.

THE TAMING OF THE DREW

CHAPTER 1

Freedom might have smelled like cow manure, but it had never tasted so sweet. I crumbled another piece of sticky maple goodness off the leaf-shaped candy I'd bought after my last pee break. Man, even the gas station candy was fancy in Vermont. The most gourmet thing we had at the Vince Lombardi Service Area was Kit Kat bars. I licked my fingers clean before putting my semisticky hand back on the wheel.

More air. Louder music. I jammed my left finger against the button on the side of the door, rolling the car window all the way down, cow poop scent be damned. Mmm. The fresh, stinky air whipped my hair, sending red tendrils smacking against my sunglasses.

As "Born to Run" blasted out of my speakers, I yelled out the window along with Bruce's growl, startling a field of particularly pungent bovine clustered near a split-rail fence.

Like any self-respecting person from New Jersey, I loved Springsteen. Actually, I was highly suspicious of anyone who *didn't* love Springsteen, regardless of their home state. I was just glad I hadn't let Dad ruin Bruce for me. Although, to be fair, could anything ruin Bruce? The man was un-ruinable.

Maybe I wasn't *born* to run—as my not particularly successful athletic career could attest to—but I'd never been more *ready* to run. Things hadn't been great at home before the Sext Heard 'Round the World, but after, it was like World War Z had erupted. At this point, I would much rather face an army of zombies than hear the name Heather ever again.

Okay. I knew Heather wasn't the *reason* my parents divorced. It was probably coming anyway. I'd gleaned enough from television to know that most parents didn't constantly scream at each other. It was more like Heather had become the blond, perky embodiment of their divorce. And I'd heard more than enough from my mom on the topic of Heather to last a lifetime.

Sometimes I wished Mom was more of a let's-repress-all-this-stuff-and-never-talk-about-our-issues kind of mom and less of a let's-share-all-the-details-of-my-personal-life-with-my-teenage-daughter kind of mom. There were things I didn't need to know. And things I could never un-hear.

Snap out of it, Cass. I shook my head, trying to clear it. None of that mattered anymore. I was driving north, farther and farther away from Jersey and my parents and everything. And every mile that put a bigger distance between me and the stupid Ruth's Chris Steak House where Heather worked was a mile I relished.

Ruth's Chris Steak House. What did that even mean? What was a Chris Steak House? Was Chris a preparation of steak? It wasn't Ruth Chris's Steak House, so it wasn't her last name, whoever Ruth was. It made no sense.

I turned the volume up even louder, blasting all thoughts of Heather out of my brain. I definitely wasn't in Weehawken anymore, and that was the important thing to remember. Hell, even just a quick glance out the window confirmed I was way out of Weehawken. I knew Jersey had farms, because of all the tomatoes and stuff that showed up in the grocery store with their cheery JERSEY FRESH! labels every summer, but there weren't any near where I lived. Vermont was serious farm country. Gently rolling hills, bales of hay, big red barns, tall silos, and even a couple weathered farmhouses complete with wraparound porches and gingerbread detailing on the eaves. And, of course, cows. So many cows, lazily flicking their tails back and forth as they grazed in the summer sun.

When I'd imagined making my professional theater debut, I never imagined cow country. I certainly wasn't complaining—I was only a couple weeks out of high school and about to grace the stage of Vermont's only professional outdoor summer Shakespeare theater. And yeah, that may have been a lot of qualifiers, but it was still a real theater. My stomach tumbled over into a nervous happy flutter. A real theater. I'd only ever been in plays at school or theater camp before. But out of all the people who'd auditioned for this internship, I was one of the chosen ones. And now I was being paid to act—a meager amount, but still—just like a real job. Just like I'd always wanted. I knew, of course, that out of the millions of people who wanted to be actors, very few actually were. But getting this part made me think that maybe, just maybe, I could be one of those few. Now all I had to do was act my face off.

The road curved, cutting away from the fields and gradually climbing as it arced toward the small mountain range I saw to my right. As I turned the car around the bend, the trees by the side of the road got denser. It was like from farm to forest in a heartbeat. Everything was so green and lush, I felt like I'd rolled right into Narnia.

I passed a wooden sign nailed at the start of a dirt road: LAKE DUNMORE THATAWAY. Crap! Assuming, of course, that Shakespeare at Dunmore was actually at Lake Dunmore—which seemed like a pretty safe assumption—that was my turn. I swerved quickly to the right, just barely making the turn, which of course sent my maple candy flying off the passenger seat. Noooooo! Not my sweet maple goodness!

I bent down to get the candy—five-second rule—when something hit the back of my car. The force of the collision jolted me forward a few inches. I screamed in a not very dignified way, sat upright, and threw the car into park. And in the process, I smushed the maple candy into a pale brown goo. I quickly wiped it on a crumpled Burger King napkin in my cup holder. Awesome. I'd gotten into a car accident over candy, and now I couldn't even eat said candy. I'd gotten into a car accident! Oh my God. I'd been driving this thing for less than a day, and I'd already been in an accident! I was so dead.

Oh, crap, crap, crap. Crap on a stick! I turned the car off and smacked my head against the steering wheel. You know what this was? This was karma. I had accepted Dad's don't-hate-me-I'll-let-you-drive-my-old-car-to-Vermont-and-keep-it-there-all-summer bribe, and now the universe was punishing me. I'd accepted that bribe under false pretenses. I did hate him. I just wanted the vehicle he'd cast off after his midlife crisis insisted he chauffeur *her* around town in a brand new Beemer.

I screamed again. A heavily bearded guy in a plaid shirt was knocking on my window, and he looked *pissed*. Was this how *Deliverance* started? I'd never seen it. Now, I wished I'd had. It probably contained some tips I could have used. At least *one* person always survived. That was how horror movies worked. So, there's always a chance. Unless you have glasses. In which case, you're screwed.

He knocked again and he still looked pissed. I took a deep breath, unbuckled my seat belt, and opened the door.

"So, you want to tell me what the hell happened?" the guy demanded, crossing his arms. From what I could see underneath the heavy beard, he was much younger than I'd originally thought—he might even have been close to my age.

"Why don't you tell *me* what the hell happened?" I jumped out, shut the door behind me, and crossed my arms right back at him. "Unless I'm mistaken, *you* rear-ended *me*."

"Technically accurate, but—"

"Yes," I interrupted, "actually, in every way accurate. If someone hits you from behind, the accident is that driver's fault."

"Not if the front driver stops suddenly for no apparent reason."

"Nah-uh. A basic rule of the road requires that a driver be able to stop safely if a vehicle stops ahead of said driver. If said driver cannot stop, he didn't leave enough space between himself and the vehicle before him. Ergo, your fault." Thank you, Ideal Driving School.

"Did you just *nah-uh* me?" he asked incredulously.

"Yes. Yes I did. And then I dropped some knowledge. And then I *ergo*-ed you. Boom."

"Did you just *drop the mic*?" The incredulity continued.

"Dropped the heck out of that mic." My hand was still frozen in mid-air. "Bringing back an old-school burn. Old-school burn on you."

"Cool hand gesture."

What a smartass.

"I can think of a different hand gesture that would be more appropriate right now," I muttered. Curling my hands into tight fists, I could practically feel my middle fingers itching against my palms. But I wouldn't let those birds fly. After all, I was a lady.

"I'm sure you could." He narrowed his eyes at me, like he was afraid I was one step away from going full-on reality TV villain or something. Which I so was not. I had never ripped out anyone's weave. Ever. "Regardless of technical fault, you were still driving irresponsibly."

"I was driving perfectly responsibly." My nostrils flared— a surefire tell that I was lying. Luckily, this weirdo didn't know that. Or that I'd crashed the car for maple candy.

The car! I pushed past him and ran to check the fender, wedging myself in front of his filthy Jeep Grand Cherokee. I squatted down, running my hand along the back of my car. No bump. No dent. Not so much as a scratch or a flake of silver paint missing. Holy flying gumballs. I had seriously lucked out.

"There's no damage," I heard from behind me. "I checked."

"No damage to the fender, maybe." I quickly stood up and turned, crossing my arms defensively again. Generally speaking, I preferred not to be standing butt-out when confronting people. It's really hard to have the upper hand that way.

"I think you mean the bumper," he corrected me. "The bumper is the part of the car at the rear designed to absorb the impact of any collision."

"Thanks," I said. "That was a really enjoyable lesson on car parts. Quite timely and absolutely necessary to this conversation."

"So, we're done here?" He shoved his hands in his pockets.

"Not done! I haven't decided if I'm suing you yet."

"*Suing* me!" he exclaimed. "For *what*? Look, the car is fine."

"*I'm* not fine! I could sue you for emotional damage! Or whiplash! Owww, my neck . . ."

"Oh, please," he sneered. "Save that performance for the academy."

"You could at least apologize, you asshat."

His eyebrows rose a little at *asshat*. Whoops. Once again, my temper had gotten the best of me. I took in a deep breath and exhaled slowly. Flying off the handle wasn't going to win any arguments.

"Fine. I'm sorry I was driving perfectly normally and a collision occurred that was technically my fault but was actually your fault."

"Great apology, bro," I snorted.

"Are we done *now*? Or have you decided to sue me?"

"Not going to sue you. If for no other reason than that would require exchanging contact information. And I have no desire whatsoever to contact you ever again."

"I can assure you, the feeling is mutual."

"Great. See you never."

"Great."

We were still standing on the side of the road glaring at each other.

"Try not to rear-end anyone else today."

"Try to drive like a normally functioning human."

"Thanks. Drive safely."

"I don't think I'm the one who needs a reminder to drive safely here."

Okay. That was enough glaring, even for me. I stomped back to my car, slid into the seat, and slammed the door.

What a ridiculous douchewaffle. Obviously I wasn't going to sue him, since that meant Mom and Dad would find out I got in a car accident, even one that wasn't technically my fault, and I sure as hell didn't want to lose the car. So why did any words remotely related to legal action pop out of my mouth? Something about that guy just got under my skin. But here was the important thing: I'd had an incredibly lucky break. The car was fine, I was fine, and I'd just seen Señor Pantalones Locos drive off in my side mirror, never to be seen again. It was over. Time to move on. I put the key in the ignition and carefully eased back onto the road.

After rounding another bend, heading deeper into the forest and under the shade of the trees, I was immediately distracted by a squirrel. A GIANT squirrel. The King Kong of anthropomorphic squirrels. It was even taller than the roof of the Bait 'n' Bite General Store it stood next to. The squirrel was dressed in an old-fashioned red-and-white-striped bathing suit and held a sign that read WELCOME TO LAKE DUNMORE: HOME OF SOME-MORE SUMMER FUN!

Wow. Now there was something you didn't see every day.

CHAPTER 2

Pulling past the Bait 'n' Bite, I turned the corner and came face to face with the shores of the lake. It was enormous, and beautiful—a perfect oval of deep blue water, still as glass, ringed on all sides by cabins. I passed a tiny pebbly beach with Adirondack chairs bordering a makeshift marina with kayaks and canoes waiting on shore. I loved the way the cabins disappeared into the woods as they marched up the side of the mountain. It was almost like something out of a fairy tale, like Snow White should be hiding out in one of those cabins with the Seven Dwarfs. I half expected Little Red Riding Hood to go skipping past me at any minute. And there was my turn—luckily, no last-minute swerving mishaps involving maple candy this time. At least these directions were pretty easy to remember. Black Bear Pass had a way of sticking in one's brain. If I'd been looking for a street sign, I would have missed it—the only road demarcations seemed to be painted planks of wood nailed onto posts. There, at the end of the dirt road, stood an old white house on the shore of the lake. From the front it looked like any normal building, but the back half of the bottom level was in the water, like some kind of boat garage. A wooden sign in front proclaimed it to be the BALD MOUNTAIN SCHOOL BOAT HOUSE. I pulled into the driveway and parked.

Grunting, I managed to yank my huge duffle bag out of the trunk. Slinging its strap over my shoulder, I resisted the pull to topple to the ground and crunched my way over the gravel toward the front door. The house's white paint was cracked and peeling in more places than not, but the bright green shade on the shutters gave the whole place a cheery look. It didn't look rundown so much as—well used. I pushed the screen door to the front of the house, careful not to put my palm through a softball-sized hole in the middle. The door creaked noisily open.

"Hello?" I called cautiously, my eyes adjusting to the relative darkness inside. All I could see was wood. Wood floors, wood paneling, wood ceiling. And on top of that, the wood paneling on the walls was almost completely obscured by wooden oars of all shapes and sizes. This whole place was like a beaver's fantasy.

"Welcome, stranger." A pale girl with a heart-shaped face and bright blue bob made her way down a narrow set of wooden steps. That was the most vibrant hair color I'd ever seen in my life. She shone in the relative darkness, an electric beacon. "You must be Cass." She pulled Pokeball-shaped earbuds out of her ears, tucking them into the pocket of her cardigan. I nodded. "Our last arrival. Points for insouciance. Our extremely informational meeting is imminent. I'm Langley," she saluted, raising a dark brow sardonically above the rim of her cat's-eye glasses, "your stage manager and overall SAD servant."

"Sad? You're a sad servant?"

"S-A-D. Shakespeare at Dunmore. You'll need to pick up the acronyms quickly around here. And considering the intern stipend they not so generously bestowed upon me, factored against the insane hours and amount of work this job requires, I'm basically an indentured servant. It's theatrical debt bondage. Only not as fun as it sounds."

I stared at her blankly. It didn't sound particularly fun.

"Ooookay," she sighed, clearly thinking her biting sarcasm was lost on me. "You're checked in. I'll give you the tour."

"Great."

She had the kind of sense of humor where I wasn't quite sure if she was mocking me or not. Or if she was attempting to be humorous.

"So, we're in the storage room now, which is ultimately useless to you unless you have a penchant for sporting life jackets as a fashion statement."

"Not out of the water." I watched an industrious spider spinning a web between two oars.

"Don't wear these ones in the water," Langley shook her head. "The Bald Mountain Prep School uses this place to train their crew team during the school year and as storage in the summer. And, of course, to make rent money off homeless actors — on the condition that we stay the hell away from the boats. Which, incidentally, are through the doors on my left. Not that you need to know. Door at the end of the hall leads to the world's smallest kitchen. Good luck claiming your fridge space. Follow me."

Behind her, I struggled up the creaky wooden stairs with my bag, barely squeezing through the narrow passage. Upstairs, it was far more spacious.

"This is the Actor Lounge," she announced as we hit the top of the stairs, arriving in a room with two mismatched floral couches, a TV, and a foosball table that had been unsuccessfully duct-taped together. "This is where you guys hang out. This or the kitchen, if you can fit. Nowhere else. See the sign on the door back there?"

A wood-paneled door on the other end of the room bore a handwritten sign that read SAD ACTORS KEEP OUT!

"Anywhere that says 'Keep Out,' keep out, 'kay? Pretty self-explanatory."

"Got it," I nodded. "Mind if I ask why?"

"Oh, you know . . ." She led me out of the lounge and down a narrow hall. "We're lucky Bald Mountain lets us use the place at all. Usually they board it up in the off-season, but we got them to open the downstairs and this wing for us. But it's easier to keep anything we're not using boarded up, you know? That way we don't have to clean it. And, you know, mice."

"Wait, what?"

"This is you." She jerked her thumb at a door that had the names Cass, Amy, and Heidi cut out of magazine letters and taped on it. Like an artsy ransom note.

I hoped she'd been kidding about that whole mice thing. Not that I'm afraid of mice or anything; I would just prefer not to share my living space with them. Those things poop everywhere.

"This is the girls' room. The boys live at the other end of the hall. I'm upstairs in the attic—holler if you need anything, and I may respond. If I don't have anything better to do. But I'll hear you—the walls are thin. I'll leave while you get acquainted with your fellow captives. Meeting on the lawn in fifteen."

As Langley popped in her earbuds and walked toward the lounge, I pushed open the flimsy wooden door, which creaked noisily. Like everything else in this house. Inside, a girl who looked like a teeny-tiny fairy tale princess was sitting on a rollaway cot, sobbing silently but profusely. Fat teardrops spilled out of her big blue eyes, clung to her thick dark lashes, and landed on the tip of her perfect button nose. A very tall, thin girl in a peasant top had draped one long, elegant arm around the princess's shoulders, copper bangles clanking up and down her wrists. The two of them looked up.

"H-h-hi," the tiny blonde sputtered, and blew her nose into a Kleenex. White crumpled tissues dotted the floor like gross, mucus-filled snow.

"Come on in," the tall girl waved me over with her free arm. "We're having kind of a rough day."

"I'm r-r-ruining our first m-m-moments together as r-r-roommates," the blonde sobbed. "This is not good memory making!"

"No, no, sweetie, it's fine," the other one said soothingly. "It'll be funny in like a week, I promise." She smiled, crinkling the dusting of freckles across her nose. "I'm Heidi. You must be Cass."

"Yup. Hi." I dropped my bag next to a set of bunk beds lined up next to the wall. The bottom bunk had stuff strewn over it, so it looked like the top for me. I walked over toward the girls on the cot.

"S-s-sit," the short one sniffled. "I'm Amy."

"Hi." I sat on the other side of Amy. "This is probably a stupid question, but are you okay?"

"N-no," she sighed. "No, not at all." She picked the cell phone up out of her lap and handed it to me. I read the series of text messages on the screen:

Connor: its ovr
Amy: Y???>
Connor: we gradu8d an I wanna hook up with hotsluts
          @ skool

Gradu8d? I stared at the text, puzzled for a few minutes.

"Your boyfriend broke up with you because he wants to 'hook up with hot sluts' in college?" I asked incredulously.

This kicked off a fresh round of sobs.

"He did it today," Heidi whispered, "just as she crossed the border into Vermont. That's when she got the text."

"What a douchebag," I muttered murderously. Who would *do* something like that? Somehow, the depths to which the male species would sink continued to surprise me. "Okay, firstly, saying something so crass makes him a total douche. Secondly, he broke up with you via text, which is like, douche move one-oh-one. But most importantly, you could never be serious about someone who uses text words like gradu-eight and misspells school and thinks hotsluts is one word. You just dodged a bullet, my friend."

"I don't want to dodge him; I love him." Amy sniffled. "He may be a bullet, but he's my bullet."

"Maybe . . . maybe it's time to let the bullet fly away," Heidi offered, making a flapping, birdlike gesture with one large hand.

"Yeah, and shoot someone else," I mumbled. "I know we just met"—I folded my legs up under me—"so it's probably not my place to say anything at all, and I definitely shouldn't have just used the word 'douche' about forty-seven times, but this guy is clearly a Class-A douchebag." Forty-eight times. God, I'm classy.

"No, no, he's not! Not at all! We had some good times, too!" Amy reached over Heidi to pick up a framed photo that was laying in a partially unpacked pink floral quilted duffle bag. "See?"

I picked up the silver frame, which was engraved with A Night To Remember: Big Beaver Falls High School Prom. I studied the picture: Amy, in formal wear and a plastic tiara, was clinging to a good-looking blond guy in a plastic crown.

"That does look . . . fun." I set the frame down decidedly. I hadn't actually made it to my prom, so maybe that *had* been a barrel of laughs. What the hell did I know? "But still—"

"Wait!" she reached over me to grab another frame. "More fun!"

Amy smiled sadly at the frame, which read GO BIG BEAVERS!, and showed her in a cheerleading outfit and the guy I assumed was Connor sweating profusely in a football uniform.

"Although Cass may have been putting it a bit bluntly," Heidi said as she gently removed the frames from Amy's lap and placed them back in the bag, "I think she's right. You wouldn't want to be with someone who would break up with you for such a terrible reason anyway."

"Exactly." I nodded. "Really, why be with anyone?" I added earnestly. "Commitment is a waste of time. It only ends up like this. Being single is so much better. None of the messy emotional cleanup."

"Well, I didn't mean that all relationships are bad . . ." Heidi started.

"Sure they are." I nodded again, then realized I was in danger of going full-on bobblehead. Definitely time to stop nodding. "They all end. So why bother starting? I sure wouldn't."

"Wait a minute." Amy dabbed at her eyes. "You *wouldn't*? So, are you saying you've never been in a relationship?"

"Oh, God no!" I shot her a horrified look. Both Amy and Heidi looked slightly stunned. Clearly, neither one had ever watched her mom staple-gun half-naked pictures of her dad's new wife to every tree and telephone pole in town. Now, I knew what came after "I love you." What came next was going batshit crazy and having your teenage daughter bail you out of jail after a property damage charge. It was so much better to stay safe. Stay alone. Not open yourself up to any of that mess. I never wanted to have a cop wrestle me to the ground and pry a staple gun out of my crazed hands.

"No relationships? But . . . but why?" Amy spluttered.

"Um . . . Exhibit A." I picked up a Kleenex. "Exhibit B." I picked up another one. "And Exhibit C."

"Tissues?" Amy wrinkled her nose.

"Tears," I clarified. "So not worth it. There's no boy who is. It's better to get out before someone gets hurt. Or ends up holding someone else's used tissues . . . gross." I dropped them hurriedly. "I rest my case."

I felt like it was a little early in our friendship to get into the whole sext-printout-staple-gun-telephone-pole-jail-bailout explanation.

"Or maybe," Heidi said gently, "you should just choose someone nicer next time."

"Good luck with that." I shook my head sadly. "Every guy is a giant toolbox. No matter how nice he seems at first. I promise you this."

"That's not true." Heidi squeezed Amy's shoulder before mouthing the word "nicer" to me behind Amy's back.

"Choose someone who's *less* of a giant toolbox then, maybe," I amended brightly, attempting to be conciliatory. Nicer, as instructed. "I mean, comparatively. If you have to. And just don't get too invested in the whole situation. Protect yourself and you won't get hurt."

"Maybe the boys here will be nice," Heidi suggested hopefully.

"Oh, because there's a strain of men *not* known for their total douchebaggery—actors."

Heidi shot me a warning look. Amy's lower lip wobbled dangerously.

"Just kidding. I bet they're *super.*" I grimaced. But, like, a nice, friendly grimace. "Should we go check 'em out?"

"It's just about time for our informational meeting anyway." Heidi glanced down at her watch.

"Just a minute!" Amy bolted up from the bed and sprang to her mirror, performing a quick makeup rehab. Seconds later, you couldn't even tell she'd been crying. "Ready," she announced, a look a grim determination on her flawless face as she spritzed herself with a bottle of "Touch of Pink" by Lacoste.

"Where are we going?" I asked as Heidi unfolded her limbs. Standing, she was even taller than I'd thought. She could have easily rested her chin on my head.

"We're meeting on the lawn," Heidi replied, "and then, we're off to points unknown."

I still wasn't entirely sure how to navigate this maze of a house, but Heidi, explaining that her flight from Boulder had gotten in hours earlier, knew where she was going. Amy and I followed in her wake. The door to the outside world appeared after a short trip down a flight of stairs and around a corner. Langley was already at the meeting point, standing on the lawn, clutching an enormous binder to her chest.

"Welcome," she said flatly. Pretty much the least welcoming welcome of all time. God, Langley was even worse at enthusiasm than I was. "I gather from your presence here that you made it with no real problems?"

Heidi nodded her assent. Amy swiped on some lip gloss like she was girding her loins before heading into battle.

"Well, I got in a small car accident—"

"A car accident?" Amy gasped.

"No. Well, yes, I did, but I'm totally fine," I explained. "It was really minor. Some toothless yokel in a jeep almost ran me off the road, but seriously, no damage. Like beyond lucky. I'm fine."

"I'm from New York. Hardly a yokel," an all-too-familiar male voice announced from the back of the room. "And I'm pretty far from toothless."

I turned. I would have recognized that insane growth of facial hair anywhere. It was the guy from the jeep, grinning through his heavy beard, displaying an irritatingly full set of teeth.

"You!" I gasped.

"Yup," he said grimly. "Me."

This was way too coincidental to actually be happening. How was this even possible? How was he here? *Why* was he here? It made no sense.

"How's your neck?" he asked, all fake solicitousness.

"Fine. No thanks to you." I glowered. Okay. Regroup. I took a deep breath. Time to play it cool. I would not be defeated by some lame-ass hipster lumberjack. "And you said you're from New York?" He nodded warily. "Ah, well that explains why you can't drive."

"New Yorkers are the best drivers in the world," he shot back.

"Maybe in a world that consists solely of Boston and New York," I replied.

"Please," he said. "*You're* criticizing *my* driving? You had practically stopped in the middle of the road and were slowly veering into oncoming traffic."

"There *was* no oncoming traffic. I had slowed down for . . . reasons." Don't say maple candy. Don't say maple candy. Don't even *think* about maple candy. Anymore. "And the last time I checked," I picked up steam, "there was no minimum speed on one-lane dirt roads. Ramming into someone in a no-passing zone, however—"

"No-passing zone?" The stupid toothy non-yokel was getting louder, and the visible parts of his face had turned red. "There *are* no no-passing zones on one-lane dirt roads, because there are no lane demarcations. That's the whole point of a one-lane dirt road; you can pretty much do whatever you want!"

"Because *that's* a great traffic law!" I realized I was shouting, too, but I didn't care. "Everybody, go ahead and do whatever you want! Who cares what happens! Talk about a New York attitude—"

"New York attitude?" he parroted. "New York attitude! What does that even *mean*?"

"It means—"

"Enough!" Langley barked. We stopped yelling at the same time and turned to face her. The rest of the cast must have arrived. Five pairs of eyes stared at us like we were a volatile reality show. "Sorry to break it up when things were getting interesting, but we've got places to be. You can do more . . . socializing . . . later."

I snorted, as the jeep guy muttered, "No, thanks."

"Everyone." Langley pulled six strips of silk in bright jewel tones out of her binder. "Please choose the silk that speaks to you and your aura," she read off her binder, "and tie it on."

"Like a blindfold?" Amy asked querulously.

"Or a ninja?" one of the other boys asked in a slight Southern drawl. I turned to look at him and nearly got whiplash. Holy hotness, Batman.

"Like a blindfold," Langley replied.

"Are you joking?" I arched an eyebrow.

Heidi was already tying on an amethyst blindfold. "Close the eyes to see," she smiled serenely. "Classic trust exercise for ensemble building."

I preferred to trust myself *with* my eyes open, thank you very much. I disliked these moments when, all too often, theater games turned into amateur psychology. Shudder. Couldn't we just run our lines or something?

"This is clearly a joke," the toothy non-yokel said.

"Not a joke," Langley insisted. She seemed a little *too* amused that we were all about to blindfold ourselves. Hmph. "Choose a color."

"None of these really work for me," a third boy complained, as he held various strips of fabric against his cheek and discarded them disdainfully. "This palette is awful. I hate jewel tones."

"I think it's supposed to flatter your aura, not your skin tone," I replied, unable to keep the sarcasm out of my voice. How could a piece of fabric speak to your aura? I was pretty sure I didn't have an aura. And that poly-silk-blends couldn't talk.

"Whatever you pick, it'll flatter your insides, not your outsides." Heidi tried to pat his arm, but missed, as she was blindfolded, and pawed the air. "Besides, the only important thing is that we can't see. That's how we build trust."

The boy with the Southern accent tied a turquoise blindfold around Amy's shiny hair before tying a sapphire blue one around his own head of sandy blond hair. How chivalrous. Heaving a sigh, the indecisive boy picked up the topaz yellow strip between two fingers, considered it at arm's length, and eventually resigned himself to tying it on. The toothy non-yokel took emerald green, and I was left with ruby red. Fantastic. Now my head looked like it was on fire.

"Honor system," Langley said. "We're trusting you to say you can't see. Get it? Cuz it's a trust exercise. Can you see?"

"No," I said honestly, amid mumblings from everyone else to the same effect. I groped around in front of me until I grabbed onto someone surrounded by a little cloud of what I recognized as "Touch of Pink." Amy.

"From now on," Langley said, "silence. Form a chain. Lay on Macduff. And cursed be he who first cries 'hold, enough!'"

CHAPTER 3

Generally speaking, I'd prefer not to have *Macbeth* quoted at me while I am visually incapacitated. Way too macabre. I walked right into a sandalwood-scented blur that must have been Heidi. She grabbed my wrist, then felt her way down until she clasped my free hand firmly. I heard everyone shuffling around, and we must have formed a satisfactory chain, because we gradually began shuffling away. Next, I heard what sounded like a car door opening, and I was lifted along and up into something so high it must have been a van. I was wedged between Heidi and Amy. My eyes watered at the potent cocktail of sandalwood and Touch of Pink. Good thing I only smelled like Powder Fresh deodorant, or it would have been unbearable in there.

The van started and bumped its way out of the driveway. I wondered idly if this whole summer theater apprenticeship thing was a front and I'd actually been kidnapped. Nothing broke the silence except for the soft crunch of tires on gravel,

Amy's nervous giggles, and Langley's infrequent shushing. I had no idea how long we were in that van. Being naturally impatient, everything always seemed longer to me than it actually was. And it seemed even longer because I couldn't see anything. Kind of like how Space Mountain seems like such a long roller coaster, because you have no idea where you're going. Nevertheless, many bumpy, blind minutes later, the van ground to a halt. I heard the door open once more, and I was pulled out, scrambling until my feet hit solid ground. The group shuffled along something that felt similar to the gravel driveway back at the Boat House until I walked straight into Amy, who'd stopped cold. Heidi walked into me, and then, with much shuffling and bumping, everyone gradually came to a stop.

"Drop hands," Langley instructed. "Remove your blindfolds."

I took mine off. We stood at the base of a mountain that climbed toward the sky, stretching endlessly onward and upward, covered in rocky patches of grass studded with wildflowers. It must have been an off-season ski slope, because a stopped chairlift stretched all the way up it, looming over our heads like a big metal monster.

"Tie them around your heads like the warriors you are," Langley droned on, still reading off her binder without any expression whatsoever. Heidi had finished tying hers before Langley had even stopped speaking. She looked like she'd stepped straight out of the pages of a *Free People* catalog. I rolled my eyes at Amy, who scrunched her nose and chose to tie hers like a headband instead. One pointed look from

Langley, though, and she sheepishly changed it. I tied mine ninja-style, while the boy with the yellow ribbon tied his with a spectacularly gorgeous bow, then twisted it so the bow sat a rakish angle to his brow. The stupid jeep guy was still staring down Langley. Heaving a mighty sigh with an even more obnoxious eye roll than mine had been, he eventually tied his sash sloppily around his head.

"Your journey begins," Langley read, "at the base of this mountain." She gestured somewhat woodenly toward the off-season ski hill. I had a feeling that whatever strange script she was reading from had a "gesture to mountain" stage direction. "Your journey this summer, like your journey on the mountain, will be uphill. Rigorous. But together you will ascend." On "ascend," her arm pointed to the peak of the mountain.

We stared at Langley. We stared at the mountain.

"So . . . ascend!" she repeated, gesturing again.

"Like, up the mountain?" Amy asked.

Langley nodded. "Like up the mountain."

I stared. So it wasn't, like, a rock-climbing wall, but it was still pretty steep. Definitely more of a rigorous hike than a casual stroll.

"This is a joke, right?" I asked. Langley had to be joking. I'd been involved in some weird theater exercises before, but this one took the cake. Langley shook her head grimly in response. "This has got to be a joke. There's a chairlift up this mountain for a reason."

"What, you can't handle it?" That idiot who almost ran me off the road poked his head out of the line to face me. "Afraid of a little hike?"

"Um, no," I contested hotly as I tied my ninja band tighter. "I can absolutely handle this. *I* was joking."

"Sure you were." He smirked.

"Watch me."

I started up the mountain, stomping every step, churning up little eddies of dust and rocks in places where the grass had been worn away by other insane, suicidal hikers on forced marches.

"Enjoy the death march, suckers!" Langley cackled as she hopped back into the van. Part of me wondered if she'd invented this whole thing on her own just to mess with us.

The rest of the group followed less angrily in my wake. Heidi ascended like a graceful, long-limbed mountain goat, simultaneously picking flowers, weaving them into garlands, and practically skipping up the 90 degree incline. Even with her stops for flowers, she was rapidly outpacing the rest of us. We straggled behind her in a clump. Man, that hill was *steep*. Not that I was going to let anyone, particularly plaid-clad bad drivers, see how much it was making me sweat. I kept on going, propelled by nothing but sheer force of will and a desire to prove that cretin wrong.

"Eek!" Amy pitched forward over a boulder, falling neatly into the arms of the Southern boy, who had zoomed to her side at nearly superhuman speed to catch her.

"Don't worry." He grinned. "I got you."

"Gosh." Amy blinked up at him. "That was like Edward Cullen-fast."

"Who?" He furrowed his brow.

"Oh, um, never mind. How embarrassing." Amy blushed.

THE TAMING OF THE DREW

When I blush, I look like a tomato. Amy somehow managed to look even more adorable as the flush spread over her cheeks, which sent her gallant rescuer into his own, equally adorable fit of blushing. Good. The way things were going, hopefully that douchey ex of hers would soon be no more than a distant, unpleasant memory. This would be exactly what she needed—a nice, fun, cute summer fling with a Southern accent. Perfect.

We straggled onward and upward for who knew how long, until the tiny dot that was Heidi had stopped moving, and we eventually reached her at the summit.

"I think it's a little house," she announced, hands on hips, as she stood facing what was, in fact, a little house. Not like playhouse-little, just a small house, located about fifty feet from where the chairlift ended.

"Is it open?" the boy with the yellow bow asked.

"Dunno." Heidi shrugged. "I was waiting for you." She smiled and indicated the woven flower headband and long flower necklace she was now sporting, which she must have made while she waited.

"Well, there's only one way to find out," the Southern boy drawled, as he stepped toward the door. "Shall we?" Heidi nodded. He knocked three times on the door, loud and sure.

"Enter," a voice wafted from within, as the door seemed to open of its own accord, releasing a heavily perfumed cloud of incense.

"You have got to be kidding me," the toothy non-yokel mumbled.

"Ladies first," the Southern boy smiled, tipped an imaginary hat, and held the door as Heidi, Amy, and I trooped through, followed by the boys.

A tiny woman with a long, thick gray braid sat cross-legged on top of a table, a bongo drum nestled in her lap, which she beat at even, rhythmic intervals. A goateed man in his thirties stood behind her, arms folded across his chest. They were both wearing black turtlenecks and some type of weird, flowy black drawstring pants.

"Come. Come into the center," the woman instructed, still beating the bongos.

It was only the first day, and I had been blindfolded, thrown into a van, forced to climb a mountain, and was now choking on incense in a tiny room while listening to an impromptu bongo concert.

"Move to the rhythm," the woman instructed. "Move! Begin walking in a circle."

As we walked in concentric circles, I took the opportunity to inspect where we were. This must have been some kind of ski outpost in the winter, because although the walls were now draped in even more jewel-toned silks—that boy with the yellow sash must have been thrilled—they didn't completely obscure the framed photos of ski teams beneath them.

"Now feel the music!" the woman instructed. Easy. "No, no keep moving!" she amended. Oh, right. I started walking again. "Begin to feel it. Really feel it. Let it inform your body. Your movements. Break free of your circles. Break free of your steps. Break free of your *selves*. Move across the space in any way you see fit. Dance, dance, DANCE!"

Heidi was now leaping about like a gazelle who'd been trained by Alvin Ailey; the rest of us were shuffling around somewhat awkwardly, like middle schoolers dancing free-style at a bar mitzvah. Amy had decided to stick to twirling, which she was executing beautifully until she got dizzy and had to sit down.

"Slow as the bongo slows." The woman started to slow down the rhythm. Thank God. This was about as much bizarre theater-game time as I could take. Don't get me wrong. I love acting. I love it more than anything else. But I love being on stage, attacking scenes, making character choices. Not bongo dancing. Incidentally, bongo dancing was not featured at all in Weehawken High's recent production of *Anything Goes*. I bet it would have really added a certain je ne sais quoi to my energetic, if not particularly skillful, tap dancing. "Slow," she continued. "Slow until you come face to face with another person."

Wait, what? I was all the way off in some corner, and the closest person to me was . . . no. Oh no. I started power walking toward someone, anyone, who wasn't . . . *him*.

"SLOW!" the bongo lady barked, in a tone very unlike her previous meditative one, and, grumbling mightily, I found myself face to face with my least favorite member of the Shakespeare at Dunmore Journeyman Apprentice Company.

"Wanted to be my partner so badly you speed-walked over here?" he smirked.

"Oh, as *if*," I hissed.

"Ooo, nice diss, Cher. That, like, totally hurt," he valley-girled back at me.

"Shut up, shut up, shut up!" I whispered.

"SILENCE!" One loud bang of the bongo. We both shut up. Great. I was already in trouble. "Now, look into your partner's eyes. Only the eyes. The rest of the world falls away."

My partner's eyes were rolling. To be fair, mine probably were, too.

"Now." Two beats of the bongo. "Where does their pain lie?" She repeated again, in a whisper, "Where does their pain lie?"

I didn't even need to look. He was a pain in the ass, so his pain clearly lay in the ass. Or my ass. Whatever. But I looked, because there was nowhere else to look. Hazel. Weird. They were pretty interesting eyes, at least. I couldn't really find the pain, but there were all sorts of interesting golden flecks in there.

"Where does their fear lie?" And in a whisper, "Where does their fear lie?"

This time, my hazel-eyed partner snorted audibly, then tried unsuccessfully to pass it off as a cough.

We went through hurt, anger, and finally love in the same fashion. Definitely no love lying in those weird hazel eyes. Unless love looked exactly like skepticism.

"Form a circle in the center of the room."

Finally. I had been smirked at enough for one day. I shot hazel-eyed beardy my best death glare before shuffling with everyone else into the middle of the room. It was definitely more of an amoeba than a circle.

"Pull down your blindfolds." *Bang bang bang.* "We close our eyes to truly see."

Before pulling hers down, Heidi winked at me under her strip of amethyst silk.

"Nevin will tap you one by one. When you feel the tap, remove your blindfold. Choose your archetype, and become it. Begin to create a soundscape. "

Nevin? Archetype? Soundscape? I didn't understand 80 percent of the words in that sentence. But around me, everyone started humming, buzzing, clicking, making all sorts of strange ambient noises. I joined in.

"I am a salmon in a pool." It sounded like Heidi. "I am a salmon in a pool." Heidi. I was sure. This time, I hadn't tied my blindfold so tightly. Pretending to scratch my nose, I pushed it up a millimeter. Heidi was swimming around the center of the room for all she was worth, flopping back and forth. The goateed man tapped her on the shoulder. I quickly pulled my blindfold down before he caught me sneaking a peek.

"I am a wizard. Who but I sets the cool head aflame with smoke?" boomed out from the center of the circle. It took me a minute to place the voice, but I was pretty sure it was the boy with the yellow bow. He boomed out very loudly several more times, drowning out the bongos.

"I am a wonder among flowers." Amy. She must have been twirling around, because clouds of Touch of Pink dusted me from time to time. I sneezed. Twice.

"I am the shield for every head." Definitely the boy with the Southern accent. That was easy. And this had officially become the weirdest theater exercise of my life. Way weirder than the time we had to say "this is a pen" for like forty-five minutes in drama club.

"I am a breaker threatening doom." Knew who that was. What, they didn't have an archetype that said, "I am the jerk-face who ran into your car"? Or, "I am a potential psychopath who will almost assuredly ruin your summer"?

I felt a tapping. The goateed man was holding a piece of paper in front of my face. I chose one line of text at random: "I am the blaze on every hill."

The goateed man prodded me into the circle.

"I am the blaze on every hill."

The bongos kept getting louder. I looked over at the woman with the gray braid, who nodded encouragingly.

"I AM THE BLAZE ON EVERY HILL!"

The bongos got louder and louder, I got louder and louder, and the "soundscape" behind me got louder and louder.

BOOM BOOM BOOM.

I stopped.

"Together," the bongo-ing woman said. "I am the hill where poets walk."

We repeated, together, "I am the hill where poets walk."

"Excellent." She smiled. "Excellent. Please, retie your headbands, thespian warriors." We did. "Take seats in the circle." We sat. "No, no, let me *in* the circle." Southern boy and Heidi, who were closest to the table where she was sitting, scooted apart to make a space. She waited. "Nevin!" The goateed man walked over to her, and grunting slightly, he pulled the table, the woman still on top of it, into the space in the circle. "Thank you," she sighed exasperatedly, rolling her eyes. "No, no, don't sit," she commanded as the goateed man's knees began to bend.

So, that was it? We were done? I looked over at Amy, who seemed as confused as I was. Well, I'd discovered that I was apparently a blaze on a hill and that I couldn't find where someone's pain lay, probably because he didn't have any feelings.

"Welcome." The woman nodded to each of us in turn. "Welcome. I am . . ." — she played a little drum roll on the bongos — "Lola St. Clair." She punctuated it with a loud *bang*. Amy widened her eyes at me, and I raised an eyebrow in return. "I am the founder and artistic director of Shakespeare at Dunmore. Standing behind me is Nevin Vandergrue." She indicated the goateed man. I was willing to bet my entire internship stipend that their given names were something like Gladys Sfakianakis and Gary Czerwinski. "He will be your director for *The Taming of the Shrew*, our Journeyman Apprentice Company main stage production." Nevin inclined his head slightly.

"Many years ago, after our first five successful seasons of Shakespeare at Dunmore, I started the Journeyman Apprentice Company as a training program for young artists. We are thrilled to have you here, you bright, promising young artists on the verge. I am honored to shepherd you on your journey out of the nest that is high school as you fly off into the world at large. Here at SAD, we hope to strengthen your wings to help you fly. We begin." *BANG!*

"Uh, before we begin . . ."

What on earth could El Beardo possibly have to contribute to this conversation? If the smug look on his face was any indication, he clearly thought he had something of value to add.

"I'm assuming you know the name is completely ridiculous?"

Somehow, Lola looked more intrigued than pissed. This was insane. Had he just called the company's name ridiculous? I could not believe he had just insulted the artistic director. *To her face.* Something tapped me on my chin. Startled, I jumped in my seat as a manicured hand beat a hasty retreat out of my line of vision.

"Sorry," Amy whispered. "Your jaw was hanging open. My mom always says that's how bugs get in there."

"It's nonsensical," he continued. "Journeyman is the phase after apprentice. You can't have a Journeyman Apprentice Company. It makes absolutely no sense. First, you have to complete an apprenticeship, then after your education you become a journeyman."

"This isn't a guild, Drew," Lola replied breezily, a distinct note of amusement in her voice. Drew. Arrogance had a name. "Although, if you would like to submit a master work at the end of the season, I look forward to seeing it."

"If anything, it should be the Apprentice Journeyman Company," he argued. He was still going? Sheesh. "Then at least it would indicate a logical progression."

"Time," she chuckled. "What a linear, westernized notion."

Drew opened, then closed his mouth. Apparently he had nothing to say to that.

"Now, we progress. Logically." She winked at Drew. Ten points to Lola for unexpected cheekiness. "During these exercises, you have gotten to know yourselves, and you have gotten to know each other, on a deep, elemental level. But, of course, we must concede to the superficial as well." She clasped her hands in front of her face, as if thinking. "Name," she stated. "The character you'll be playing. Where you come from. And, so we know you best, your passions. One thing you love, and one thing you hate." She turned to Heidi. "Begin."

"I'm Heidi." She smiled. "I'm from Boulder, Colorado, and I'll be playing Baptista Minola."

"You're my father?" Amy asked quizzically.

"Who's your daddy?" the boy with the yellow bow jumped in.

Lola St. Clair held up her hand for silence. Immediately, everyone hushed.

"Yes, I'm playing Baptista Minola, who is traditionally played by a man," Heidi continued, "but traditionally, all of the parts in Shakespeare's plays were played by men. So that's nothing new. And besides, when you get right down to it, gender is just a social construct."

Lola gave her an appreciative beat of the bongos.

"Actually, if anyone is interested in discussing this further, I did my senior independent work on the performance of gender, as seen specifically through the lens of movement. Actually, this would be a really great text to work on with some of the movement-based techniques I explored, since it is so gendered. Did everyone bring movement pants?"

Silence. Heidi seemed really nice, but . . . not really my thing. Also I wasn't exactly sure what movement pants were, and from looking around the room, neither was anyone else.

I almost laughed out loud at the expression on a certain someone's face, but I held it together. Barely.

"Ah. Okay." Heidi cleared her throat. "Well, then, no pressure. Just keep that in mind. As an option. Anyway," she began again, "I love discussing the performance of gender—just kidding! Well, I do really like that, but I also love other things. Like tubing. It's the *best*. I pick tubing as the thing I love. And I hate that female genital mutilation is still practiced in parts of the world."

Heidi turned, beaming beatifically at Amy, who was staring at her, agog.

"Gosh, that's terrible!" Amy exclaimed. "Wow, who wouldn't hate that. I—"

"Name!" Lola interrupted.

"Oh, right!" Amy blushed. "I'm Amy. I'm from Big Beaver Falls, Pennsylvania—go Big Beavers!" She did a little fist pump. "I'm playing Bianca."

Well, no surprise there. *The Taming of the Shrew* is about two rich sisters—the older one is a huge pain in the ass, and the younger one is sweet and beautiful. Their father devises this scheme so that no one can marry the sweet younger sister, Bianca, until the older one, Kate, is married. So after Bianca's most ardent suitor, Lucentio, convinces this cash-strapped guy, Petruchio, to woo Kate, Petruchio marries Kate and "tames" her by basically inflicting psychological torture until she's all "women are simple, worship your husband." And this is supposedly a love story. Gag me.

You know, I still couldn't quite figure Amy out. She had certainly been popular in high school—hence the photos in the cheerleading uniform and the prom queen tiara—and here she was, at a Shakespeare internship. And obviously popular people can like Shakespeare, I'm not saying they're all vapid clones or whatever; it was just that, in my high school, no one who looked like Amy would have been caught dead in drama club. She must have been one of those weird anomalies that somehow manages to be a popular cheerleader and still does time steps in the spring musical. The rest of us, however, looked like the usual band of misfits. Actually, scratch that—the Southern guy was super hot, *and* he was a dude. Even more unusual. Hmm. Maybe this was what happened once you did theater outside of high school. The Ryan Goslings and Scarlett Johanssons of the world had to come from somewhere, right?

"I love polka dots, and I hate roller coasters," Amy finished. She turned. Oh, right—me!

"I'm Cass," I started. "I'm from Weehawken. New Jersey."

Drew snorted and rolled his eyes. I glared. I knew that snort of tristate-area prejudice well. There is nothing wrong with New Jersey!

"I'm playing—"

"The shrew," he interrupted, quiet enough that Lola couldn't hear it, but I sure could.

"They call me Katharine that do speak of me," I shot back. He may have technically been referring to my character, but I could tell he thought I was a total shrew. Rude. "I mean, I'm playing Kate," I amended, slightly less hostile, for the benefit of the group. "I hate raisins, and I love blue nail polish." I liberated my left foot from my Converses and waggled a turquoise toe.

"Very nice," the boy with the yellow headband remarked. "My name is Rhys," he started. *Reese.* What a cool name. Like a Reese's Piece. "I'm from Dover—it's just outside of Boston. And before we begin, in my defense, I would just like to say, I don't *normally* look like a gay werewolf."

He kind of had a point. When we signed the contract, there had been a stipulation about not cutting, coloring, or altering hair in any way—which specified that the boys shouldn't shave. And by the looks of it, they hadn't shaved for a long time. The only one who looked at all decent was the boy with the Southern accent; he'd grown a light beard of scruff that made him look like a sexy cowboy. Drew looked like a crazy lumberjack who'd been roaming the woods for the better part of a decade, and Rhys did, in fact, look like a gay werewolf. His beard grew most of the way down his neck until it blended into the tuft of chest hair sticking out of his mint green striped Oxford.

BANG! "Don't denigrate the facial hair!" Lola remonstrated.

"Sorry, sorry," he sighed, and blew a flop of his bangs out of his eyes. "I'm playing Hortensio, a.k.a. Loserface McGee Bianca's Suitor Who Doesn't Get the Girl. I love scratchy old Billie Holiday records and I hate an improperly steeped mug of tea." He nodded seriously. "You need to set the timer, or it's worthless. NEXT!"

"Oookay." Arrrgh. Next up was that stupid crazy lumberjack. "I'm Drew. And I'm playing . . ." Oh, please don't say it. Please don't say it. "Petruchio." Oh, no. Oh, no, no, no, no, no. This was the *worst* of all possible worlds. He was playing—gag me—my love interest. Oh, gag me with a long-ended spoon. This was even worse than the time I'd been cast opposite Jeff Butts in *Much Ado About Nothing* the winter he tried to grow a mustache.

"I'm from New York."

"The city?" Amy interrupted, eyes sparkling. "Oh, how exciting! Uptown? Downtown? Where? Oh my God, are you from SoHo? Don't tell me you're from SoHo!"

"Oh, uh." Drew colored. "I'm actually from Rye."

Now it was my turn to snort.

"It's *basically* the city," he addressed Amy.

"Rye's about as much New York City as Weehawken is," I rolled my eyes.

BANG! Lola fixed me with a stare. I shut up.

"Anyway," Drew cleared his throat, also glaring at me, "I love . . . um . . . *Sir John Oldcastle.*" We stared at him blankly. "The Elizabethan play." More blank stares. "It's part of Shakespeare's Apocrypha." He rolled his eyes, exhaling in an exasperated fashion. "That means the collection of works that are sometimes attributed to Shakespeare, but most modern scholarship has since refuted those claims. *Pericles*, for example, was once considered apocryphal, but has since been included in the canon."

Oh my God. What a show-off. You don't bust out obscure Elizabethan theatricals while playing get-to-know-you games. That's just rude. Also who *loves* Apocrypha? If it means the stuff that's been left out, it was probably left out for a reason. He probably said that just so he'd sound smart. Also probably the same reason he referred to Shakespeare's works as *the canon*. Fancy schmancy. And his tone of voice just grated on my nerves. It was like he was explaining arithmetic to a kindergartener.

Here's the truth: This small, petty part of me was pissed that I hadn't known what Apocrypha was. Of course, I knew that there was still debate about exactly which plays Shakespeare had written and that some people thought he hadn't written *any* of them — personally, I thought those people were nuts — but I'd never heard of Apocrypha. I knew it shouldn't have bothered me, but I hated that Drew knew something I didn't. It made me feel so stupid. I wished I'd said I liked something a little bit more profound than blue nail polish. That was what I chose as my defining characteristic? Blue nail polish? Real stellar first impression, Cass. God, I hoped everybody didn't think I was an idiot.

"And I hate active listeners," he concluded, satisfied.

What did that even *mean*? Who hated being listened to? I hadn't even known it was possible to come across obnoxious in a simple getting-to-know-you game. All of my suspicions about Drew had been confirmed: he was officially the worst.

"Well, alright," the Southern boy drawled, laughing slightly. "Apocrypha. There you go. Learning already. I'm Noah, and I'm from Pecos, Texas." That explained the accent. It was very Matthew McConaughey. Alright, alright, alright. "And I'm playing Lucentio." Lucentio is Bianca's suitor who marries her at the end of the play. "I love the Dallas Cowboys, and I hate wet socks."

"Excellent." Lola bopped softly on the bongos. "Excellent. The journey begins. You're getting to know each other.

THE TAMING OF THE DREW

You feel that? Feel that?" She looked at each of us in turn. Not sure what I was supposed to be feeling. Except if it was *confused*. Because that was what I felt. "That's tension. Sexual tension." Oh, Lord. I was starting to turn into a tomato again. Amy was also blushing, looking less like a vegetable, and all the boys were looking at the floor. Only Heidi was nodding, like she knew exactly what Lola meant. I bet she could have gender-in-performance-movement danced the shit out of some sexual tension. "Feel it. Use it. A group of good-looking teenagers in a house together, studying the greatest work in Western history on the war of the sexes. Yes." She and Heidi were now nodding in synchronicity. I hadn't felt any sexual tension as of yet. But if there was anything that could kill sexual tension more rapidly than your artistic director commenting on it, I couldn't imagine what it was. "Oh, yes. Nevin." She changed the subject abruptly. "Pass out the packages."

He did. I pulled apart the brown paper to look inside: There was a camo print T-shirt, and something black. Camo? We'd already climbed a mountain. What else could be in store?

"Report at oh-eight-hundred hours for Bard Boot Camp," Lola smiled.

Bard Boot Camp?

BANG BANG BANG.

"Dismissed!"

CHAPTER 4

"This all just feels a little too Patty Hearst for my taste," Heidi said as she pursed her lips and adjusted her black beret. "I'm not comfortable wearing such a militaristic outfit."

"Agreed." Amy frowned at herself in her compact mirror. "Camo is *so* 2001. What are we, extras in *Save the Last Dance*? On our way to STEPPS with Julia Stiles? Proving that white girls can bust a move?"

I yawned in agreement. A yawn was about as much brain function as could be expected of me before eight in the morning. Particularly since I'd never seen *Save the Last Dance*.

The three of us were sitting under a little tent in front of a folding table. Well, technically, I was curled up in a ball on top of said table, trying to nap, while Amy and Heidi were sitting in two of the folding chairs behind it.

We'd made it to "Bard Boot Camp" bright and early. Except for Langley, who was busy sweeping the water from last night's rainfall off the stage with an old push broom, we were the only ones there. The Shakespeare at Dunmore stage stood in a little green clearing on the shore of the lake, nestled between the gazebo in the Dunmore town square and a long reddish building that looked sort of like a barn. The stage itself was a good-sized wooden platform featuring three archways and a staircase that led up to a tiny balcony—in case of an impromptu production of *Romeo and Juliet*, one supposed. There was nothing in that valley but the birds chirping and the *swish swish* of Langley's broom.

Heidi sang a few bars from "The Heather on the Hill," her voice trilling prettily, like a bird's, on the high notes.

"Too early," I mumbled.

"Too early for singing?"

"Too early for *Brigadoon*." There should never be show tunes before noon. There's a reason matinees start at two.

"Hopefully today won't be quite so . . . extreme." Amy sighed. "That was the weirdest day of my life."

"What, yesterday?"

"Mm-hmm." She nodded. "They blindfolded us and threw us in a van! I thought I was going to wake up two weeks later in Mexico or something."

I laughed. It was nice to know I wasn't the only one who'd thought yesterday's events were entirely bizarre.

"I liked that hike," Heidi said brightly. "Seriously, one of my top five theater exercises ever."

"Can you explain to me how, exactly, hiking up a mountain constitutes a theater exercise? Not being sarcastic. Honestly wondering. How was that a theater exercise?" I asked.

"Well, um, I don't know," she admitted. "I'm not completely sure how that applied to *The Taming of the Shrew*. But it was enjoyable! The landscape on the East Coast is so different than it is back home. It's beautiful, too, but in a different way. Everything's on such a smaller scale. It was nice to be hiking, even if it was just up a little hill."

A little hill? I shuddered. Thank God Heidi wasn't in charge of picking our theater exercise hiking excursion venues. I didn't have the aerobic capacity to survive a Heidi-run Shakespeare theater.

"I just wish I hadn't picked the salmon in the pool," Heidi moaned, as the brightness suddenly drained out of her voice. "I had no idea what I was supposed to do! I was trying so hard to be a fish. But I couldn't figure out how to swim on carpet. Was I supposed to get on my stomach and flop? Or swim upright? I was so scared they'd send me home if I wasn't fishy enough."

"You were perfectly fishy. I peeked," I admitted.

"Cheater!" Amy squealed.

"Whelp, there goes all the trust I built." Heidi's pretend disappointment radiated from every freckle.

"I am perfectly trustworthy, and I don't need a salmon to tell me that. What a bunch of BS. That Lola St. Clair is . . . something else."

"Oh, she's something, alright." Heidi nodded vigorously. "But no BS. She's the real thing. Lola was a huge deal in the whole protest-theater movement."

"The what?" Amy asked.

"You know, theater as a form of social change? Like Boal and the Theater of the Oppressed?"

I nodded, like I knew what that was. I had a basic idea—the name was sort of self-explanatory. Even if I had no idea what, or who, Boal was. "She was a celebrity. A complete fixture on that scene in the village. Bob Dylan wrote a song about her."

"He did not," I scoffed as Amy whispered, wide-eyed, "Wow."

"He absolutely did," Heidi insisted.

"Gonna play my bongos all day, gonna find me a ski chalet, cover it up with jewel-tone silks, get some actors . . ." No idea what rhymed with silks. And my Bob Dylan impression wasn't very good.

"Of all ilks?" Amy suggested. "Can ilk be plural?"

"Works for me."

"It was a real song, guys! I swear!" Heidi did not seem amused by our musical creation. "But then she had some kind of falling out with the rest of the movement, left New York, moved up here, and never looked back."

"That's nuts." I shook my head. I could totally picture Lola protesting stuff in The Village with her bongos, but Bob Dylan's muse? No. It was just too much.

"It's impressive, really. She turned a tiny artist's commune in the green mountains into one of New England's most respected summer stock Shakespeare theaters, pretty much all on her own. Of course, it's not the Public, but it's nothing to sneeze at. Frankly, Lola St. Clair is a goddamn hero."

"A goddamn hero, huh?" I marveled, unable to keep a laugh from bubbling out. "That's some strong language, Heidi."

"I meant it. Goddammit." She smiled.

"Where are the boys?" Amy snapped her compact shut and checked her phone as she slid it back into her purse.

"Who cares," I mumbled and rolled over as Heidi mused, "Dunno."

"They're gonna be late." Amy checked her phone again. "It's like seven fifty-eight."

"Well, they're definitely not here. So I'm totally within my rights to go back to sleep." I closed my eyes. Ahh, sweet, blissful darkness.

Heidi sang the opening measures of "Goodnight My Someone."

That song. That *show*. If I never heard it, or anything from that score, ever again, it would be too soon. Anything that reminded me of my humiliating turn about the boards as Winthrop was slightly traumatic. Trust me—no ninth-grade girl wants to play an eight-year-old boy in a sailor suit. Those knickers were unfortunate. Some nights I still woke up in a cold sweat, lisping my way through "The Wells Fargo Wagon" in my sleep.

"First *Brigadoon*? Now *Music Man*?" I cracked an eye open to look at Heidi. "I wouldn't have pegged you for a Broadway baby. What with the whole theater of the oppressed thing. That's about as far from show tunes as you can get."

"That's the beautiful thing about theater though, isn't it?" She smiled. "It can be so many different things. It feeds so many different needs, for different people or for different sides of the same person. That's what's so wonderful about theater. It's as complex as human nature itself. That's what it's reflecting back to us, after all."

She was right. I'd never really thought about it like that, but it was just like Hamlet said: "What a piece of work is man! How noble in reason! How infinite in faculty!" And yes, that monologue was about how Hamlet totally didn't want to deal with people anymore, but even in his state he could appreciate the infinity of human possibility. No wonder Hamlet used a play *within* a play to reflect back on his uncle's own lack of humanity. Oh, Shakespeare. He never got old. Always more to discover.

It was nice to be in a place where everyone was pretty much obsessed with Shakespeare. A lot of weird stuff had happened in the brief time I'd been at SAD, but I'd never felt like *I* was weird. I felt like I belonged, somehow, already. Like Amy and Heidi would never think I was weird. Not even if I was just randomly contemplating the genius of *Hamlet* on a Tuesday morning. And that felt nicer than I would have guessed.

My eyes had fluttered closed, and I had just started to drift off to sleep, when I was rudely awoken by, of all things, a bugle.

CHAPTER 5

W/hat the what?" I muttered, sitting up, rubbing the sleep out of my eyes. "A bugle? What the hell is this, 'Taps'?"

"It's 'Reveille,'" a voice said smugly. I blinked and opened my eyes wider. Drew. Of course. The boys had arrived during my brief nap. "'Reveille' is a bugle call traditionally used to wake military personnel. 'Taps' is played at funerals."

"Just wait, I might have been right after all," I muttered, hopping off the table. The way things were going there was a pretty good chance I would kill him before day's end.

The rest of the cast was gathering in front of the stage. I walked hurriedly toward it, away from Drew.

Nevin, dressed in a black turtleneck, military beret, and camouflage cargo pants, was walking slowly through the archway onto the stage, playing the bugle. I stared at him, slack-jawed. He was seriously playing the mother-eff-ing bugle. Unbelievable. Where was I? Both Heidi and Rhys had their hands over their ears. Noah and Amy just looked confused, and Drew was rolling his eyes so rapidly he looked in need of an exorcist.

After one long, extended blast of the bugle, Nevin brought it down from his lips.

"Welcome to Bard Boot Camp, Thespian Soldiers!" he barked, coming to stand next to Langley, who leaned on her broom.

"Sir, yes, sir!" Rhys shouted flippantly.

"No back-talk!" Nevin ordered.

"Sorry, sir, sorry!" Rhys called, more meekly.

"Fifteen laps around the barn!" Nevin ordered.

We stared at him.

"Just me?" Rhys asked tentatively. "Or everyone?"

"Everyone!" Nevin thundered. "Move, move, move!"

As Langley waved goodbye, we took off in a confused mass toward the big red barn, jogging around the long building. Heidi easily outdistanced us, breaking away from the pack. I smiled smugly as I watched Drew try again and again to overtake her, but with no success, clearly desperate to be the fastest but unable to pass Heidi. Hee hee hee. *That* brought me so much joy I didn't even mind running. Noah, Amy, and I jogged comfortably in the middle, while Rhys followed behind at a more leisurely pace.

Nevin called out the lap numbers as we jogged by, until, finally, we hit fifteen, and we collapsed into a slightly wheezing circle.

"Fifteen push-ups!" he shouted.

No rest for the weary. Groaning slightly, we scrambled into positions and began.

"Your form is wrong," Drew hissed at me from across the circle.

"Excuse me?" *My* form was wrong! I looked at the two people on either side of me. Amy had her knees on the ground and Rhys was doing little more than leaning his chest in a vaguely downward direction.

"Yes. It's not a correct push-up. Which makes it not a push-up at all. The angle of your arms is wrong, and you haven't stabilized your core. Basically, for all the good that's doing, you might as well be sitting on the ground," Drew concluded. "Actually, everyone," he started speaking again, at a slightly louder volume. "Your hands should only be slightly wider than shoulder-width apart. Don't look straight down. Look slightly ahead, otherwise your body will be misaligned. Like Cass's."

"No talking!" Nevin commanded. Who knew my tormentor would become my savior? Because listening to Drew talk on top of this physical punishment was cruel and unusual. And apparently I already had a misaligned body to deal with, which was difficult enough.

"Fifty sit-ups!" Nevin barked once the push-ups were complete.

Groaning again, we rolled onto our backs. Would this never stop? When they called it Bard Boot Camp, I didn't really expect Boot Camp! Luckily, the Push-Up King declined to comment on my sit-up form. I looked over to see Amy hastily wipe away an errant bead of sweat from her brow. Rhys's bangs were flopping so madly they were almost creating a breeze. At this point, I would readily have welcomed an actual breeze.

"And now, we stretch," Nevin announced, to great relief from the group. "I will guide you through your first sun salutation."

Okay, now I could really relax. Because my mom's a yoga teacher, I was practically doing Warrior One before I could walk. She runs her own studio in Weehawken, called Yoga-booty, of all the embarrassing horrible things to call a yoga studio. But at least it meant I could let my mind wander as we went through the poses. I looked across the circle and Heidi was beaming so brightly there was practically light emanating from her grin. At least someone was happy. Unlike Drew next to her, who was having so much trouble maintaining the poses he was sweating, wobbling, and cursing under his breath. Tsk tsk. Not very yogi-esque.

As we moved into Downward Dog, I looked through my legs to see a group of guys about our age in Town Square staring at us. Hmm.

"Amy." I transferred my weight to my right foot and kicked her gently with my left. "Amy," I whispered again. She turned her head to look at me. "Look through your legs," I whispered, darting glances at Nevin to make sure he didn't hear us. Luckily, he seemed particularly absorbed in his Downward Dog.

"Ooo." She looked behind us. "Who are they?"

"No idea," I answered.

"They look cute upside down though!" she whispered enthusiastically. "What are they holding? Are those . . . skateboards?"

"Hey! Hey you!" Nevin shouted suddenly. I zipped my lips, bracing myself for a telling off. But the telling off wasn't for me. "You guys get out of here! This isn't a free show! This is our rehearsal space! OURS!"

"Hey, bra, relax!" one of the guys behind us called out. "Just enjoying the sick view!"

"Now, see here—"

"Of the lake, man, of the lake!" the guy yelled back as his friends laughed. "Lake belongs to everyone, yeah?"

"If we have even so much of a hint of trouble from you skate camp hooligans this year," Nevin threatened, "don't think I won't hesitate to—"

"Dag, bra, easy!" the guy called back. "We're on our way out, donut shop. No sweat."

In one fluid motion, they hopped on their boards and skated away. I realized suddenly that I was the only person left in Downward Dog and hastily scrambled to a sitting position. Rhys was leaning forward eagerly as if he were watching a play, while Amy was posing, trying to show her most advantageous angle. Noah leaned back, his face tilted up toward the sun, as if he hadn't really paid attention to any of that. Heidi sat in lotus position, lips pursed, while Drew kept mumbling something that sounded like "donut shop."

"All right," Nevin sighed heavily. "Let's form a circle onstage. And let's hope that's the last we see of those skaters," he added in an undertone, as all of us, including Langley, sat in a circle. Everyone was misted with a light coat of sweat except for Nevin and Langley, who was smirking in a self-satisfied manner.

"Who were they?" I asked curiously.

"Who cares?" Drew said.

"Woe to us all, there's a Skate Camp at Lake Dunmore every summer." Nevin shook his head. "Little snots shipping up for the summer to wreak havoc on the Skate Park at Camp Dunmore, under the asinine tutelage of, quote-professional-unquote skaters. They are a plague as deadly as the locusts and boils of Egypt."

Wow. That seemed a little harsh.

"But forget them," Nevin began again. "Now that we've exhausted our bodies, our minds are clear. Welcome to Circle Time." He tried to smile, but it looked more like a grimace.

"Like in preschool?" Drew asked, aghast.

"Like in Vermont's *only* professional outdoor summer Shakespeare Theater that you should be *honored* to be part of!" Nevin bellowed. Drew looked down, slightly chastened. Although, again, that was an awful lot of qualifiers. "Each morning," Nevin continued in a much gentler tone, "we shall begin rehearsal with Circle Time and an emotional check-in, where you will be free to air your thoughts and concerns, and to check in with yourselves and the group."

More psychobabble. When were we ever going to start rehearsing?

"I have a question," Amy raised her hand. "I don't know if it's emotional, but it's a concern, I guess."

"Speak your mind," Nevin instructed her.

"The, um, Internet doesn't work in the house? And there's no cell service here? And I kind of feel like I should call my parents?" Despite Nevin's best efforts to seem gentle, Amy practically cowered under his goateed grimace.

Oh, right. Parents. Well, my mom was more of the forge-your-own-destiny school of thought, so unless I called to say I'd lost a limb, I knew she'd assume I was fine. And I didn't think dear old Dad, over in Pleasant Hills with Steak House Heather, either needed or particularly wanted an update. Quite frankly, I had no desire to contact either one of them. And now I didn't have to worry about them attempting to contact me. Beautiful. Out of sight, out of mind. Just like I'd wanted. I'd have a blissful summer of Green Mountain solitude, then make my official escape to Rutgers in the fall. Which would technically send me right back to New Jersey, but there would be a crucial forty minutes between me and the parental units.

"The Internet will work if you sit on top of the freezer in the kitchen," Nevin replied.

"That's the only place?" Amy asked.

"The *only* place," Langley confirmed, raising her eyebrow. "Let's hope no one here has rich, fulfilling, MMORPG lives they'll be suddenly and brutally forced to abandon."

"Enough with the MMORPG, Langley." Nevin sighed heavily. "A new router is not in the budget."

"The MM-O-what?" I asked.

"Massively multiplayer online role-playing games. Obviously," Drew explained, irritation evident in his voice. "I thought everyone knew that."

My cheeks flushed. *I* didn't know that. God! How was I expected to know all the acronyms? This was like that time I didn't know how to pronounce *meme*, but worse. Because the way Drew explained things just made me feel like the dumbest idiot alive. I wished I could blend into the scenery like a chameleon. Or shoot spikes out of my body like a porcupine. Actually, that would be much better. Drew would probably benefit from a good porcupining.

"Anyone else?" Nevin asked.

Rhys raised his hand. "I'm really emotionally concerned about how sweaty I am."

"Invalid," Nevin dismissed him.

"You can't invalidate someone's emotional circle time!" Heidi gasped.

"Next!" Nevin prompted.

"I am extremely emotionally concerned about the invalidation of someone's emotional concern!" Heidi's hand shot back up in the air defiantly, her gray eyes flashing with indignation. "You can't set up an emotional safe space and then construct parameters about which feelings are valid and which aren't. Doing so destroys the safe space!"

"No insubordination during Circle Time!" Nevin yelled.

Drew slumped over with his hand on his mouth, like he was trying to suppress something. Amy sat silent and tense, white-lipped.

"Now, now, now," Noah drawled, placing a soothing hand on Heidi's back and rubbing it slowly. I could see her visibly relax as he touched her, her breathing coming smooth and even. Then again, I can't imagine how anything with a pulse wouldn't relax when getting a back rub from Noah. He had the kind of hands that made me think he played guitar. Very, very well. "Why don't we all just center, focus, and see if there's anything we really want to talk about."

"I have a problem with my room," Drew broke in after a few moments of silence, un-slumping. "It doesn't have a bed."

"Bullshit," I coughed.

Drew glared at me. I coughed a few more times for effect. You know, really selling that cough that just happened to sound like "bullshit."

"I was promised a single bedroom," he continued. "And it—"

"Wait a minute," I interrupted. "Why do *you* get a single? That's not fair."

"Trust me, we don't mind," Rhys exaggeratedly stage-whispered to me behind his hand.

"I have very bad allergies!" Drew contested hotly.

"Sure you do," I said dryly. "Allergies. Why exactly does that preclude you from sharing a room?"

"Because . . . because of allergies!" he insisted. "I'm allergic to feathers. And dust. Dust mites. Dust motes."

Well, that didn't answer my question. At all. I still wasn't buying it. I opened my mouth to respond, and—

"A mote it is, to trouble the mind's eye," Langley declaimed before I could say anything.

"You have your single." Nevin held up his hand for silence, completely ignoring Langley. "What's the issue?"

"It's not a bed. I was promised a bedroom. Emphasis on *bed*. I have a cot. A rollaway cot."

"Are you *joking*?" My jaw dropped. "What do you think the rest of us are sleeping on? Bald Mountain Boat House isn't exactly the Four Seasons."

"No. Invalid," Nevin shook his head.

"Wait a minute—"

"You can't just invalidate—"

As Drew and Heidi started talking at the same time, Nevin picked up his bugle and played a single earsplitting blast.

"Can we start rehearsing this damn thing now?" Nevin asked, lowering the bugle.

"Finally," I sighed.

"Preach it, sister," Langley agreed.

"Everyone! On your feet for vocal warmups!" Nevin ordered.

As we worked our way through various exercises, hitting the consonants with explosive precision on the tongue twisters, filling our diaphragms with air to exhale on vowels, long and loud and clear, I could feel myself start to come alive as my voice did, rich and round and strong.

Now, time for my favorite one. Shaking out the jaw! I clasped my hands together in front of me and shook, keeping my jaw loose, as my teeth chattered in my head.

"Actually, Nevin?"

"Yes, Drew?" Nevin sighed. I could tell his patience was wearing thin.

"That's not the optimal way to loosen your jaw. You're all doing it wrong." Oh *were* we now? Were we all doing it wrong? It was only day two, and I was already so tired of being corrected by this smug know-it-all. "If you grasp the bottom of your chin, it's much more effective. Like this."

He demonstrated. He looked insane, but it's impossible to look sane and shake out your jaw.

"Thanks, Drew," Nevin said flatly. Wrong. Hmph. I'd shake out my jaw however I damn well pleased.

"Uh, Heidi," Drew interrupted again.

"Mmm?" She paused mid-shake.

"That's still wrong. You're not letting your jaw relax enough to really keep it loose."

"I'll keep working on it. Thanks." She smiled wanly. Whoa! That was as close to frosty as I could possibly imagine Heidi being. Clearly, I wasn't the only one Drew was getting to with his know-it-all ways. Even the supremely serene Heidi was having her patience tested. God, if *Heidi* was having problems working with Drew, then there was no hope for me. No one had ever called me serene. Or patient.

Once our voices were limber and warm, Nevin instructed us to sit again. "Now, this is the point where we'd have a read-through of the script in a normal rehearsal process," he began, "but since you all came to Dunmore off-book—as you better have done, or woe to you"—he glared at each of us in turn—"we shan't be simply reading today."

"If you're not off-book, we're not opposed to corporal punishment," Langley piped up cheerily.

"Well put." I had the feeling that although Langley was kidding, Nevin wasn't. "So we're having a script-less read-through. A non-read-through."

"A line-through?" Amy asked.

"NOT A LINE-THROUGH!" Nevin thundered as Amy quailed in fear. "What I mean by that"—he cleared his throat—"is don't just recite the lines by rote. Explore them.

Enjoy them. Start testing the theatrical waters. Understood? Begin."

Heidi closed her eyes and took a deep breath. She began, her voice ringing out over the valley:

"Gentlemen, importune me no farther,
For how I firmly am resolved you know;
That is, not bestow my youngest daughter
Before I have a husband for the elder."

Before I knew it, Rhys was delivering my cue line, as one of the suitors imploring Baptista (a.k.a. Heidi) to marry my sister Bianca (a.k.a. Amy) despite Baptista's best efforts to get someone to marry Kate (a.k.a. me). I took a breath, and with as much sass as I could muster, I said:

"I pray you, sir, is it your will
To make a stale of me amongst these mates?"

And we were off. Everyone knew their lines perfectly, and as we progressed, the show got better and better as everyone relaxed. The only surprises came when we discovered that in addition to company managing, Langley was playing a few of the minor roles, including Bianca's suitor Gremio. Hmm. I wondered what the hell they were going to do with that hair. That definitely wasn't a hue they'd had in Shakespeare's day. And the biggest surprise of all came in Act One, Scene Two, with the introduction of Drew as Petruchio. And as much as it pained me, I had to grudgingly admit that he was good. Really, really good. Dammit.

Although, the only thing worse than him actually being good would have been if he was insufferable *and sucked*. I could put up with insufferable if it meant I got some quality acting in exchange.

We flew through the script. I was enjoying myself so much that I was almost surprised when we reached the end and Noah said wryly, "'Tis a wonder, by your leave, she will be tamed so."

Clap.

Clap.

Clap.

CHAPTER 6

Well done." Nevin stood up and finished his slow clap.
"Oh, well done," Langley echoed. "I commend your
pains, and everyone shall share in the gains!"

"The gains she speaks of are lunch," Nevin added. "We're
taking an hour. Langley will point you in the direction of feed,
and I expect you back promptly in sixty minutes for Bard Boot
Camp: the Text Session!" Fire blazed in his eyes. "Dismissed!"

Nevin turned and went out the way he came in, through
the arch. Maybe he lived back there. Like a troll under a
bridge.

"Come on, peeps." Langley stood up. "I'll show you to the
Bait 'n' Bite. There's a deli inside."

"What else is there?" Drew asked.

"You know, regular grocery stuff, pretty decent ice
cream . . . there's a pizza parlor annex. . . ." Langley started
walking, and we followed.

"No, I mean, what other options are there?"

"That's pretty much it." She shrugged.

"Our only option is the Bait 'n' Bite?" He sneered, like the words tasted bad in his mouth.

"You're no longer in the big city of . . . Rye," I said dryly. Was he too good for sandwiches? Who didn't like sandwiches? What a prima donna.

"It's still New York," he muttered mulishly as we followed Langley down the road.

When we approached the Bait 'n' Bite, a couple of familiar-looking figures were draped over the porch in front of it.

"Amy." I sidestepped over to poke her. "Are those—"

"The skater guys." Her eyes grew round.

"Biblical plague," Drew sniffed.

"Where you're concerned, a few boils might improve things," I said sweetly.

"This is ridiculous. You can barely make it up the stairs," Drew grumbled, pushing his way through the skaters and marching up to the Bait 'n' Bite.

"Hey, easy, homes!" one of the skaters called as the rest laughed. I was pretty sure it was the same one who had talked back to Nevin.

Langley, Rhys, Noah, and Heidi followed in Drew's wake. Amy and I hung back slightly, slowly approaching the stairs. Clearly, we were both thinking the exact same thing: it was time to make contact.

"So, what are you?" the same skater addressed me, eyes raking over my Camo T-shirt. "You Girl Scouts, or something? Cuz I'd take some cookies."

"We're a little old for Girl Scouts, don't you think?" I said tartly.

"Duuuude, watch out." Another one with enormous, lengthy dreads leaned forward. "This one'll schralp you!"

"Oh my God, is that a rat?" Amy squeaked, pointing to dreads-guy's shoulder. Sure enough, there was a furry little creature perched on his shoulder.

"Easy, Betty, it's a ferret," he explained, as the ferret dove into his dreads. Gross.

"Oh, uh, it's Amy, actually," she corrected him.

"Well, Amy, I'm Taylor." The first guy who spoke tipped his hat up farther as he introduced himself. "This is Ferret. Behind me are Skittles, Thiago, JJ, and Ragner."

Each waved in turn. They were an interesting bunch. Skittles was swallowed up by an enormous splatter-paint hoodie, Thiago's hand-knitted cap was pulled so low you could barely see his eyes, JJ was shirtless, and Ragner was blonder than Amy.

"Hei hei." Ragner smiled. "Meget hyggelig."

"See this guy, Betty?" Taylor slung his arm around Ragner's shoulder. "He's, like, the Prince of Norway."

"Ooo, a prince . . ." Amy's mouth formed a perfectly round O.

"He said 'like' the prince," I whispered.

Her *ooo* rapidly transformed into a more wistful *ohh*. "But maybe that means like an earl or something," she whispered back.

"Or something," I agreed. They were all definitely something.

"What's your name, Red?" Taylor turned to me, and smiled. He was so tan his teeth were blindingly white. Actually, all of him was kind of blinding. He shook his shaggy blondish hair out of his eyes, highlights glinting in the sun like he'd just stepped off the beach. Taylor was probably the hottest guy I'd ever seen in the flesh. Emphasis on flesh—he had amazingly well-defined arms under his graphic tee. And I was willing to bet everything else was pretty well-defined, too.

"Cadet Cass," I saluted.

"Wait, are you guys really military?" Ferret furrowed his brow. "Is this like some Charlie's Angels shit?"

"Oh no, you've blown our cover," I said sarcastically. "Now the mission's been compromised."

"Jigga-whaaaaa." Ferret's jaw dropped.

"She's messing with you, bra." Taylor laughed. "Who's been schralped by the Betty now?"

"I hope you end up on the wrong end of an ass-knife, Griffith!" Ferret grumped as the ferret snuggled consolingly against his cheek.

"Ass-knifes only happen to BGLs like you, knuckle-dragger." Taylor smirked. "Who's been nutted at the last two X-Games?"

"Your mom, Griffith," Ferret sulked. "Your mom got nutted." He retreated around the corner of the Bait 'n' Bite while the rest of them laughed.

So maybe I only understood about half of what was being said. But I understood that Taylor—Griffith—whatever—was undeniably hot.

"If you're no angel, Cass" — Taylor turned to me — "what are you doing way up here in the middle of the woods?"

"We work at Shakespeare at Dunmore."

"What, you an actress, Red?" He straightened.

"We both are," Amy said.

"Dag, that's ill, Betty!" He leapt off the steps to join me in the dirt at the bottom. "This shit is mad timely!"

"Speaking of mad timely." I looked up as a new voice interrupted. Langley was standing at the top of the stairs, chewing contemplatively on half a sandwich. "You guys had better order your sandwiches or you won't have a lunch break."

"But we're —"

"Now, Cass," she warned, making her way down the stairs, ducking neatly under Skittles's arm as he tried to block her path. "We've still gotta walk back."

"Fine, fine," I acquiesced, as Noah, Rhys, Drew, and Heidi made their way down the stairs, Drew glowering darkly as Heidi shot us disapproving, mom-type looks. Or the kind of looks I imagine other people's moms would shoot. Mine would probably have been trying to do a flip trick on one of their skateboards by this point. Or she would have, before she went crazy and did nothing but lock herself in her room, listening to Norah Jones for hours on end. When, you know, she wasn't destroying public property.

"That your warden?" Taylor asked.

"Hot warden," Skittles commented. Clearly, as evidenced by his hoodie, the man was attracted to bright colors. Langley must have been his perfect woman.

"Kind of our warden, I guess." I shrugged, as Amy and I moved up the stairs to get our sandwiches. Langley waited at the bottom, tapping her watch while masticating her sandwich.

"Wait, Cass." Taylor grabbed my wrist, bringing me face to face with surprisingly clear blue eyes and warm, tanned skin. "I've got some ill shit to talk to you about. Ill important shit." He nodded, like that explained anything.

"Sandwich!" Langley yelled.

"Cass, let's go." Amy tugged on my arm nervously. "I really, really don't want to be late."

"Do you enjoy getting me in trouble?" I asked Taylor, placing my free hand on my hip.

"Redheads are nothing but trouble," he said softly, pulling on one of my springy red curls and watching it bounce. He pulled a Sharpie out of his baggy shorts and before I could stop him, on the underside of my forearm, he wrote TAYLOR GRIFFITH. SEGUNKI CABIN.

"SANDWICH!" Langley yelled again.

"Find me, Red," he whispered as Amy pulled me into the store. "Or I'll find you."

"Bowser!" one of the guys outside howled. Then they all did this weird *bow-ow-ow* dog howl, like a pack of wolves. Sexy wolves, but still. Strange.

"Ohhhhh emmmmmm geeeee." Amy exhaled as the doors to the Bait 'n' Bite swung shut behind us. "H. O. T. T."

"Has their hotness robbed you of the ability to speak in anything but letters?"

"Pretty much." She nodded as we approached the deli counter.

"Understandable," I agreed as we surveyed our options.

"Taylor certainly seems to like you," she remarked after we'd ordered, a twinkle in her eyes.

"Doubt it." I shrugged as I walked over to claim my turkey sandwich. "He didn't even ask for my number."

"Obvi," Amy said smugly as she picked up her sandwich. "This place is a total cell phone dead zone, remember? There's no point in getting your number; he can't call you. Instead he did something much more . . . indelible." She poked my arm.

"He probably was just looking for something to tattoo." I blushed as we pushed open the door. All the skaters had cleared out in the time we'd been getting our sandwiches. As soon as we hit the ground, Langley started speed-walking back to rehearsal, the rest of us trailing behind.

"Nah-uh." Amy shook her head. "Don't you see? It's so romantic! Like old-fashioned times!" She clasped her turkey sandwich to her heart. "Deprived of cell phones, he has to make bold statements to declare his love! To fight for you! To *say* what he feels instead of typing, bravely exposed without the cover of text messages!"

"You're kind of a nut, you know that?" I arched my eyebrow.

"You're kind of a skeptic." She slung her arm around my shoulder as we walked. "But I'll convert you. Love is *fun*, Cass."

"*Fun!*" I snorted. "I *know* you've read enough Shakespeare to know that is just not true."

"Oh, come on. Romeo and Juliet had, like, four whole acts of super fun times before the really serious shit went down," she teased. "Live a little."

By this time Heidi had wound her way to the back of the group, demanding a full update. Unlike Amy and me, however, she wasn't so convinced that meeting the skaters had been a good thing.

"I still think they're trouble." Heidi shook her head as we approached the rehearsal space.

"Why? Because Nevin said so?" I asked. "Who cares what he thinks?"

"No, it's just a . . . feeling." She shook her head. "And I'm usually very intuitive about people."

"Thanks for the warning." I started tearing into my sandwich. "But I'm pretty sure I can fend for myself."

Heidi looked dubious, but Amy and I were too busy devouring our sandwiches to be too concerned.

We had more than enough time to eat and make it back to rehearsal. When we returned, Nevin stood in the middle of the stage holding a slim stack of sheets of paper, a few heavy books at his feet. Once we hit the stage, he instructed us to sit and handed the papers to Langley, who passed them around the circle. I looked down at mine.

Ugghhhhh.

It was my least favorite part of the entire play. Really, the only part of the play I didn't like. Kate's last monologue. After she's been "tamed," she gives this whole terrible speech about subservience and obeying your husband and placing your hand below his foot and how women are weak and all this other horrible bullshit. I hate, hate, hate it.

"You undoubtedly recognize what you see before you," Nevin said. "Each of you has one of your monologues from the play. Langley will pass out pencils. Mark out everything in iambic pentameter. Scan it for rhythm and meter. Look up any words you don't know in these dictionaries." He gestured to the books at his feet. "You will know these monologues better than you know yourselves!"

A bit dramatic. But it was what I was coming to expect from Nevin. Dutifully, I grabbed a pencil from Langley and began dissecting the hated text. When you scan something, you mark it into syllables, making notes of which syllables are stressed. Like in Shakespeare, all lines go ba DUM ba DUM ba DUM ba DUM ba DUM. And if it doesn't work out like that, it means he's trying to tell you something—like maybe your character is really emotionally choked up or something. It's important to find the very few places where things don't scan out, because they almost always have a special meaning.

We all worked diligently, almost in complete silence, except when I inadvertently muttered particularly offensive lines under my breath. "I am ashamed that women are so simple," I grumbled. "Place your hands below your husband's foot . . . ridiculous."

After what felt like hours had passed, Nevin stopped us and had us clear the stage. We were now going to perform our monologues for each other. Rhys went first. After he finished,

Nevin asked him questions about it, encouraging all of us to share our opinions. Everybody else went through the same thing. Heidi. Noah. Amy. Drew, thankfully, had not been given the monologue in which he calls Kate "my ass," but instead the one where he describes how he's going to tame the shrew. As he finished the monologue with "He that knows better how to tame a shrew, now let him speak," I had to grudgingly admit—again—that he was really good. He had that unnamable magnetic quality that drew you to him onstage; you had to watch. And weirdest of all, he was even funny. Onstage Drew couldn't have been more different than offstage Drew.

Then it was my turn. I hopped on stage and recited the monologue, my tongue trying to rebel as it formed the stupid words.

"Now, why are you saying this?" Nevin asked after I'd finished.

"I have no idea."

"You don't understand?" he asked.

"Oh, I understand what the monologue's saying," I clarified. "I just don't understand why I—she—Kate—me— whatever—is saying it. The Kate we've known for the past five acts would never say this. Never. It feels like a betrayal of her character." I folded my arms. "I hate it."

"Thoughts, everyone?" Nevin opened the field to questions.

"A concession to a patriarchal time whose gender norms our modern minds can't condone or process," Heidi began eagerly. Someone was ready to discuss gender in performance.

"I think it's about a foot fetish," Rhys piped in. "You know, all that 'place your hand below your husband's foot' business."

"I agree with Heidi. I think it was just a different time," Noah nodded.

"What if she's speaking out of love?" Drew asked, tilting his head to the side.

"Love?" I spat. "That's your idea of love? Total submission?"

"No." He shook his head. "Right before, Petruchio bet these other guys that his wife would be the only one who comes when called. And it turns out, she is the only one who comes. Why? Because she's got his back. That's what you do when you love someone. You back them up, even if you don't always agree with them. You're there when it matters. And despite the hell they put each other through, by the end of the play, Kate and Petruchio love each other. So even if she might not believe what she says, she says it, because she knows it's important to him. She would put her hand under his foot if he asked, but at the same time, she's also trusting him not to."

Total silence fell over the rehearsal space. That was remarkably introspective and almost sentimental, especially considering the source.

"Upon further consideration," I swallowed throatily, "I think she's just being sarcastic."

"All valid theories many scholars have posited. Except for the foot fetish." Nevin stroked his goatee thoughtfully.

"Kate's realized what their game is," I continued, picking up steam. "What all these men want. And the only way to win their game is to give them what they want, but in a way so over the top that she knows that she's mocking them. After all"—I looked straight at Drew—"Kate gets the last word, doesn't she?"

Silence. Ha! For once, Drew had nothing to say.

The shrew was right. There was no better victory than getting the last word.

CHAPTER 7

"Oh my god," Amy whispered.

All six of us were standing stock-still, staring at the detritus in front of us. We'd reported bright and early for rehearsal, but there was nothing bright about what greeted us that morning.

"Apocalypse theater," Rhys lamented. "This is disgusting."

The grassy area in front of the stage where the audience would sit, once we had one, was covered in trash. Mangled pizza boxes. Half-eaten peppers and onions. Plastic bags coated in some oily brown substance I couldn't name—and didn't want to. It was absolutely foul.

"How did all this trash get here?" Heidi asked.

"It doesn't just smell like trash." Amy wrinkled her nose. "It kinda smells like . . ."

"POOP!" Rhys screamed. "There's a big giant poop! Right in front of the stage! Oh God, what if this is my entrance? And there's poop!"

"Who did this?" Amy asked, ashen.

"It was the skaters!" Drew claimed. "Just like Nevin warned us. They threw trash everywhere, and then they—they—"

"They ate half of it, vommed the rest up, and pooped in front of the stage?" I finished skeptically. "That seems highly unlikely."

"Yep, that kind of fecal matter only comes from a critter," Noah said evenly, squatting down to examine it. "Bear, by the looks of it. Explains the trash, too. Must've gotten into the dumpster behind that big ol' barn and come over here to enjoy himself."

"How nice for him that we provided this bathroom," I grumbled.

"Bears must *hate* Shakespeare." Rhys shook his head sadly.

"You think this was some kind of bear-thespian hate crime?" I asked archly.

"Or just some kind of thespian hate crime," Drew muttered.

"You're not still clinging to your insane skater theory, are you?" I pointed to the poop. "Noah's right. No human made this. This thing is the size of a cow pattie. Or a Boston cream pie."

"Oh, gross." Amy blanched. "I'm never eating a Boston cream pie again."

"I'm not sure I'm ever eating again." Rhys had turned a rather unbecoming shade of green. I just hoped he'd keep it together. I could not deal with human barf on top of bear barf. There are limits to what even the not-particularly squeamish among us can endure.

"Producing waste is part of the cycle of life," Heidi said consolingly. "It's natural. What comes out of the earth goes back into the earth. All this litter, however . . ."

Langley walked through the archway, holding a trash bag, a shovel, and several pairs of latex gloves.

"That better not mean what I think it means," I murmured.

"What does it mean?" Amy asked.

"It means they expect us to clean up all this shit," Drew answered. "No way. Absolutely not."

"Captain Negative is right." Langley started handing out the gloves. "We have to clean all of this up."

"Where's Nevin?" I asked.

"Nevin's not coming out to start rehearsal until all the trash and, uh, poop, is gone."

"This is ridiculous," Drew muttered. I hated to admit it, but I kind of agreed with him. I couldn't believe they were making us clean up bear poop! Maybe there was no one else to do it, but this was so not in the apprenticeship description.

"I'm allergic to latex," Drew said as Langley held out a pair of gloves.

"No you're not!" I challenged. "You are so unbelievably full of shit—"

"Guess who's not full of shit—that bear! Well, not anymore." Rhys giggled, clearly becoming hysterical at the prospect of having to come in contact with the horrors before us.

"You're just too lazy to pitch in and help!" I continued.

"Latex allergy is a real thing," Drew countered.

"Oh, I know it's a real thing." I held out the glove. "I just don't believe you have it."

"I'm not putting that on." He stared down the glove.

"Fine." I took it back. "Have fun scooping up poop with your bare hands."

"Your bear hands!" Rhys made claws. "Get it? Bear hands?"

"Too soon." I shook my head.

Langley, Rhys, Amy, and I started gingerly picking up trash with our latex-gloved hands and pitching it into the garbage bags. Heidi and Noah, as the only two people not completely repulsed by it, took up the shovel and started scooping the poop away. Drew, arms folded, watched the events take place. With each piece of decomposing pepper I picked up, I got madder and madder. How dare he just sit back and watch? What, did he think he was better than the rest of us? Who was he, to stand there and not help?

By the time we finished, I just couldn't take it anymore. I pulled off my gloves and marched straight up to him.

"You are an unbelievable asshole, you know that?"

"Why? Because I wouldn't clean up shit?" He snorted in disbelief. "What's the problem? Sheriff Woody and Jessie the Yodeling Cowgirl took care of it."

"Don't call them that," I spat at him, looking over at Noah and Heidi rinsing off the shovel in the lake. Luckily they were far enough away that they couldn't have overheard. "What on earth could have possibly given you such an enormous sense of entitlement that you didn't think you should have to help?"

"None of us should have had to do it." He shook his head. "It's not our job. They're not paying—well, intern stipending—us to clean up trash. We all should have refused. Together. Then no one could have made us."

"What was that you said?" I cupped a hand to my ear. "We're interns. That's right. We're not in the Actors' Union. We're not Tony nominees. We're not Meryl Streep. We are at the very bottom of a very big pile in this industry. And to work your way up, sometimes you have to deal with shit. Literally." I dropped the gloves at his feet. "If you can't handle it maybe you're on the wrong career path."

I spun on my heel and marched back toward the stage. Seriously. Who did he think he was? Being part of a show was all about being part of a team. Ensemble building, as Heidi would have said. We all needed to work together. And honestly, if we didn't clean this all up, who would have? At the end of the day, this was our show. Our space. We were responsible for it. Except someone clearly wanted no part of teamwork or responsibility. What a lazy jerk. Although not quite as lazy as Nevin, who emerged from behind the archways as Langley marched toward the dumpsters, trash bag slung over her shoulder like the Santa Claus of garbage.

I crossed my arms over my chest and glared at Nevin. He held a canvas tote bag that undoubtedly contained something torturous.

"Obstacles to great art are innumerable and often unforeseen." Nevin stroked his goatee meditatively. "And often times unpleasant. Well done clearing the hurdle before you," he said approvingly, as if this had been some sort of theater challenge. Despite my impassioned speech to Drew about cleaning up shit, I was really not pleased with the whole situation. Nevin, unfortunately, seemed impervious to my usually effective death glare. I glanced over at Amy, who seemed on the verge of tears and kept furtively sniffing herself, trying to detect if any of the trash odors had settled on her.

Langley returned, garbage disposed of. "Time to hand 'em out, chief?" she asked Nevin.

"What did I tell you about 'chief'?" Nevin muttered in a threatening undertone. "And yes, Langley," he said at full volume, "you may hand the women their corsets."

"Aye, aye, Cap'n." From the look on his face, Nevin seemed to like *cap'n* even less than *chief.*

"Cor-whats?" I asked.

"Ooo!" Amy clapped her hands with delight as Langley pulled out a white satin brocade corset with thick straps and a faint flower pattern. Small hooks and eyes marched up the front and nylon laces crisscrossed the back. Amy eagerly reached out for it as Langley handed it to her.

"Okay now." Heidi held up her hands. "Let's just take a minute now, shall we, before we force our natural bodies into these unnatural shapes? This—this garment," she said disdainfully, "represents centuries of the subjugation of women. It represents female enslavement at the hands of the male gaze. It represents everything our mothers, and their mothers, and their mothers and sisters, have fought to free us from—"

"Forget about subjugation, that just looks really uncomfortable," I interrupted as Langley held out a red brocade corset in my general direction. Red. Again. Shocker. "Why do we have to wear those?"

"Rehearsal corsets are necessary to give you the proper posture and bearing of a woman of Shakespeare's time," Nevin said evenly. "They're not optional. They will inform your characters."

"This confinement will inform our inner characters," Heidi said sadly. "Inform them in incarceration."

"A woman of Shakespeare's time wouldn't have known that," Nevin said.

"A woman of Shakespeare's time wouldn't have been on-stage," I countered. "What's with the sudden concern for historical accuracy?"

"Won't you stop whining and put on the damn thing?" Drew groused.

"I don't see you having to spend a summer without breathing!" I retorted. "I bet you'd whine, too!"

"We're wasting rehearsal time," Drew said shortly.

Sulkily, I snatched the red corset out of Langley's hands. I turned it over, looking at the tag. It read: TARTE TATIN TEMPTATIONS. Historical accuracy my ass. This was a Halloween costume or some kind of weird sex underwear.

"Just put yourself in the mindset of a woman in the late sixteenth century," Nevin said soothingly to Heidi. "You wouldn't have known anything else. This is your life."

"For historical accuracy?" Heidi cocked her head. Nevin nodded. "Oh, process. Fine, for historical accuracy," she sighed, and held out her hands. Langley gave her a corset just like mine and Amy's, but in purple. "Forgive me, sisters"—Heidi shook her head as she held it up—"for they know not what they do."

Drew rolled his eyes. "Can we do something now? Like rehearse, maybe?"

"In good time," Nevin said. "Langley, help the ladies, please."

We loosened our laces and undid the hooks. I pulled the corset over my tank top like a vest, eyes lingering on the dark smudge of Taylor's name that a shower hadn't quite erased, and did up the hooks in the front.

Was I really going to find him? "Taylor Griffith, Segunki Cabin" had been blazed into my brain, but I wasn't sure how I felt about wandering into a rando camp to stalk down a man. That seemed like behavior more befitting of . . . Heather. I was no predatory blonde. I tossed my head, resolute. If he wanted me, he could come find me.

We formed a little corset train. Amy laced up Heidi's, I laced up Amy's, and Langley laced up mine. With each yank of the nylon strings, I could feel my lungs collapsing.

"How are we supposed to breathe in these?" I gasped. "Breathing's kind of important when you're acting. Because you're, you know, talking and stuff."

"It'll force you to use your diaphragm," Nevin retorted. "Tighter, Langley."

"Oh, sure, lungs are overrated," I grumbled, unconsciously yanking Amy's strings a little tighter than was necessary. She yelped.

Nevin marched up and down the line, commanding us to pull tighter. I could hear Heidi whimpering softly at the front.

"Tighter, Cass," he ordered.

"Isn't this tight enough?" I exclaimed, pointing to the sides of Amy's corset. "These bitches are straight up meeting."

"Adequate," he nodded. Really, there was nowhere else for that corset to go! That was as tight as it got. The pale yellow cotton of her sundress was all bunched up, and her shoulder blades looked uncomfortably close together. "Tie them up. That's good enough."

I tied Amy's strings in a sloppy bow and tucked the extra length inside her corset. Corsets are weird. They are not sexy. Sure, they push up your boobs and make your waist look smaller, but that extra waist has to go somewhere. You end up with a weird blob of back fat and all of your displaced waist shooting out under the corset. It doesn't matter how skinny you are, it just happens. And it's gross. Luckily, Langley then pulled three long, black rehearsal skirts out of Nevin's canvas bag, which covered the corset-produced muffin top hanging out over my shorts.

"So, what do the boys have to wear?" I asked once I'd pulled my skirt over my head.

"Boots, but we won't need those until we get closer to opening," Nevin said. "They're fine for now."

"Can you help me muster up a little feminist outrage here?" I asked Heidi.

"I am a woman of my times," Heidi muttered, like a mantra. "It is fifteen ninety-four and I know naught but what I know."

"Thanks for your help," I sighed.

"Now that the ladies are finished discussing their wardrobe, can we start?" Drew raised his hand. Ugh, that smug, patronizing—

"I couldn't agree more," Nevin said. "Actors, to the stage."

Nevin and Langley retreated to the small tent where they sat behind a table, Langley's binder opened before her, poised to take notes. Everyone but Drew was in the first scene, so he had to sit backstage all alone. Too bad for him.

Noah entered, and Nevin spent a long time going over his monologue about why he was new in Padua and what he was doing there. Then everyone else entered, Heidi explaining why no one could marry Amy until someone married me, and we were off with a bang.

Early rehearsals often have more to do with traffic patterns than with acting. Nevin was mostly concerned with blocking the first few scenes, making sure everyone knew where they were going and that no one ran into each other. Once we'd blocked the first fifteen pages, we went through them several times, focusing more on the relationships between the characters and the language of the text. I was having such a good time I almost forgot about the sharp pain in my ribcage. By the time we broke for lunch, it had subsided into a dull ache.

"Are we supposed to eat in these?" I asked Langley skeptically as the group started moving toward the Bait 'n' Bite.

"You don't have enough time to get in and out. It's too much of a pain in the ass. I'm certainly not following you around playing wardrobe assistant," she replied.

"You know what else is a pain in the ass? Going out in public dressed like this," I muttered.

"Come on, they're not that bad," Amy said consolingly as she swiped on some lip gloss. "They're kind of pretty!"

"Pretty embarrassing," I replied. "I hope those skaters aren't there."

"Why not?" Amy asked, surprised. "I was hoping they would be! Hello, cleavage city!"

"I don't want them to think we dressed this way intentionally! We look like Goth girls going to the prom."

"We look like imprisoned sisters of an unenlightened age," Heidi chimed in.

Amy rolled her eyes good-naturedly and looped her arms through mine and Heidi's, like we were in *The Wizard of Oz*. "I think we look hot," she said, smiling. "So, Cass, did you track down Taylor like he asked?"

"What, was I supposed to climb out the window last night?" I laughed. "If he wants me so badly, he can come find me." I tossed my head, shaking my hair back from my face. Mm-hmm. Miss Independent. That's me.

"He certainly seems to have left his mark on you," Amy said with a twinkle.

"Literally," Heidi added dryly, rubbing the grayish smudge on my arm where he'd written his name.

My heart sped up a bit as we approached the Bait 'n' Bite, but there was not a skater to be seen on its faded porch. No. Bad Cass, I reprimanded myself. I was not going to let myself get all freaked out about some guy. Because no guy was worth that. Even one as hot as Taylor Griffith.

"The vegetarian options in the Bait 'n' Bite are sadly lacking," Heidi said once she'd ordered her LT sandwich.

"Maybe this'll be the summer you turn carnivore." I grinned. "Extra bacon on mine, please," I told the bored high schooler behind the deli counter who was eyeing our corsets strangely. Heidi shook her head and glared with exaggerated disapproval.

After collecting our sandwiches, we headed back to the shore of the lake, forming a little circle to eat lunch in. I lowered myself awkwardly to a sitting position. That stupid corset made even basic movement difficult.

I don't think I had ever in my life not finished a sandwich before, but it felt like my stomach had evaporated along with my waist. I wrapped the rest up to eat later and dropped it in my bag. Heidi had been right—this corset was an unholy prison. I would mow that sandwich the minute I was free.

CHAPTER 8

Lunch break was criminally short, and before I knew it, Langley was herding us back to rehearsal. We spent the first part of the afternoon blocking further into the play, preparing for a later run of what we'd done so far.

Several hours later, when it was time to do the run, I followed the rest of the cast onstage and looked out over the field, surprised to see Taylor Griffith and the skaters sitting on top of a picnic table in the middle of the town square. If I'd expected anyone to come see this sloppy first run, it was Lola St. Clair—who had apparently disappeared—not the skater boy brigade. I pinched Amy surreptitiously, and she elbowed me back in response.

I hadn't known it was possible for anyone to look sexy while eating a giant bag of Cheetos and chugging Red Bull, but damn, that boy looked good. He and the others sat on the picnic table and watched us for most of the run. I could see Nevin glancing over at them agitatedly the entire time, but since they weren't technically in his rehearsal space, he couldn't get up and yell at them. Needless to say, it was not my best work. It was all a little bit distracting. Particularly when Taylor decided to take off his shirt.

Unfortunately, by the time we finished the run, wrote down Nevin's notes, packed up our things, and helped Langley clean up the rehearsal space, the skaters were long gone. But I was far too excited about my liberation to be upset by their absence. I ripped the corset off and breathed deeply. Ah, bliss. I dug through my bag like a rabid badger and shoved my sandwich in my mouth.

"Hungry?" Drew smirked.

"Shmmeruppf oddint aff wrrr corsh odunnoow!" I hissed through a mouthful of sandwich.

"Shall I compare thee to a summer's day? Though art more lovely and more temperate!" Drew quoted sarcastically and strode away.

"He is *so annoying*!" I thundered once I'd swallowed.

"Don't pay any attention to him. You are perfectly lovely. And you let your appetite be free!" Heidi said fiercely. "Appetite for life, appetite for food. Society tells us we women should deny ourselves, but it is time to be hungry! Hungry for everything!"

"Don't worry, I won't let that asshat ruin my sandwich," I vowed as I swallowed my last bite and crumpled the wrappings into a ball.

"Should we go back to the house?" Amy asked somewhat breathlessly. I looked up from my sandwich wrappings ball.

Whoa. She was glowing like she was lit from within. I'd never before seen someone whose eyes were literally sparkling.

We quickly walked back to the boathouse and the group dispersed, wandering to the kitchen or the lounge. Noah invited us all to join him on a run, but everyone demurred. Fitness. Meh.

Amy always had a bit of the Disney Princess thing going on, but right then she was especially out of control. Her walk back to the boathouse had been more of a skip. She kept humming and sighing at random intervals, gazing dreamily into the distance. Something was up.

"All right, Cinderella," I asked once the three of us had made it safely into our room and I shut the door behind. "What's up? I'm half expecting you to burst into song and for cartoon birds to alight on your fingertips."

"I wouldn't be surprised if they did." She giggled. "Oh, Connor breaking up with me was the best thing that ever happened to me. I think"—she blushed, eyes shining—"I think . . . I think I'm in love!"

"Love!" Heidi clasped her hands to her chest with delight.

"*Love?*" Oh, brother. "While I am completely thrilled that you're over Douchey McTexterson, I think it would be in your best interest if you dialed it down like five hundred notches."

"Oh, psshh, don't listen to her." Heidi waved one of her giant elegant hands in my face. "There's nothing more beautiful than falling with an open heart."

"Emphasis on falling," I muttered. "When did this start? When we saw the skate guys at the Bait 'n' Bite? They looked good today, tanning on the picnic tables."

"No, no." Amy shook her head. "Don't get me wrong, the Prince of Norway is super hot and everything, but, um . . . no . . . it was at rehearsal . . ."

"Ohhh." Heidi's eyes lit up with understanding. "Noah is really nice, isn't he?"

"As nice as a guy can be, I guess," I shrugged. "And damn if he doesn't have that sexy cowboy thing going on."

Heidi nodded enthusiastically.

"Wait—what?" Amy crinkled her nose and blushed. "No, no, it's not Noah. He's really nice, and he's cute, and all, but it's—it's Drew," she sighed, blushing harder.

"Oh," Heidi said, her voice wavering as she tried to smile.

"No," I said flatly. "No, no, and no. Absolutely not."

"Wait—what—why?" Amy's lip wobbled dangerously.

"Did you even talk to him?" I asked.

"Yes! Well, sort of," she hedged. "I'm not sure it counted as a conversation, exactly, but words were exchanged, so I think that—"

"No. Not a Drew," I said firmly. "Anything but that. Not a Drew!"

"What do you mean, 'a Drew'?" Heidi asked.

"Yeah. What's 'a Drew'?" Amy chimed in.

"A Drew, a Drew—you know! A Drew!" I said emphatically. "You know the type." The girls stared at me blankly. I heaved an almighty sigh. "Seriously? Were you doing theater under a rock?"

"Under a Boulder," Heidi said, poker-faced. "Boulder, Colorado."

Amy giggled.

"Guys, focus." Now was not the time to be distracted by location-based puns. "A Drew is a guy who's always been the only moderately cute, straight, single guy in every drama club, musical, or play. He's the guy who's always had all the girls fighting over him, just because there aren't any other options. He's the one who gets the lead in everything, just because there are fifteen girls for every guy auditioning. It's not fair! They don't have to try, those Drews of the world! They don't have to work for anything! They just get whatever they want and they think they deserve it, which results in the most arrogant, obnoxious, entitled assholes the world has ever known!"

The girls were staring at me.

"Maybe it's time for a cleansing breath?" Heidi suggested.

"He's not an arrogant, obnoxious a-hole!" Amy said, sniffling slightly. "He's complicated. And intense. And—and passionate."

I don't know what the eff Mrs. Potts was singing about, but *this* is the tale as old as time. Nice girl falls for angry asshole and convinces herself he's just "intense" and "complicated," when really he's just a mean jackass.

"Passionate is just a nice way of saying psychotic!" I continued. "Did you guys read *Wuthering Heights* in school?"

"So romantic," Amy sighed, as Heidi nodded. "Oh, Drew is *just* like Heathcliff!" Amy clapped her hands with delight. "So brooding!"

"My point exactly!" I crowed with triumph. "Heathcliff is *not* romantic. He's insane. He's a certifiable psychopath! He hanged a dog. *Hanged* a *dog*, Amy!"

"*Drew* didn't hang a dog!" Amy contested hotly.

"We don't know that! We don't know anything about him!"

"Why don't we just take some deep, calming ocean breaths," Heidi interrupted, "and go play some National Parks Pictionary?"

"Is that even a thing?" I asked.

"It is indeed a thing." Heidi nodded, standing up. "And it's just the thing we need!"

Heidi ushered Amy and me out of the room like an efficient Girl Scout troop leader. Still glowering slightly, Amy and I followed her to the Actor Lounge, settling in on opposite ends of the dilapidated floral couch, eyeing each other somewhat warily. Rhys was the only other person in there, but he hastily closed the Edith Wharton novel he was reading when Heidi announced Pictionary.

"Parlor games!" he cheered with delight as Heidi pulled National Parks Pictionary out of the cabinet under the TV.

"Is this really all there is to play?" I eyed the game skeptically. "Because it kind of sounds like the worst game ever."

"I think you mean the best game ever!" Heidi chirped.

"It's the *only* game here," Rhys said in a low tone. "No Scrabble, no Boggle, no Taboo, no nothing. I checked. I ran a wicked game night back at Andover. If I'd known things were going to be this bleak, I would have brought my own stash."

"Look at this!" Heidi pulled off the box top and started going through the cards. "We get to draw all sorts of fun words like deciduous . . . and, and . . . conifers . . . and, and . . . the Tuskegee Airmen!"

"I don't know what any of those are," Amy whispered, and I nodded in grim agreement.

"Learning," said Heidi, "is part of the fun."

Well, Heidi may have been wrong about National Parks Pictionary being the most fun game ever, but she was right that it made Amy and me forget that we had been quasi-fighting. As Rhys and I took on Amy and Heidi, trying with little success to draw the Organic Act of 1916 or Gneiss, everyone collapsed into laughter. No one guessed a single picture the entire game.

After a couple rounds, Noah returned from his run and the five of us trooped into the tiny kitchen to make a communal dinner of mac and cheese. I caught Amy glancing hopefully toward the door the entire time, but Drew never showed up. Thank God.

We brought the mac and cheese out onto the lawn and all ate straight out of the same pot, fighting each other with forks for the cheesiest morsels, talking and laughing nonstop until long after the fireflies came out. It is a truth universally acknowledged that theater people never run out of things to talk about.

Many hours later, after Noah had produced a guitar and we sang until our voices were hoarse—I had been so right about his guitar-playing hands—we drifted into the house and off to our bedrooms. I pulled on an old faded NJ Devils

T-shirt and some plaid pajama shorts and climbed up to my bunk. I tried to get comfortable on the extremely thin mattress, tossing and turning, listening to Heidi's gentle snores and the low drone of the mosquitoes outside the screen window. Ugh, Drew. That smug, pompous, arrogant, obnoxious asshole! Why did he think he was too good to scoop poop like the rest of us? Was he too good to eat mac and cheese with us, too? I fumed, flopping back and forth, my legs tangling in the sheets. What could Amy possibly see in him? He was a good actor who knew a lot about Shakespeare, but that alone did not ideal boyfriend material make. If only I'd been able to convince her to direct her attentions elsewhere, but that had failed spectacularly. There was no way she could ever be happy with him. *No one* could ever be happy with him. Unless, of course, he was a totally different person. A much better person. With a way better personality.

I sat up straight in bed, nearly whacking my head against the ceiling in the process. An idea had hit me with all the subtlety of a thunderclap. It was either pure genius or pure madness. Either way, it meant I would get to spend the summer torturing Drew—and nothing could be better than that. This was going to be the most hilarious summer *of all time.* I hastily scrambled down the ladder to the floor by Heidi's bed.

"Heidi!" I shook her, pulling on the sleeve of her organic cotton-hemp-blend fair trade pajamas.

She muttered, "Lalita sahasranama."

"Are you dreaming in Sanskrit?" I asked, stunned.

"Hmm?" Heidi woke up. "Lalita sahasranama," she repeated.

"That *is* Sanskrit," I confirmed.

"How do you know Sanskrit?" Amy asked, sitting up and rubbing her eyes.

"My mom. She's a yoga teacher. That's where I get my rudimentary knowledge of Sanskrit. And deep sense of calm and inner peace," I added sarcastically.

"Cool." Amy smiled.

"Namaste." Heidi folded her hands into a prayer position.

"No, no, not Namaste time, war time!" I pulled her hands apart.

"Oh, no. War, no." Heidi pulled her hands away and stuck them back together.

"No! Uh, not war!" Damn. I'd forgotten my audience. "Uh . . . woman empowerment!" I grabbed her wrists and shook them around in celebration.

"Sisters unite!" she cheered.

"Right, right, unite!" I echoed, then whirled around to the other side of the room. "Amy," I announced, walking toward her like a lawyer on *Law & Order.* "You are sure, beyond the shadow of a doubt, that it is Drew you are 'in love with'?" I air-quoted.

"Beyond a shadow of a doubt!" She clasped her hands in front of the TOUGH COOKIE printed on her pink tank top and pulled her matching pajama pants–clad knees into her chest. "I love him, Cass, I know it. I do! And I know you'll come to see how amazing he is—"

"I think, Amy," I interrupted her, "that you'll come to see how amazing he *could* be." I smiled. "Let's review the situation, shall we? Tell, me, what is it that you so like about your special beloved?"

"Um . . . okay." Amy stared at me, clearly unsure why I'd awoken her in the middle of the night to interrogate her about her crush. "Well, for one, he's sooooo talented. How could you look at him onstage and *not* love him? That was when it started. From the very first line of his monologue, boom—it was like something exploded in my chest. I couldn't look away."

"I concede that he possesses a modicum of talent." I nodded. That was indisputable. He was good. Very good.

"And he's sooooo cute."

"He's not hideous." I shrugged. Honestly, it was hard to tell anything under that beard. He might have been a god. Or he might have been the elephant man. Who could say?

"And he's soooo smart," she added happily. "He knows so much stuff. Connor thought school was so stupid; he never tried or anything. But Drew is, like, absolutely and completely totally brilliant."

"I guess . . . but wasn't it a *little* obnoxious, the way he was pushing all that obscure Shakespeare terminology in everyone's faces on the first day?" I asked.

"The way he explained it was so condescending." Heidi's voice was rich with disappointment. "Learning new things should be celebrated, not treated as shameful."

Oh, Heidi. Sweet, innocent Heidi was unintentionally proving to be a brilliant accomplice. Walk into my web, said the spider to the fly . . . or however that thing goes.

"We-elll," Amy hemmed and hawed. "I guess that was a little much."

"Oof." I grimaced, struck by another way to add some fuel to the fire. "Remember the way he *corrected* everyone in warmups?"

"Oh, the jaw shaking!" Heidi cried. "If you have a tip, share it as something to explore. Don't tell everyone they're wrong. And the push-ups, too! I heard him admonishing you, Cass. Honestly, you were doing your best. It's effort that should be rewarded, not the end result."

"I was just trying to do my very best push-up." I shook my head sadly.

"I know you were." Heidi patted my arm. "It's hard to build upper body strength."

"And wasn't it ridiculous that he didn't help out with the bear situation?" I widened my eyes in exaggerated disbelief.

"Well . . ." Amy looked even more unsure.

"That was truly ridiculous." Heidi was looking as close to pissed as I could imagine her being. "No one should fault a bear. It's an innocent creature, doing only what it knows how to do. Excreting waste is part of the very definition of a living organism! And the bear didn't know it was littering. Everyone should have pitched in to clean up that trash. It was the only decent thing to do."

"The only decent thing to do," I repeated with as much gravitas as I could muster. "And why didn't he hang out with us tonight? Where was he, huh? Isn't this supposed to be an ensemble?"

"That's what theater is all about!" Heidi pounded her fist on the bunk bed. "Creating and celebrating the ensemble!"

"Well . . ." Amy whispered.

"And doesn't he *always* have something snarky to say?" I added. "Like when we were struggling into our corsets, wasting his precious time?"

"Okay, fine." Amy held up her hands in defeat. "I admit he's not perfect."

"Ah, but what if we could *make* him perfect?" I crowed in triumph. I snatched something out from under our bunk bed. "Now, what do you see here?"

"My script?" Heidi answered.

"This isn't just a script." I grinned. "It's a manual. A manual on how to end the war of the sexes and to create the perfect mate."

Amy looked confused. So did Heidi. I had to think fast. I didn't want to lose my unwitting ally.

"I thought you said the whole 'taming' thing was sexist. You know, like in your monologue," Amy said hesitantly.

"Well, yeah, sure, it's sexist if you tame a woman, but not if you tame a man," I said smugly.

"That's a double standard. The whole point of equality of the sexes is *equality*." Heidi looked dubious.

"Fine! Sexist, schmexist, whatever! It *works*!" I jumped on the bed next to Amy. "Would we *still* be performing this play five hundred years later if there wasn't a nugget of truth in here? A big-old golden nugget?"

"She has a point," Amy said in Heidi's general direction.

"Listen, we just gotta do what the script says, and we can make you the perfect boyfriend!" I said.

"The pursuit of perfection leads to nothing but grief," Heidi warned.

"Okay, fortune cookie, could you cool it a minute?" I implored Heidi. "The perfect boyfriend," I whispered to Amy. I could see her eyes glowing. "You can keep everything you like about Drew and change all the bad parts! By *taming* him. All guys need a little bit of work, right? This is just a shortcut. We follow this script, and voila! The perfect man!"

"I don't get it," Heidi interrupted, crossing her arms over her chest.

"What's to get? You just agreed with me that he's been acting like a complete and total jackass all week. This will *work*. Pranks, tame, better, boyfriend, boom!"

"I'm lost," Amy interjected.

"I mean it doesn't make any sense," Heidi continued. "What purpose is this serving? Why is playing a bunch of Shakespearean pranks on Drew going to make him fall in love with Amy?"

"Well, it's not—I mean yes, but no," I amended, noticing Amy's panicky face. "Amy doesn't need our help making Drew fall in love with her. That's obvious. Have you ever had a problem getting a guy before?"

"Well, um, no."

"Knew it, homecoming queen." I smirked. "That's not the point of this. They'll get together on their own; I'm not worried about that." I waved my hand dismissively. "We

just need to tame all the obnoxiousness out of Drew before they do. Otherwise, you'll be stuck with yet another
epic douchebag of a boyfriend. No one here wants Connor
two-point-oh." Amy shook her head vigorously. "Just look
at the play. It wasn't all the tricks that made Petruchio and
Kate fall in love. The spark was always there, even when
they thought they hated each other. All the sleep deprivation and the starvation just made her a lot nicer. Taming
works. Get it now? It doesn't just make sense, it makes *perfect* sense!"

"But you love him, don't you?" Heidi prompted Amy.
Well, that settled it—I'd lost Heidi. But I could tell Amy was
intrigued. "Why would you want to change him?"

"It's not that I want to change him, it's just that—let's be
real here. I may be a romantic, but I'm also a realist. *Every*
guy needs a little bit of work. You should have seen Connor
before I got to him." Amy rolled her eyes. "He ate everything
with his hands. And I mean *everything.* It was disgusting.
He was obsessed with pudding cups." She shuddered. "Ick. I
could never enjoy a pudding cup again. So why not put the
work in before we start dating? That way I can just enjoy the
finished product!"

"Hmm . . ." Heidi narrowed her eyes at me. "What's in it
for you?"

"Who? Me?" I tried to approximate some Precious Moments figurine-esque portrait of innocence. If Heidi figured
out how excited I was by the prospect of tormenting Drew
all summer, this whole operation was sunk. But honestly,
who wouldn't be excited by the prospect of playing a bunch

of Shakespearean pranks? I'd never successfully pranked anyone. I'd been the victim of four years of expert prankage courtesy of the Weehawken High tech crew, but I'd only ever been the *prankee*, not the *pranker*. If we could pull this off, it was going to be *so* epic. "I am shocked! Of all people, Heidi, I thought you would recognize this as the truly selfless gesture it is."

"Uh-huh." She crossed her arms.

"I am serving humanity by making the world a better place. How? By helping Drew along on his path to self-discovery. Showing him how to grow and develop, to evolve into the best version of himself he could be. Just like the Buddha! Yes, a bearded, thespian Buddha, on that sweet, sweet road to enlightenment." Man, I didn't even know where this was coming from anymore. I was on fire! "And, of course, I'm helping a friend." I slung an arm around Amy's shoulder. "Doesn't Amy deserve the best possible boyfriend? And as her friends, shouldn't we help her find him? Or, uh, make him?"

"He's not a robot." Amy wrinkled her nose. "Or a science project."

"Of course not." I patted her genially on the back. "He's a guy. And he's about to become the perfect guy."

"The perfect guy," she repeated.

"We just tame this Drew, and he's all yours."

"Alllll mine." Amy grinned. "Let's do it."

"Oh what a tangled web we weave, when first we practice to deceive!" Heidi wailed.

"That's not Shakespeare," I said, and smiled in triumph.

CHAPTER 9

had been unprecedentedly quiet at rehearsal today. During every scene I wasn't in, I crouched backstage, poring over my script, highlighting every trick Petruchio played on Kate and making notes in the margins. That thing was a gold mine, chock-full of interesting tips and tidbits. Sleep deprivation, food deprivation, destruction of personal property—Petruchio was like some kind of crazy sixteenth-century rogue CIA agent! Realistically, I probably couldn't keep Drew up every night with a trumpet. Or hack up all his clothes with a bread knife. Then he'd know it was me, and secrecy was of the utmost import if I wanted to maintain any kind of decent onstage relationship with him while at Dunmore. Because as much as Drew annoyed me, I wasn't about to sacrifice my performance to make his life miserable. So I'd have to be way craftier than Petruchio had been. Luckily, there is more than one way to tame a shrew. And more than one way to keep said shrew from sleeping.

Which was why Amy and I were sitting on our bedroom floor, bribe at the ready, waiting for our accomplice as Heidi paced nervously back and forth.

"I still think it's a bad idea. We should just stop it now before we even start." Heidi traced even, concentric circles around us. "Well, maybe he's not coming anyway," she added hopefully. "Is he late?"

Amy checked her cell phone. "Barely five minutes. That's still on time. Kind of."

We jumped as three quick, sharp knocks at the door interrupted us. I hastily sprang to my feet and opened the door. Rhys tried to sidle inside but was met with some difficulty as he had a pillow shoved up his shirt.

"Somebody knock you up?" I asked.

"My papa always warned me to keep outta the backs of pickup trucks!" Rhys wailed in a Southern accent once he'd made it into the room.

"That's not very stealthy! You said you'd be *subtle*. What if someone had seen you?" Heidi worried.

"Well, someone did. I ran into Noah, NBD," Rhys replied breezily.

"You ran into *Noah*?" Amy squeaked. "What did he say? What did you say?"

"He was looking at me, and I was like, 'What?' and he was like, 'What's goin' on there?' and I said, 'Sodium bloat. Too many hot dogs. Water retention. Tragic.'" Rhys smiled. "And I actually did eat a bunch of hot dogs today, so, not even a lie. Completely genius, right?"

"Genius would have been *not* being seen." I rolled my eyes. "But good enough. I doubt Noah will say anything." I held out my hand, waiting as Rhys pulled the pillow out of his shirt.

"Noah might," Heidi said. "He seems very honest. And forthright. And if he suspects that we stole Drew's pillow, he *might* say something because it's not right—"

"But he won't suspect," I said, "because no one will ever notice it was gone. How much time do we have, Rhys?"

"He just got in the shower. So you've got time, but not much."

I quickly peeled off the navy pillowcase and tossed the pillow to Amy.

"It's amazing, isn't it?" she said as she handed me her pillow and started pulling a pink polka dot pillowcase over Drew's old pillow. "My pillow's full of feathers and his is all hypoallergenic, but they look exactly the same."

"Thank God you both shop at Target," I agreed, stuffing Amy's feather pillow into Drew's navy pillowcase. And thank God Drew had let slip that tiny detail about his feather allergy. Let's see him get a good night's sleep in his luxurious single room *now.*

"You got the goods?" Rhys asked.

Wordlessly, Heidi handed him the bag of Sour Gummi Worms we'd bought at the Bait 'n' Bite.

"A pleasure doing business with you, ladies." Rhys smiled as he shoved Drew's new feathery pillow up his shirt and took the bag of worms. "I look forward to my next assignment."

Rhys waddled stealthily out of the room, and Heidi shut the door behind him. "I still don't like this."

"Come on, Heidi, it's just a couple feathers. And he probably made up that allergy anyway just to get a single. Most likely it won't even do anything," I said.

"Oh, come on, Cass, he didn't make that up," Amy scoffed. "Who would make that up? What a weird thing to lie about!"

"What if he *is* really allergic and his throat closes up?" Heidi had a genuinely concerned look on her face.

"What? No. I'm sure he'd move to a couch or something before it got that bad." I waved my hand, dismissing Heidi's concerns. I'd honestly never even thought about it, but it couldn't be that serious, right? I ignored the nervous, guilty burble in my stomach. "It's not *that* big of a deal. We're just teaching him a lesson. A couple of teensy little lessons. Nobody's gonna get hurt."

"We'll see." Heidi sank grumpily to the floor.

"Think of it like . . . summer camp pranks. Totally innocent. Some summer fun!" I said it with all the enthusiasm I could muster, but enthusiasm's just not my thing.

"I've decided on my terms," Amy interrupted.

"What terms?" I asked. "We already started. The plan is in motion. Phase One is complete. It's too late for terms."

"You meet my terms, or I pull out."

"Oh, wow, terms. That sounds complicated. We should probably just stop," Heidi said hopefully.

"Fine, give me your terms." I crossed my arms and glared.

"You're helping me *make* the perfect boy, so I'm gonna help you *get* your perfect boy." Amy smiled wickedly.

"What are you talking about?" I could feel a violent blush, bane of my redheaded existence, creeping up my neck.

"I'm talking about Taylor Griffith, Segunki Cabin." Amy bounced to her feet. "Let's go!"

"What, right now?" I asked, slightly panicky.

"What about curfew?" Heidi asked.

"What, are you chicken?" Amy challenged playfully. "Buk-buk-bakaw! Buk-buk-bakaw!"

"One, I am not chicken, and two, that sounds nothing like a chicken."

"Don't tell me you're all talk and no game, Cass." Amy poked me in the ribs.

"Oh, I've got the game," I affirmed. "Isn't it just kind of . . . desperate? Heading over there and chasing him?"

"Not desperate! Gutsy! Brave! Bold! Listen, Cass," she said seriously. "You're helping me be bold, and now I'm gonna help you. Bold moves!"

"Bold moves," I agreed.

"Curfew?" Heidi asked again.

"We have a curfew?" I asked.

"It's in the contract," Amy said. "But who's in charge of checking that anyway?"

"Langley," Heidi answered.

"Right. And Langley's not gonna turn us in. I don't think she's even older than us." Amy stepped into her flip-flops.

"Me neither. And I think she's on the see-no-evil-hear-no-evil managerial plan," I said. "Plus, she never takes her iPod earbuds out long enough to hear any evil. Or curfew breaking."

"Exactly!" Amy clapped her hands together with delight.

"What about your whole no-relationship thing?" Heidi asked.

"I'm not saying Cass needs to marry the guy." Amy rolled her eyes. "She said no relationships, not no shenanigans."

"Shenanigans?" I had a feeling Taylor Griffith was nothing but shenanigans.

"Shenanigans, Cass. You in?"

"I'm in." I started pulling on my sneakers. I liked this new, bold Amy, and I certainly wasn't about to wuss out in front of her. I noticed Heidi strapping on her sandals next to me. "You coming, too?"

"Someone has to keep an eye on the two of you," Heidi said grumpily, but I could tell by the twinkle in her eye that there was more to it than that.

I guess we were technically sneaking out, but it was so easy it didn't really feel very sneaky. Someone was watching *Cool Runnings* in the lounge, but aside from that, the place appeared deserted. It was totally silent apart from our quiet footsteps and the vague sounds of the Jamaican bobsled team fading away into the distance as we made our way down the stairs and out into the night.

"This door doesn't lock, does it?" Heidi asked as she shut it very quietly, trying to minimize the creaking as much as humanly possible.

"Better not." I shrugged. "Or we're sleeping on the lawn."

"I don't think so, or they would have given us a key, right?" Amy theorized.

"Exactly. And why bother with a lock, anyway? This doesn't appear to be a particularly high crime area," I said as we crunched our way down the gravel driveway and onto the dirt road. "It's not like they have to worry about someone breaking in to steal our collection of vintage life jackets."

Amy giggled as Heidi strode confidently into the dark. I don't know how she knew where she was going, because I couldn't see anything. Once we'd left the small radius of the glow of the houselights, it was absolutely pitch-dark, and the ground was deceptively uneven.

"Eek!" Amy squealed. "I almost wiped out. How are you guys walking okay? I can't see *anything.*"

"Me neither." All I could see was overwhelming darkness. I studiously ignored a rustling sound in the bushes, refusing to even let the word "bear" enter my mind.

"This is ridiculous," Amy muttered, rustled around, and then produced a small circle of artificial light. "Flashlight iPhone App," she announced proudly.

"Genius," I admired.

"If I was really a genius I'd have thought of it before we left," Amy snorted in an amusingly un-Amy-like fashion.

"Are you guys coming, or what?" Heidi called out from somewhere in the darkness.

"How did she get so far ahead of us?" Amy marveled as she tilted her phone up to reveal the road ahead.

"I think she's part gazelle." I shrugged as we jogged to meet up with Heidi. "So, uh, who knows where we're going?"

"Me! Straight up the road to Camp Dunmore," Heidi said, pressing onward into the dark.

"It's not that far," Amy chimed in. "Didn't you see the Lake Dunmore map in your Welcome Packet?"

"Oh, yeah," I said vaguely. I'd skimmed that thing. Most of it, anyway.

Heidi led us up the dirt road, following the curve of the path along the lake. I made sure to stay in the faint circle glow of Amy's cell phone. The closer we got, the more Amy kept giggling uncontrollably. I couldn't blame her. There was something dangerously fun about feeling like we were breaking the rules, sneaking out into the night. Although, I guess, technically we *were* breaking the rules. Like Scarlett O'Hara, I had a feeling that I was the kind of criminal who would feel worse about getting caught than about committing the crime. Which maybe wasn't such a great character trait, but hey, at least I was self-aware.

Heidi turned abruptly to the left, away from the lake and into the woods.

"Is this Camp Dunmore?" I asked.

"Think so." Amy tilted her phone upward and revealed what looked like a wooden archway with letters on top. We walked through the archway and into the woods, now following a much smaller path, riddled with stones and roots.

"What if everyone's asleep?" I asked nervously, the full realization of what we were doing finally hitting me. "What if we find Segunki Cabin and it's totally dark and no one's there and then we just look like huge losers?"

"Oh my God, Cass, chill out," Amy giggled. "It's, like, ten-thirty. No one's asleep. If I didn't know any better, I'd think you were *ner-vous* about seeing *Tay-lor*," she sing-songed.

"Please," I snorted. "I hope you know me better than that by now."

"I'm starting to think I know you better than you know yourself," she laughed.

"I'm starting to think I found the cabin," Heidi said.

I peered ahead. In the middle of the woods, there was one cabin with lights burning brightly in every small window, a faint hum of thumping bass emanating from within.

"Well, they're definitely not asleep. It's go time," Amy said, grinning, as she pushed her way in front, sprinting up to the cabin. Heidi and I jogged to catch up with her. The minute we hit the front porch, the door swung open.

CHAPTER 10

Heeeeeeey, my ladies!"

A buff shirtless guy in dangerously low-riding track pants pushed the door open, a red plastic cup clutched in his free hand. A riot of noise and light poured out into the quiet Vermont darkness. The three of us exchanged glances.

"This way to paradise, Betties!" he proclaimed, and turned around, walking back into the cabin. "JJ" was scrawled in permanent marker on his back.

"And this must be JJ," I murmured. "What a clever way to save time on introductions."

"Too bad I left my marker at home," Amy sighed.

We followed him in. I was pretty sure it was the same guy who had been shirtless at the Bait 'n' Bite. Did he even *own* a shirt?

Inside, the place was packed with guys in hoodies and littered with empty beer bottles and crushed red plastic cups. The music was so loud it drowned out all conversations;

I could see peoples' mouths moving and hands gesticulating, but couldn't hear anything. The floorboards vibrated pleasantly under my feet with the thump of the bass.

"You guys, volumes this loud can cause permanent damage to the inner ears," Heidi said, wincing. "It could ruin our ability to match pitch."

"Lighten up, Grandma," Amy joked, jostling Heidi in the ribs.

"Who is this, anyway?" I asked.

"It's CKY." Taylor Griffith had emerged seemingly out of nowhere to answer my question. "Camp Kill Yourself," he elaborated.

"Clever," I approved. "Very thematic. Is that your general attitude towards Camp Dunmore?"

"Usually." He leaned in conspiratorially, until I could feel his breath tickling my neck. "For some reason, I feel a lot more like living tonight."

"Oh God." I rolled my eyes. "Is this your usual level of cheesiness? Or do you feel less need to try because we're in the backwoods of Vermont?"

"Could this be? The Bowser himself? Schralped again by the sickest Betty in this godforsaken state!" JJ crowed, pounding his bare chest like Tarzan. "If I didn't see it with my own eyes, I wouldn't believe it! Bow-ow-owwww!"

Heidi raised her eyebrows at the dog howls. I could tell she was not impressed.

"Smooth, JJ," Taylor said, as JJ gulped his beer and busted out a resounding belch.

"Don't tell me the girls in L.A. fall for that shit." I poked him playfully in the chest. It was solid as a rock.

"Actually, they usually do." He straightened, and I thought I might have seen a gleam of admiration in his eyes. "How did you know I was from L.A.?"

"Aren't *all* skaters from L.A.? All the real ones, anyway. Not the ones sliding down the bike rails in the Shop Rite parking lot."

He laughed. "Gotta start somewhere, yeah? That's where I used to be."

Amy coughed discreetly.

"Oh, Taylor, you remember Amy, right?" I said.

He nodded, as Ragner the Norwegian possible-prince zoomed to Amy's side, raised her hand, and kissed it.

"*Vi møtes igjen, Prinsesse,*" he murmured, as Amy blushed. If Ragner the pretend-prince kept this up, we might end up scrapping this whole Drew scheme. Although I would certainly miss the opportunity to spend several weeks torturing Drew. Maybe I could even make him cry. Wouldn't that be a beautiful sight?

"And this is Heidi." I dragged her into our circle. She was looking extremely uncomfortable and in danger of edging toward the door.

"It really is Charlie's Angels." Taylor smiled, and I couldn't help but notice the nice way his eyes crinkled.

"Access to some kind of secret Betty stockpile. I like it!" JJ yelled from across the room as he vigorously pumped a keg, refilling his cup.

"Lemme introduce you to the guys, new Betty," Taylor said, addressing Heidi. "I'm Taylor. We've got JJ, Ragner, Skittles, Ferret, and Thiago." Taylor looked around. "I guess Thiago's still out back playing Stump."

"Who are all these other people?" I asked.

"Sheep and yoinkers." He shrugged. "Who the hell knows? Locals. Guys who help out with camp, run the skate shop, that kind of shit."

When he said guys, he meant it. I looked around the room and realized we were the only girls there.

From the corner of the room, Ferret walked toward Heidi, like a moth drawn to a flame. She turned and walked toward him with the same purpose, until I realized it wasn't Ferret himself she was seeking out. It was the creature draped around his neck. Heidi seemed far more enamored of the actual ferret than of the human who shared his name. The ferret deserted his owner and began blissfully twining himself around Heidi's neck as she stroked his tiny furry head, whispering sweet nothings into his little ferret ears. Ferret pushed his dreads back to get a better look and continued staring at Heidi with awe.

"May I get you ladies some liquid refreshment?" JJ asked. "Refreshment of the beer kind?"

"I *never* put toxins in my body," Heidi declared emphatically, stroking the ferret tenderly. Human Ferret stared at her for a solid minute, then bolted toward the kitchen. Maybe her beauty had overwhelmed him or something.

"Here, Cass, lemme grab you a beer," Taylor said as he walked off to the fridge.

"Cass," Amy whispered, "we're not supposed to drink."

"Well, duh. We're underage. It's against the law."

"No, I don't mean legally." She shook her head. "Did you read *anything* in the Welcome Packet? Drinking at SAD is a fireable offense. And the SAD directors reserve the right to randomly administer breathalyzers and drug tests."

"You seriously think Lola St. Clair has a breathalyzer lying around?" I asked skeptically. "She can't even be bothered to show up for rehearsal, let alone administer a random drug test. Are we entirely certain she still exists?"

"Oh, please. She *exists*, Cass. She just hasn't been particularly, well, present. And breathalyzer or not, better safe than sorry. This party is so not worth getting fired for." Amy flipped her hair dismissively. "They don't even have stuff for making cocktails. I should show them how we do it in Beaver Falls."

I had a feeling Amy had been way more into the party scene at her high school than I had been at mine. The drama dorks at Weehawken High had occupied the social rung only slightly above the Mathletes, AV nerds, and chess club kids. Consequently, I spent most of my weekends watching *Rocky Horror* in someone's basement while eating SmartPop. Yes, it was a thrilling existence.

At that moment, Ferret returned with what appeared to be, somewhat improbably, a steaming hot mug of green tea. Heidi sipped it appreciatively as the ferret nuzzled her cheek.

"It's my favorite brew," he explained. "It's sencha, which is a Japanese green tea, specifically one that's made—"

"Without grinding the tea leaves!" They finished the sentence in unison, grinning at each other.

"Sencha's one of my favorites, too," Heidi agreed warmly. "If I had to only pick one tea, though, I'd have to say I'm an oolong girl—I tend to prefer the Chinese teas. But there's just something about a nice sencha."

"It's mellow, you know?" Ferret and Heidi were nodding at each other, smiling broadly. Amy and I exchanged glances. *There are more things in heaven and earth, Horatio, than are dreamt of in your philosophy.* Like Hamlet said, life was weird.

"Here, Cass," Tyler said, handing me a cold beer bottle, cap already off. "I got you one of the good ones," he added with a wink.

I accepted it and took a sip. A *small* sip. Definitely not enough to show up on any impromptu breathalyzer. Still, I did my best to avoid Amy and Heidi's disapproving looks. I'd already broken more rules in a couple days at Lake Dunmore than I had in my entire high school career. I felt somehow simultaneously exhilarated and extremely uncomfortable.

"You want, blondest Betty?" JJ asked, holding out a red cup.

"No, thanks," Amy said disdainfully, flicking her eyes toward the cup. "That'll just slow me down. Who's in charge of the music around here?"

Ragner executed a small bow and led her over to an end table that held a lamp, an iPod docking station, and a mountain of empty Doritos bags.

"So, are we the only girls you could convince to show up?" I asked. "Why are there only guys here?"

"Well, we scoped out the town, and we're not so much into the barrels. And if you ignore the jailbait, it's like a fucking barrel shop out there," JJ moaned dramatically.

"I haven't seen any barrels," Amy said quizzically as she started scrolling through the music on her iTunes. "Oh, wait. Do you mean the pickle barrel at the Bait 'n' Bite?"

"I don't think they mean literal barrels." I cocked my head, thinking. Because that would be crazy. "What's a barrel?"

"You know." JJ puffed out his cheeks and stomach, and started waddling around, miming something.

"Penguin?" Amy guessed as she put her iPhone into the docking station. "Santa! Fat Santa! Fat people?" she finished, a question in the arch of her eyebrow.

"Wait a minute. There's no other girls here because you thought they were too . . . fat?" I asked, appalled.

"That is—that is horrible," Heidi sputtered. "The pressure on female body image in this country—the impossible standards of modern media—"

"Not just fatties. Also jailbait," JJ added helpfully. "You Betties are all eighteen, right?"

"Stop being a chode, man." Taylor rolled his eyes at JJ. "C'mon, let me show you out back, Cass. Sick view."

I wished I could dismiss JJ as easily as Taylor had. There was a sick, sour taste in my mouth that had nothing to do with one sip of illicit beer. But that wasn't Taylor's fault—he couldn't help who was on his team. I certainly wouldn't want anyone assuming I was anything like Drew simply because we were forced to spend the majority of our waking hours together.

The CKY cut out and was instantly replaced with Rihanna, blaring at an even louder volume than before.

"It's on, bitches!" Amy screamed gleefully as she jumped on top of the coffee table, kicked off a bunch of empty Rock Star energy drinks and Cheetos bags, and started busting out what looked like a choreographed routine.

Heidi covered the ferret's teeny-tiny rodent ears as Ferret escorted the two of them toward the front porch, where I had a feeling he was gonna get an earful concerning his friend's gross attitude about women. And then maybe some further stimulating conversation on the nature of tea leaves. Ragner, and most of the rest of the guys at the party, were gathering around the coffee table Amy had turned into a stage, cheering and pumping their fists.

"Come on." Taylor grabbed my hand, squeezed, and my heart sped up. "Let's go outside."

"Hells yeah, you *take* her outside, Bowser!" JJ crowed.

"Come on, man, hamster the fetus act. Shove it," Taylor said, and something in his tone finally silenced JJ. Or maybe it was whatever "hamster the fetus act" meant. "Ready?" Taylor asked.

I nodded and let him pull me through the party, past the kitchen, and out back.

"Why does he keep calling you Bowser?" I asked.

"Oh, it's just a nickname." He shrugged.

"What does it mean?"

"You don't know who Bowser is?"

He inferred from my blank stare that no, in fact, I did not.

"You know, from Mario?"

"Oh!" Realization dawned. "That big turtle guy who's always kidnapping Princess Peach?"

"Nailed it." He shot finger-guns at me.

"But why do they call you Bowser?"

"Cuz I'm the king, Betty. King of the Koopas. Bow-ow-ow!"

From all around, more male voices joined in on the howling chorus of bow-ow-ow. I couldn't see them in the dark, but I could hear them. It was slightly spooky.

"But he's the bad guy."

"Who says, man? Why should some weird-ass tiny plumber in overalls get the girl? I'd rather be a badass turtle king covered in spikes any day."

Huh. Interesting analysis of the Nintendo universe. I felt like I had just been handed some valuable insight into the soul of Taylor "Bowser" Griffith, but I wasn't quite sure how to interpret it. Was it troubling that he identified with the villain? Maybe not. After all, I'd never felt much like a princess. I'd much rather be Tamora than Lavinia. Although that was a horrible example, because everyone in *Titus Andronicus* dies in a spectacularly gruesome fashion, so I wouldn't want to actually *be* anyone. But I had a feeling Taylor might somehow know what I meant.

Something sharp and heavy whizzed through the air in front of us, landing with a resounding *thunk* in a piece of wood.

The crowd outside, again all male, cheered uproariously. We'd gotten close enough to see a small figure in a knitted cap acknowledge the roar of the crowd with a neat wave.

"Sick shot, Thiago!" Taylor applauded.

"What the hell is this?" I asked, moving closer to the stump to investigate. "Did he just throw an axe at us?"

"Not at us, at the stump. Mellow out, Betty," Taylor laughed. "You never heard of Stump?"

"Actually, no, I wasn't raised in a lumberjack camp," I replied tartly.

"I'd never heard of Stump 'til I got to Vermont, either," he confessed, "but it's ill as shit. You put a bunch of nails in a stump, then throw an axe at the stump, trying to like hammer the nail into the stump. Totally sick, right?"

"Yeah . . . sick." Privately, I thought it sounded sick in the non-skater way—namely, really stupid and dangerous. They were really close to the house and were standing in a crowd of people. Plus, they were drinking. How easy would it be for an axe throw to go haywire? I didn't want to sound like a wuss, though, so I kept my thoughts to myself and hoped we passed by Stump as quickly as possible. Thankfully, Taylor started leading me away from the house into the woods.

"Thiago's like some kind of Stump genius. Maybe it's like the national pastime of Brazil."

"Maybe." Although I was pretty sure it wasn't. "This party's crazy." I shook my head. "The camp doesn't mind?"

"I dunno." He shrugged. "We're way far away from the campers, so why would they care? We might as well be in New Hampshire. And we're supervised. Technically."

"What do you mean?

"Well, our manager's here. How the hell else would we get beer?" he laughed.

"Manager?"

"Every pro skate team's gotta have a manager."

Wow. These guys may have been a bigger deal than I realized. I had just thought they were skateboarders. I hadn't realized they were, you know, professional.

"Back up a minute. Your manager bought you beer?" I asked, dumbstruck. This made the authority figures at SAD look downright strict.

"He straight up had to. We're all still underage. Well, 'til next month, then JJ'll be twenty-one. You ever heard of Donovan Rayne?" he asked, his voice rich with expectation.

"Um . . . no."

"Come on." His jaw dropped open in disbelief. "Donovan Rayne? *The* Donovan Rayne?"

"Still don't know who that is."

"Wow, you don't know *anything* about pro skating, do you?" Taylor asked, laughing.

"Sorry." I shrugged. I really didn't. Pro skating hadn't made much of an impact in Weehawken. Or maybe it had, like back in the '90s or something, and I'd just missed its heyday.

"Nah, don't apologize. It's kind of . . . refreshing." He smiled. "Well, Donovan's our manager, and he used to be, like, the biggest skater in the world. Then an injury ended his career. The only thing he'd ever known how to do, you know? Gone. In an instant."

"I can't even imagine." I shook my head. What would I do if I couldn't act anymore? I had no idea. It was the only thing I'd ever wanted to do my whole life.

"Shit, I almost ended up like him." Taylor stopped. We'd come to a clearing where log benches surrounded a long-dead fire pit. He led me over to a bench and sat.

"You did?" I asked, settling down next to him, resting my beer in the sandy ground.

"Really bad snowboarding accident when I was fifteen. Stupidest shit I ever did. I shouldn't have been snowboarding. Thought it was the same as skating, but it's not—it's different. Broke my back and the doctors weren't sure I was gonna walk again, let alone skate."

"Holy shit," I breathed. "Taylor, I'm so sorry, that must have been awful." Almost involuntarily, I moved closer to him.

"But Donovan, man, he was a fucking champ. He'd been my manager since I was twelve—"

"Since you were *twelve*?" I interrupted. "That's so young! You've been a pro skater since you were *twelve*?"

"Yeah. Donovan saw me skating in a parking lot and kinda took me under his wing. And then, after my injury, he did all the physical therapy with me. We're talking hours in the hospital. Practically taught me how to walk again. If it wasn't for him . . . well, and for my mom."

Taylor broke out into a wide, embarrassed grin, and it was so cute I almost threw up in my mouth. Then I *really* almost threw up in my mouth because I just described something as "cute" and that something was a boy who I was suddenly feeling strangely vulnerable around.

"So many of my teachers wanted to fail me, but my mom made sure I didn't. She made sure I got my homework, that I *did* my homework, that I graduated. I didn't really care much about school since I turned pro, but it was important to her, so . . ."

"And did you?" I prompted. "Graduate?"

"Yep, last year." He took a swig from his beer bottle, then set it down. "Right on time, like any normal eighteen-year-old."

"I just graduated. Just last month."

"No way." He smiled. "Congrats, Cass. You're probably going to college though, right? You seem really smart."

"Um, yeah. I am. Going to college. Not 'I am really smart.' I mean, I wouldn't say that. I mean, thanks."

I felt a red-hot blush creep up my neck. Boy-induced blushing? "Cute"? Who *was* I? Hopefully it was dark enough that he couldn't tell I was *blushing*. Oh, gross. Less blushing, more talking. "I'm going to Rutgers? In New Jersey?" Why was that coming out like a question? It wasn't a question. I had somehow transformed into one of those horrible up-talking girls.

"You're okay now, right?" I asked. Time to steer the conversation away from me and my increasing bizarreness.

"Hell yeah. By now, shit, I've broken almost every bone in my body. And I'm still skating."

"A pro skateboarder," I mused. "What does that mean, exactly? Like, how does this work? People pay you to just travel around, skateboarding?"

"Pretty much, yeah." He nodded. "From Tulsa to Tokyo. All over the place."

"That's crazy." I shook my head. "You must have girls in every city." I laughed, thinking how ridiculous I was being. He must have made a million girls all over the place feel all stupid and blushy.

"No, I don't."

"Oh, please." I rolled my eyes. "You don't have to bullshit me, Taylor."

"No bullshit, cross my heart." He made an x movement over his chest. "Seriously, Cass, I don't."

"I'm not a typical girl, Taylor, you don't have to make me feel special."

"I know you're not a typical girl." He reached out one long, tanned finger and tucked a springy red curl behind my ear. "And that's why you are special."

My mouth dropped open. Someone had just called me "special" and I didn't feel even a little bit like vomming. Actually, I felt like the opposite of vomming. I felt all warm and fuzzy like I was wrapped in my mom's favorite organically sourced cashmere blanket. My heart was beating about a million miles an hour, and my whole face felt warm—especially where Taylor's hand still lingered on my cheek. He started pulling my face toward his, and his startlingly blue eyes disappeared as his long lashes closed over them. I closed my eyes, too, leaning in closer, and closer, and—

"CASS!" Amy shrieked. "I GOT YOU SOME SUNGLASSES!!!!"

Startled, I leapt away from Taylor and rolled right off the log into the ashy dirt surrounding the fire pit. Really graceful, Cass. I hastily picked myself up and tried to dust the ashes off my butt. Taylor mumbled a rather colorful stream of curses under his breath.

Amy burst out of the woods like a colorful comet, decked out in an entirely new outfit. She was wearing a giant T-shirt emblazoned with GANGSTA RAW PRO SKATE in neon graffiti lettering surrounded by splatter paint. The shirt was so long it covered her sundress, and she was also wearing a matching backwards baseball hat. Not only did she have a pair of sunglasses propped on top of her hat and tucked into the collar of her T-shirt, but she was clutching two giant fistfuls of extras.

"Oh my God, Taylor, your friends are so super nice. Look at all this stuff they gave me!" she squealed, shoving several pairs of dark blue sunglasses into my hands. "They didn't really dance, though. Lame."

"They probably just didn't want to slow you down, Betty," Taylor said evenly as he stood, but I could tell whatever moment had passed between us was over. Part of me was pissed at Amy for interrupting, but part of me was relieved, too. I had started to feel way too mushy and vulnerable for my liking.

"What's Gangsta Raw, anyway?" Amy asked, squinting quizzically at the tiny GRs on the sunglasses.

"It's our sponsor. They make skateboards, skate shoes, clothes, sunglasses, energy drinks—all sorts of shit."

"And you get all sorts of that shit for free?" I asked.

"Yeah. More than we can give away."

"Well, I'm glad you gave it away to me!" Amy attempted to clap her hands with glee, but only succeeded in knocking her handful of sunglasses together. "Well, now that we've collected our souvenirs, it's time to go, Cass. Don't wanna get in trouble."

"You got a curfew, or something?" Taylor joked as he escorted us back to the cabin.

"Unfortunately, we do." I grimaced. We'd missed it by a long shot, but still, better late than never.

"*Finally*," Heidi sighed as we made it to the porch, gently handing the ferret back to Ferret. "We should have been in bed *hours* ago."

"Thanks for the lovely evening, boys!" Amy trilled as she and Heidi started dragging me down the steps and onto the path away from the camp.

"So, that's it, Cinderella? You just turn back into a pumpkin and bounce?" Taylor shouted as we disappeared into the night.

"You know how it works, Romeo!" Amy yelled. "Find her tomorrow!"

Shaking with laughter, the three of us sprinted down the path, filling our lungs with the crisp night air.

"So . . . you and Ferret, huh?" Amy said slyly, poking Heidi in the ribcage as we wound our way back toward our front lawn.

"Are you kidding me?" Heidi exploded with outrage. "He was *disgusting*!"

"Really?" I was shocked. "But it seemed like it was going so well, with the small mammals and the tea and everything." If I was going to guess Heidi's type, that would have been it. "You're not into the dreadlocks and stuff?"

"He *threw away* a bottle!" Heidi fumed. "Didn't recycle it. Just threw it right in the trash. Disgusting," she muttered, shaking her head. "Just disgusting."

"I'm not gonna fight you on the disgusting front," Amy agreed.

"The ferret was nice, though," Heidi amended.

As we made our way back to the boat house, Amy and Heidi kept talking, but I didn't say anything. All I could think about was Taylor. Had he been about to kiss me before Amy appeared? I thought so. No, he definitely was. I mean, I *hoped* so. Oh, God. Suddenly being kissed by Taylor Griffith seemed like the most important thing that could possibly happen this summer. Who was I turning into?

The door slammed. Too late, I realized *I* had slammed it.

"Oh, shit!" I cursed fervently. Served me right for daydreaming like a stupid idiot about someone's practically perfect smile and alarmingly hard chest muscles.

We froze in the kitchen. Miraculously, the only sound was our breathing—the house was silent. Wordlessly, we scampered up the stairs and leapt into bed.

I fell asleep, dreaming of blue eyes and tanned skin.

CHAPTER 11

"Where were you last night?" Drew asked the next morning at rehearsal, unfolding a crumpled tissue from his pocket and dabbing at his rather red, runny nose.

My heart started racing. There was no way he could know, right? About us sneaking out? Or about my one, tiny, infinitesimal sip of beer? God, I was regretting that now. Amy was right; drinking at that party was so not worth getting fired for. I didn't even *like* drinking. I never drank. Until some guy handed me a beer and all of a sudden I did? I felt like such an idiot. And worse, that I'd done something just to impress a guy, not because it was something I actually wanted to do. Consequences. There were going to be Consequences with a capital C, like I was in a health class movie. Oh, why hadn't I just said no?

"Um, I'm not sure what you're referring to. I was in the house."

"Interesting." Drew scratched his thick beard. "For some reason, I couldn't sleep last night. At all. When I went into the lounge to make sure that stupid *Cool Runnings* video was off, your room was quiet. Suspiciously quiet."

"You were *listening* at our door?" I puffed my chest out, trying to summon up some outrage to deflect his suspicion. Unfortunately, he didn't seem particularly deterred. And also, had he just called *Cool Runnings* stupid?

"I don't *try* to hear you, it's just impossible to avoid all the shrieks, giggles, clicks, and whistles that emanate from inside your room. It's like living down the hall from a dolphin habitat."

"Oh, for the love of—"

"And then," he interrupted, "in the wee hours of the morning, still not sleeping, I heard the front door slam, and a rather distinctive 'oh, shit.'"

"Again, I'm not sure what you're referring to," I said, chipping away at my blue nail polish, trying to stay cool. "And how can an 'oh, shit' be distinctive, anyway?"

"'Her voice was ever soft,'" he quoted, "'gentle and low, an excellent thing in a woman.'"

My jaw dropped as Drew punctuated the line from *King Lear* by blowing his nose like a trumpet into his crumpled tissue. Was that a compliment?

"Well, it's low, anyway." He shrugged. "Not so much with the 'gentle' and 'soft.'"

"What, low like a *man* voice?" I fumed. Okay, definitely not a compliment.

"ONSTAGE, lovers!" Nevin thundered from across the field. Unfortunately, that meant us. I shuffled onstage mulishly, following Drew. Saved by Nevin. I really didn't want Drew to continue that line of questioning.

Heidi and Rhys were standing upstage; it looked like Heidi was henna-ing his arms with a Sharpie, so they'd apparently been hanging out up there for a while. Amy, perched next to Noah on a bench downstage, broke character to wave.

"Drew, what are the rules about sunglasses?" Nevin yelled. "It's bright out."

"The handbook is *very* clear on the issue of sunglasses."

"Maybe I wasn't the only who didn't read the handbook," I muttered. Much to my surprise, Drew chuckled.

"OFF!" Nevin roared.

"Fine, fine," Drew muttered as he folded up his Ray Bans and stuck them in his back pocket.

"Holy shit!" I gasped, as Heidi dropped her Sharpie and it rolled across the stage.

Drew's eyes were a mess. A red, puffy, disgusting mess. He had giant dark circles under his eyes, his lids were puffy as marshmallows, and his eyes were so red I could see all the little bloody veins crisscrossing the whites of his eyes, which had turned from white to an unhealthy pink. I knew this had been the plan all along, but looking at him, I couldn't help but feel bad. It just looked so . . . painful.

"What happened to you?" Rhys asked, staring at Drew in shock.

"Jesus, man, are you okay?" Noah asked as he leaped over the bench and walked toward Drew.

Amy was studying her ballet flats with an unusual amount of focus, seemingly trying to look anywhere but at Drew.

Heidi's brow was wrinkled with concern, her guilty eyes boring into mine. She was biting her lip, worrying it back and forth between her teeth.

"I don't know what the hell happened. Let's just get on with rehearsal, okay?" Drew barked.

Just when I was pretty sure Heidi was about to say something incriminating, Drew blew his nose again and tossed his tissue offstage into the grass. Heidi narrowed her eyes as she pursed her lips disapprovingly. Saved by littering! Knowing Heidi, she probably considered itchy eyes a just punishment for despoiling the earth.

"What's going on up there?" Nevin asked as he charged toward the stage.

"Drew has pink eye," Rhys volunteered.

"It's not pink eye!" Drew protested. "It's, I don't know, allergies or something. But it's not pink eye."

"Sure." Rhys looked skeptical. "Don't touch my stuff."

"I'm not a leper, and I don't have pink eye!"

"In light of your . . . issue," Nevin interrupted, "you may wear your sunglasses. Only for the duration of this medical emergency."

"How benevolent of you," Drew muttered darkly as he unfolded his sunglasses and slammed them onto his face.

I was officially a horrible person. Why didn't Shakespeare write any scenes where Petruchio soliloquized about how guilty he felt for messing with Kate? I had a lump in my stomach just like the time I'd eaten a whole funnel cake and gone on Kingda Ka at Six Flags Great Adventure.

The next few hours of rehearsal were not my finest. Because I couldn't concentrate, I couldn't absorb any of the blocking, which meant that Drew had to steer me around the stage, which only made me feel guiltier. Every exasperated sigh he let out as he grabbed my elbow and pulled me around the stage was like a painful reminder of what I'd done to his eyes.

When we broke for lunch, I had never felt less like eating.

"My stomach is killing me," I moaned dramatically as I collapsed in the shade next to Heidi and Amy.

"I know, these corsets are the worst," Amy clucked sympathetically as she dug around in her giant purse. "Have a Wheat Thin."

I clutched half-heartedly at the box she proffered.

"I have a feeling it's not just the corsets," Heidi said knowingly. "It's your conscience. We have to stop, Cass. We're hurting him. He may be a litterer, but this is wrong. And you know it is. You know it in here." She poked me in the chest, finger tapping against my corset.

"We—we're gonna stop?" Amy asked. "We can't! Let's be real. He's *so* not boyfriend-ready yet."

"We can't stop now," I whispered as I started nervously munching on Wheat Thins. "Because, otherwise, what was the point? We just tortured him for no reason. We at least have to keep going until we get results."

"Torture? Never a good way to get results," Heidi admonished me. "That's not a path sane people follow."

"It's not torture; it's simply playing pranks. Just like silly, stupid, fun summer camp pranks," Amy said. "Or at least it's supposed to be. Right, Cass?"

"Right." I nodded vigorously. "We just went a little too far this time. And it's not like we disfigured him on purpose. We'll keep going; we'll just scale it back a little. No more pranks that could possible cause bodily harm."

"Promise?" Heidi asked skeptically.

I held up my pinky for her to pinky swear. She looped her finger in mine, fixing me with a serious gaze.

"We can't stop now," Amy said as she tossed her hair. "I *need* him to be my perfect boyfriend. He looks extra yummy with those sunglasses."

"And that mountain man beard," I added helpfully.

"Oh, stop it." She swatted my arm. "It's only temporary. And it's for his *art*. Very Daniel Day Lewis."

"Very *Bridget Jones's Diary*," I agreed.

As Amy and Heidi laughed, I could feel the knot of guilt in my stomach start to unravel. Everything would be fine. We just had to reevaluate our methods—that was all.

After lunch, Nevin decided to work on a scene Kate and Petruchio weren't in, sending me and Drew backstage to wait until he was ready for us.

"Seriously? Wait backstage? Again?" Drew groused as he sank down to sit with his back against the flat wall, legs stretched out into the muddy grass that comprised our very glamorous backstage area. "It's like they're not even trying to manage our time effectively. Why call everyone in if they're not going to use us? Why make us sit backstage and do nothing?"

"I'm sorry, do you have somewhere else to be? A pressing appointment in the green mountains of Vermont?"

"No, I just have . . . stuff . . . to do. Stuff I'd rather do than just sit back here." He mumbled something that sounded like "itching" and lifted up his sunglasses to rub at his eyes, like a grumpy, sleepy bear. "I don't even understand how this happened."

"How *what* happened?" Boy, if I was planning to carry on with my life of crime, I'd really have to work on my nonchalance.

"This, genius." He gestured toward his face. "I'm so careful about buying hypoallergenic everything. I haven't had a reaction like this in a while. I don't understand what it could possibly be."

"Well, um, isn't it obvious?" I knew this line of questioning was in no way accusatory, but my heart started beating a little bit faster anyway. "It's an old house. And it's not particularly clean. There's dust everywhere. Who knows what kind of crap is floating around in the air?"

"That's probably it. Shitty old house. I'm surprised that leaning tower of crap hasn't been condemned yet." He shrugged, then folded his arms like he was trying to keep from scratching at his eyes. I could see his hands balled into tight fists. "God, this is such a waste of time."

"Do you even *like* acting?" I asked skeptically, eager to distract him from his itchy eyes. "Because it kind of seems like all you do at rehearsal is complain."

"Of course, I like acting," he said, looking surprised. "It's the only thing I've ever wanted to do."

"Me, too," I grudgingly acknowledged that we had something in common. Gross. "When did you know?"

"What, that I wanted to be an actor? I was six," he said as he scratched his beard. "My dad and I were going to play with the Nerf football in the park. My dad's kind of a football nut—he was sort of a big deal in college. We were both wearing matching Scarlet Knights T-shirts, if you can believe it," Drew scoffed. "I can't believe I let myself get coerced into a matching outfit. Even if I was only six. That's no excuse."

Scarlet Knights? Drew's dad had gone to Rutgers? That was crazy. Hopefully Drew wouldn't be stopping by campus to pick up any more T-shirts in the next four years.

"But when we got there," Drew continued, "the park was full of guys running around in funny-looking outfits, carrying swords. There was one really tall guy standing in the middle of the group, talking. 'We few, we happy few, we band of brothers: for he today that sheds his blood with me shall be my brother.'"

"*Henry V.* The Saint Crispin's Day speech, right?"

"Yup." He nodded. "It was some summer Shakespeare group rehearsing in the park. I sat down in the middle of the field and watched the whole thing. My dad kept trying to get me to leave, but I wouldn't budge. I'd never seen anything like it. It was like a movie, but *real*. The swords, the language . . . everything. It was incredible. Even if I didn't know what half of it meant. I thought it was about Rice Krispie Treats, not Saint Crispin."

"An honest mistake."

"But I knew I *loved* it. I spent the rest of the summer running around with a plastic sword, stabbing things, shouting, 'These wounds I had on Rice Krispies Day!'"

I laughed. I mean, that was funny.

"That's when I knew I wanted to be an actor. And much to my dad's chagrin, that meant that my glorious football career was over."

"Oh." I swallowed uncomfortably. I could tell he had meant it as a joke, but the tightening in his voice was unmistakable. There was definitely something complicated there. Or maybe I was just extra sensitive to complicated dad situations at the moment. "I'm sorry."

"It's not a big deal. My dad doesn't want me to be an actor—not exactly a tragedy of *Hamlet* proportions. What about you?" he asked brusquely, changing the subject. I could tell he wished he hadn't said anything. "When did you know?"

"It's kind of a similar story." I shrugged. "The Shakespeare Theater of New Jersey came to my school and did *Midsummer*. And Titania had really, really red hair, just like me." I smiled, remembering how cool I'd thought Titania was. "I'd always been teased for being a redhead. Probably all redheads are. But here was this redhead, who wasn't just a fairy, but a *queen*. A super powerful queen. Watching her onstage, she seemed like she could do anything. And then after, when I tried out for my first school play, when I was onstage, I felt like I could do anything, too. Just like Titania. Even though I was wearing a homemade cow costume, it didn't matter. I was one invincible cow."

"You were a cow?"

"I was *the* cow. My first show was a dramatic retelling of 'Old McDonald's Farm.' I've tried to destroy all the evidence, but there might be an incriminating video lurking somewhere in our basement."

"I bet you made a fine cow." He smirked.

"I was a very method cow. I got sent to the principal's office for only communicating by mooing in class."

"What a rebel."

"They were trying to stifle my creativity! I couldn't let the man mess with my process."

"KATE!" Nevin bellowed, and I dutifully made my way to the stage. That was almost a pleasant conversation. How bizarre.

Drew didn't end up doing much for the rest of rehearsal, and I could practically feel the heat of his anger rolling off him as Nevin called us together to meet before he dismissed us. Although I wasn't as big a proponent of yoga as my mom, if ever someone needed to do yoga, it was probably Drew. He was headed straight for a rage-induced hernia. At the very least, he could stop criticizing Rhys for taking too much time with his exits and entrances. These all-day-long rehearsals were taxing enough without contending with someone's pissy mood. This was a far cry from the couple hours of after-school rehearsal I was used to, and it was exhausting. Besides, it wasn't Drew's job to police the blocking, anyway. It was so annoying, the way he always acted like he was in charge. Why couldn't he just listen to Nevin and mind his own business like the rest of us?

"The play," Nevin announced, "will be blocked by tomorrow. Then we start runs. We open in a week."

Everyone buzzed a little with nervous energy. We all knew when the show was opening and knew that we'd only signed up for a two-week rehearsal process, but it still felt like everything was moving unbelievably fast. At school, we'd rehearsed shows for months. But in the real world, where time was money, and space was usually money, rehearsal processes were much, much shorter. Wow. One week. And where was Lola St. Clair in all of this, anyway? Did she really have so much faith in Nevin that she wouldn't even bother to come see how the show was progressing? This was her company after all. You'd think she would have been more concerned with our production than our ability to move to bongo music or to register sexual tension, but evidently not. That first day had been so surreal that sometimes I wondered if Lola St. Clair had been a figment of my imagination. Or a company-wide hallucination.

"We have one week to create a transformative experience for the fine art–loving citizens of Vermont, the summer tourists who flock here from Boston in droves, and, of course, your friends, family, and loved ones."

Family. Would mine be here? Ordinarily Mom would never miss a show, but I'd been completely ignoring her since I got here. And I hadn't exactly been talking to her a ton even when we were sharing the same house. I wondered if my dad would come. Probably not. He'd made it to graduation, but he'd missed *Anything Goes*, so why should this be any different? And even if he did come . . . I wasn't sure I wanted to see him.

Amy elbowed me sharply in the ribs, breaking my train of thought. I looked up, past Nevin's head. Taylor Griffith was sitting on top of the picnic table by himself, messenger bag slung over his shoulder, skateboard resting near his feet. He waved. *He waved!* At me! Oh, God, now was not the time to freak out.

CHAPTER 12

"Somebody's *blushing*," Amy whispered as Nevin droned on about the importance of enunciating consonants and getting enough sleep.

"Shutupshutupshutup," I hissed as I tried to wish away my telltale blush. Honestly, he'd occupied way too much of my brain space since the moment I was pretty sure we'd almost kissed. Brain space that should have been occupied by consonants. And sleep.

"All alone, without his posse. Verrry interesting," Amy purred. "I think that makes it a date."

"Itsnotadate," I hissed again through clenched teeth. "He clearly just really likes that picnic table."

"Shh!" Heidi shushed us on my other side. "Major denial, Cass," she added.

"SLEEP!" Nevin concluded with a flourish. "REST! Be ready to work. Go, and SLEEP! You're dismissed."

Finally. I sauntered as casually as I could over to my bag, trying to play it cool as I ripped that stupid corset off. Ah, sweet freedom. My T-shirt was ridiculously wrinkled from the corset, but it would have to do. It's not like I had any other options. Besides, I wasn't exactly sure what constituted an impressive date outfit. And anyway, it wasn't a date.

Taylor jumped off the picnic table, picked up his board, and strode through the grass to meet me.

"There she is," Taylor announced. I could feel the rest of the cast exchange glances and raised eyebrows—well, except for Amy, who just looked rather smug. "The coldest story every told. How could you play me like that last night?"

"Shh!" I clapped my hand over his mouth, looking around in panic. Thankfully Nevin had left. "What are you doing?"

"Last night. Mystery solved," Drew sighed. "How uncreative."

"Relax, Red, I'm just playin'." Taylor chuckled as he removed my hand from his mouth.

"Really? Because it sounds like you're trying to get me fired."

"Not here, I get it, I get it. No sweat, Betty. Let's bounce."

"Where are we going?"

"You'll see." He smiled, and my stomach did this weird happy flutter. I was in serious, serious trouble. I had a feeling I would have followed him if he'd proposed a trip to the Lake Dunmore Waste Management Facility.

As I started to follow Taylor away from the theater space and toward the woods, I felt someone grab my wrist, roughly. I whirled around, coming face-to-face with Drew's hazel eyes, flashing angrily.

"I hope you know what you're doing."

"Actually, I do know what I'm doing." I yanked my arm back. "Thanks for your concern," I added sarcastically.

"Cass, I don't give a shit what you do with your personal life. But don't be stupid. Are sleepovers with Fall-Out Boy here really worth screwing up the show?"

"I didn't sleep over—"

"I don't care what you did or didn't do," he interrupted me. "I just know that if you traipse in and out of the house at three a.m., you run a legitimate risk of getting kicked out, ruining the show, and screwing everything up for me. And everyone."

"I'm sure *everyone* really appreciates your concern." Of *course* he had said "me" first. Lest I forget that the sun orbited around Drew. "But I can *handle* this."

"I hope so."

"You comin', Red?" Taylor called from across the field.

"Absolutely!" I yelled back, turning on Drew and stomping away toward Taylor.

God, Drew made me so angry! Who did he think he was, trying to control my life? What right did he have to interfere? It was absolutely none of his business. Completely infuriating. What a smug, patronizing . . .

"Dag, Red, slow your roll," Taylor exclaimed. "You're, like, leaving a trail of steam behind you."

"Sorry," I sighed. "He's just . . . so . . . frustrating!"

"Who? That guy?"

"Yeah. Drew. He's an idiot. And definitely the last thing I want to talk about right now."

"Already forgotten, Red," he said breezily. "We have some serious, serious business to discuss."

"Serious, huh?" I had no idea what that could entail. A boarding emergency? A declaration of his everlasting love? I snorted.

Luckily, Taylor didn't seem to notice and continued to lead me down the path winding around Lake Dunmore, which followed the shoreline. He turned abruptly away from the lake and onto one of the small dirt paths that led deeper into the forest. After a few twists and turns, the wooded area opened into a small clearing.

It was so beautiful it almost didn't seem like it was real. Wildflowers dotted the tall grass, adding splashes of yellow, white, and blue to the green expanse. A couple of butterflies floated lazily from stem to stem. There were probably mosquitoes and bees, too, but I didn't see them. I felt like one of those kids who fell out of the closet and into Narnia.

"This is beautiful," I exhaled quietly.

"Sick, right?" Taylor agreed. "Come here, Cass."

Taylor lay down in the middle of the field, and I joined him, careful not to get too close, but close enough that he could reach out and touch my hand. If he wanted to.

"Wow."

White puffy clouds floated along in the deepest blue sky I'd ever seen. The leaves on the trees along the edge of the clearing rustled in the wind. The sun shone gently down, bathing me in warmth.

"This is my favorite place at Dunmore," Taylor said, and then, much to my surprise, he reached over, grabbed my hand, and squeezed it gently. I squeezed back, unable to fight the giant grin that broke out on my face. "It's the reason I love coming back every year. Teaching the little ones tricks is cool and all, but being up here is just the best. I can, like, breathe here, you know? It's the air or some shit. It's different."

A stomping, thrashing sound not unlike a wild bull on a rampage startled me into sitting up abruptly.

Drew bulldozed into the clearing, a baseball bag slung over his shoulder.

"You have *got* to be kidding me," I muttered. He was like that tiny raincloud that followed Eeyore around—always there, making everything worse.

"Excuse me," Drew cleared his throat loudly, and looked somewhat flustered as he marched across the field, indubitably squashing butterflies and ladybugs and other cute things as he cut a path of destruction through the wilderness.

"No sweat, homes," Taylor called casually at Drew's retreating back. "Think you've got a stalker, Red."

"Hardly," I scoffed. "We *hate* each other. I'm just unlucky."

"That luck of the Irish not doing it for you?" He reached out one large, tan hand and ran it through my long red hair, casually winding one of my curls around his finger. A delicious shiver ran down my spine.

God, he had such an effect on me. And by the look in his eyes, I could tell he knew it, too. I *had* to get it together. I was not the girl who could be turned to a pile of mush by a boy. I refused to be that girl.

STEPHANIE KATE STROHM

"The Mackays have been in Jersey since the Revolution. And besides, we're Scottish. So, we have no luck. Just the curse of the haggis."

He laughed. "The curse of the haggis, sounds epic. Aight." He cleared his throat. "It's time to get serious." He fixed me with that liquid blue stare, and it took all the strength I had not to melt immediately. Guys should not have been allowed to be that attractive. It just wasn't fair. "Brace yourself, Cass. Because this is some seriously sick shit coming at you right now."

I nodded. I couldn't quite tell if I was bracing myself for a good thing or a bad thing, so I tried to keep my face neutral.

Taylor unbuckled the messenger bag slung over his shoulder. I did a double take when I realized the small insignia on the front read PRADA. Whoa. I wasn't much of a purse girl, but even I knew enough to know that I was presently in the company of the most expensive bag I'd ever seen. This skating business must have been way more serious, and more lucrative, than I'd thought. Suddenly I felt self-conscious about my wrinkled T-shirt and free Grand Prix Weehawken tote bag.

"Check it," Taylor announced as he slapped a thick packet of paper down on the long grass.

"Looks like a script," I said curiously, as I leaned over to pick it up.

"That's cuz it is, Mama."

"*Prove It or Do It*," I read the title out loud. "It's a screenplay?"

"Yeah." He nodded vigorously, excitement sparking in his eyes. "My manager wants me to expand my brand. Into

THE TAMING OF THE DREW

like movies and shit. And whatever megacorp it is that owns Gangsta Raw just bought a production company. They want me to play the lead in this movie."

I flipped to the next page.

"Ryan," I read off the first description on the list of characters. "Eighteen. Southern California golden boy. Tan, toned, attractive. Amateur skater with dreams of making it big. Edgy. Attitude."

"Sounds just like me, right?"

I nodded. I mean, it did.

"I thought it would be easy as shit," Taylor continued, "because it's basically me, right? But when I say the words, they sound all stupid and awk. And now I can't tell if it's because the script is bad, or because I can't act for shit. That sucks, right?"

He ran his hands through his hair, leaving the sun-golden strands sticking straight up. He sighed heavily.

"I just . . . I just don't wanna do any stupid shit, Cass. It'd rip my cred to shreds. Trash my rep. You know?"

"I get it. Cred is important." I knew what he meant. When I got to do my first movie—I hoped one day I would—I sure wouldn't want it to be something stupid.

"I've been skating too hard for too long to become a joke." His shoulders slumped.

"Well." I scooted closer to him. "Can I do something to help?"

"I hope so." He lifted his head and smiled right at me, sending a shot of adrenaline coursing through my veins. "That's why I wanted to talk to you. You're an actress, right?"

STEPHANIE KATE STROHM

"Yes. Well, I mean, I'm not professional or anything, not yet. I mean I haven't even started college—"

"Doesn't matter," he interrupted. "You're good, Cass. I listen to you when you're rehearsing, you know? I'm not just eating Cheetos and watching you do yoga. Although I admit that part *is* mad enjoyable."

He winked, and I turned beet red.

"And you're saying all this crazy old shit and I don't know what any of the words mean, but somehow I know exactly what you're saying, you know? *That's* how I know you're a good actor. Because you get the feelings across even when you're not saying normal words. And if you can understand Shakespeare, I figure you know what's good. Cuz he's supposed to be, like, the best, right?"

"Yeah, he's pretty good," I joked. Talk about an understatement. I wondered what Old Will would think of *Prove It or Do It*. Or Taylor calling his work "crazy old shit."

"So, maybe you could read the script for me, tell me if it sucks?"

"Sure, I can read the script. But remember, I'm not an expert or anything. I don't know that much about movies—"

"I'm sure you know enough. You probably read mad scripts. And I can tell you don't pull any punches. I trust you. You're the only person right now who's not trying to make money off me," he muttered darkly. "I just don't wanna be pushed into looking like an idiot cuz it'll make a bunch of dickwads in suits a butt-load of money."

"If it sucks, I'll tell you." I nodded. "I promise."

"I knew you had my back, Red." He smiled. "And then if it doesn't suck, maybe you could give me, like, some acting lessons or something? Make sure I don't sound like a moron."

I was really flattered. No one had ever asked *me* for acting lessons. I'd *taken* plenty of acting classes, but I'd never *taught* one before.

"I could, but just so you know, I've never taught—"

"Enough with the undersell, Red!" He laughed. "You are like the opposite of a claimer. I've never seen anything like this. Own it."

"Okay, okay, fine." I laughed, too. "I'll read the script, and I'll give you acting lessons, and *Prove It or Do It* will be frigging awesome, okay?"

"That's more like it!" Taylor fist-pumped triumphantly. "Now, we just gotta figure out your payment—"

"My payment?"

"Yeah, I'm not asking you to do something for nothing. That shit's not right. Come on, there's gotta be something you want."

Something I wanted? God, was there ever something I wanted. My mouth went dry as Taylor stretched, lifting up his T-shirt and exposing a couple inches of rock-hard abs.

"Speechless?" He raised one eyebrow. "Well, I'll think of something," Taylor smiled naughtily, and the thoughts that popped into my head made me turn bright red again.

"Let's just say you owe me a favor." I swallowed.

"I'll owe you as many favors as you want." He smirked. "We have a deal?" Taylor held out his hand for me to shake.

"Deal."

I took his hand and shook, but instead of letting go, Taylor used my hand to pull me closer to him. He raised his left hand to cup my chin and tilt my head toward him. Holy shit. It was happening. It was really happening.

As Taylor kissed me, a sensation like a million pop rocks exploding slammed through my body. His lips were slightly chapped, but somehow it felt nice, and he smelled like summer at the beach—sunscreen and sunshine and coconuts.

I knew I should have been focusing on the kissing, since it was really good kissing, but there was this part of my brain that kept screaming, *The hottest guy in the world is making out with* you! *He picked* you, *Cass Mackay!* It was hard *not* to think about it. I just couldn't believe that someone so hot wanted *me*. I thought these were the kind of guys that went for the Amys of the world, the petite blond prom princesses. But no. He'd picked me.

I was so preoccupied with the kissing and my internal monologue that somehow I hadn't noticed that Taylor had maneuvered me onto my back on the grass. Things were progressing a little fast. As I tried to figure out the most democratic way to slow this down, something kicked my leg.

"Eh-hem."

I rolled away from Taylor and bolted upright, momentarily panicking that it was a bear or some other wild animal. Nope, it was worse. Drew. I should have known. He seemed to have a knack for ruining my life in the most spectacular fashion.

"Can I help you?" I asked acidly.

"Daaaag, bra, can't you see I'm busy?" Taylor groaned as he flopped dramatically onto his stomach.

"You have to go back to the house." Drew cleared this throat. "Actually, *we* have to get back to the house. We're having a text session. Rehearsal. Something."

"After hours?" I asked skeptically. "That has happened approximately never."

"Believe me, I'm not thrilled either. But it's happening."

"Fine, fine." I sprung up to my feet, trying to surreptitiously clean any grass off my back.

"You might wanna . . ." Drew made a vague gesture around his upper arms, then might have blushed. It was hard to tell with his beard.

"What?" I looked down at my arm. "Oh, for Pete's sake, it's just a bra strap." I slid my two turquoise bra straps back into place. Hmm. When did those get down there?

"Cass, you're not seriously leaving?" Taylor popped up and confidently slung his arm around my waist.

"Unfortunately, I am."

"But shit was just getting interesting." He turned me around to face him and smiled. I felt my knees start to go weak. Every time he smiled at me this warm melting-butter feeling spread through my body.

"We're late already." Drew tapped his watch.

"Yup, got it!" I barked. Jesus, he was annoying. Did his brain not develop the part that registers regular human social cues? I just needed three minutes to say goodbye, like a decent, civilized human being.

"You're really going with this lame-ass?" Taylor jerked his thumb at Drew, who glowered.

"I can't miss rehearsal. It's important. It's like skate . . . practice." Was that what they called it?

"Okay, Red, I get it." Taylor nodded and leaned forward to whisper in my ear. "You keep leaving me brokenhearted. But I know you'll make it up to me eventually."

A shiver ran down my neck as his breath tickled my ear. Suddenly, he grabbed my face with both his hands and pulled me toward him, kissing me forcefully. But almost too forcefully. Like he was trying to prove something.

I had a feeling this kiss was more for Drew's benefit than mine, which was totally unnecessary. It's not like he had anything to worry about there. Taylor broke away and pressed the script into my hands.

"Take good care of her, homes!" he called as he settled back into the grass. Drew practically dragged me back down the path to the lake.

"How did you find out about this unplanned rehearsal anyway?" I asked as we trod down the path. "Don't tell me you get cell service here." Then I really *would* have to kill him. Life couldn't be so unfair that the universe would reward Beelzebub with service in this dead zone.

"No, of course not. I took one of the walkie-talkies with me."

"Walkie-talkies? They still make those?"

"Of course they do. There was a really old pair in the boathouse. I took one and left one with Langley. You should always have a way to contact people when you go into the woods. It's not safe to go alone. Or with someone you don't know that well."

"This is hardly the woods. We're fifteen feet from the path. Maybe ten minutes, tops, away from town. And what's that supposed to mean, anyway?" I asked suspiciously. "Someone you don't know that well? Do you mean Taylor? I've known him exactly as long as I've known you. Should I be worried about my wilderness safety alone with you?"

"No, of course not," he scoffed.

"Don't you see how *ridiculous* you're being?" I was trying to keep my temper under control, but it was just impossible. Every time Drew spoke two words I wanted to throttle him. "There's no difference between you and Taylor—"

"On the contrary, there is a *huge* difference," Drew interrupted emphatically.

"No shit, Sherlock!" I exploded. I mean, one was super-hot, the other was a deranged troll. And who says "on the contrary" outside of PBS specials? I took a deep, cleansing yoga breath like Mom had taught me, tried to get my temper under control, and started again, gritting my teeth. "What I *meant* was that I don't understand why you have such a problem with him."

"I have a problem with anything that impacts the show negatively."

"Taylor hasn't impacted the show in any way! Positive or negative."

"Not yet," he prophesied darkly. "And he called me a lame-ass."

"You were *being* a lame-ass," I insisted, and we fell into a disgruntled silence. Nothing but the low buzz of the mosquitoes and the soft crunching sounds as Drew clomped over the grass.

"What's with the baseball bag?" I asked eventually. I'm not good with awkward silences. Even when they're hateful, I just feel this need to fill dead air. "You couldn't find anyone to play with you?" I asked with mock-sympathy. "Somehow, I'm not surprised."

"It's not for baseball—"

"Cass!" A female voice shrieked. At least Drew hadn't been lying about rehearsal. Although, admittedly, that would have been a strange thing to lie about. The rest of the cast was sitting in a circle with Nevin, scripts in the grass at their feet. Amy waved vigorously at me, and I left Drew in the dust as I sprinted to sit between her and Heidi.

"What were you doing?" Amy asked, eyes darting back and forth from me to Drew, who took care to sit as far away as possible from me on the other side of the circle. "Was this part of the plan? Did he mention me?" she added excitedly.

Before I could figure out how to say no in a way that wouldn't hurt her feelings, Heidi elbowed me in the ribs.

"I thought you left with Taylor," Heidi whispered, confused.

"It got complicated," I grumbled. "Can I share your script?"

Wordlessly, Heidi slid it over to me. I flipped it over, picked up her pencil, and wrote on the back: IT'S TIME FOR PHASE TWO.

I raised my head and glared at Drew across the circle. He wouldn't know what hit him.

CHAPTER 13

awoke to a blood-curdling scream, then smiled and stretched. The vertebrae near my shoulders gave a few satisfying pops. It was going to be a good day.

"Eeeyaaa!" Amy shrieked as she rolled out of bed, pushed her pink "Princess" eyeshade up to the top of her head, and grabbed her perfume off the dresser, brandishing it like mace.

"Nice reflexes." I grinned as I climbed down from the top bunk, careful to avoid Heidi's long limbs hanging off the tiny bed at improbable angles. "I actually feel a lot safer with you as a roommate now."

"I googled bear safety tips after that bear pooped on our stage. If it's a black bear, you want to spray a fog into its face. With mace, or, uh, Touch of Pink."

"You think a bear could make it up these stairs?" I asked as I gently jiggled Heidi's calf to wake her up. "How did she sleep through that scream?"

"I thought it was a bird call," Heidi said dreamily as she stretched, arching her large feet gracefully.

"Bears are *excellent* climbers," Amy said seriously as she replaced the perfume on the dresser and tossed her eyeshade on her pillow. "And this building doesn't lock."

"Let's go see the fruits of our labors," I said gleefully as I rubbed my hands together. I couldn't *wait* to get downstairs.

Barely pausing to slide my feet into flip-flops, I flew down the stairs. Amy padded softly behind me in a pair of pink fuzzy slippers. I jumped the last couple steps and landed with a thud, skidding as my Devils Hockey T-shirt flapped like a sail.

"What's wrong?" I asked as I burst breathlessly into the kitchen, using every last ounce of my acting abilities to wipe the huge grin from my face.

Drew stood in the middle of the kitchen staring despondently into an open cereal box, as Noah nodded sympathetically over his shoulder while slurping a bowl of Cheerios. Rhys was perched on top of the freezer surveying the scene disdainfully.

"The *mo-oh-ost* disgusting thing," Rhys moaned between bites of what looked like a Brown Sugar Cinnamon Pop Tart. "No one is safe anymore."

"What happened?" Amy asked a little *too* innocently, her voice pitched several octaves too high for credibility. I elbowed her subtly in the ribs.

"Some . . . stupid . . . mouse . . . thing . . . my food," Drew muttered unintelligibly.

"Looks like we've got ourselves a critter." Noah shrugged before drinking the last of his cereal milk out of the bowl.

"A critter?" Amy squeaked. Much better.

"LOOK!" Drew thundered as he shoved his cereal box in my face.

If I hadn't created that "mouse" hole in the cardboard box myself, or known that the poop pellets were actually Heidi's modeling clay, I would have been totally grossed out.

"Out of my face, please." I swatted the box away.

"What's going on?" Heidi arrived in the kitchen, belting a kimono around her waist.

"A mouse pooped in all of Drew's food," Rhys announced, pretending to vomit over the side of the freezer.

"A mouse pooped in *some* of Drew's food," Noah said fairly, adding his bowl to the tower of dishes in the sink. "Looks like the little guy burrowed his way into the boxes, ate a whole bunch, and left some presents behind."

"Thanks for the play-by-play," Drew said snidely. "Who cares what it did? It ruined everything. All my freaking food."

"All creatures need nourishment," Heidi said kindly. "His need is no less important than yours. The mouse didn't mean any harm."

She was so compassionate, I wondered for a moment if Heidi had forgotten that there wasn't actually a mouse— that *we* were, in fact, the mouse. Or maybe she was just displaying her excellent acting chops.

"The mouse's nourishment is really not my chief concern right now," Drew said sarcastically, scooping all the mouse-tainted boxes off his portion of the shelf and dumping them into the trash. I was so proud of the little mouse-holes I'd created I was almost sad to see them go. It had been a long time since I'd done any arts and crafts.

"Someone say something about a mouse?" Langley popped her head in the door.

The six of us nodded.

Wordlessly, she thrust a can of Lysol disinfectant wipes at Heidi, who happened to be closest to the door, before disappearing again.

"Don't be late for rehearsal!" Langley called as her voice faded away.

"What I don't understand," Drew said meditatively, looking at each of us in turn as he folded his arms over the BACK TO THE FUTURE logo on his T-shirt, "is why the mouse only touched *my* food. It doesn't make any sense. Mice can't distinguish between who owns what. They don't have that kind of brain capacity."

"Maybe the mouse is also gluten-intolerant?" I suggested innocently, assuming that explained the inordinate amount of quinoa and rice flour products on Drew's shelf.

"Mice aren't—"

"He simply ate his fill and moved on, taking no more and no less than what he needed," Heidi interrupted. "Yes, we could all learn something from this little mouse—"

"Thank you, Grandmother Willow," Drew snapped. "Well, wouldn't want to be late for rehearsal!" he chirped with fake enthusiasm. "I'll worry about starving to death some other time."

He stomped out of the room while the other boys trailed behind. Amy snatched the Lysol from Heidi and hopped gracefully up onto the counter.

"Eww." Amy wrinkled her nose with distaste. "'Poop'"—
she air-quoted—"aside, these cabinets are super dirty. Like
disgusting."

"What do you expect?" I asked as she slid off the counter
and dropped the nearly black Lysol cloth into the trash. "Stu-
dents and actors live here. Not exactly two groups known for
their domestic skills."

She laughed, and we tramped up the stairs.

"I still feel bad," Heidi sighed heavily.

"Heidi, he can buy new food!" I exclaimed as we poured
into our room and I started digging around for something
clean to put on. "That was like some cereal, pasta, and a box
of crackers. Not that much."

"I feel bad that a mouse had to take the blame." She
pursed her lips. "An innocent creature. What if Langley sets
up a trap, and we're responsible for *murder*? Rodenticide!"

"Langley's response to a mouse was Lysol. I think any
mouse that may or may not exist in this house is totally fine."

Not surprisingly, Drew was in a particularly foul mood
at rehearsal. The torrent of rage he unleashed when Noah
crossed downstage of him instead of upstage probably would
have made anyone but the remarkably even-tempered Noah
cry. Even Nevin appeared taken aback, and he wasn't exactly
an old softie.

"Do you think it's working?" Amy whispered anxiously
backstage where we hid in safety, peeking around the curtain
as Drew continued ranting about people not knowing the
blocking this close to opening. "If anything, he just seems . . .
grumpier."

"That's just the first phase," I said with more confidence than I felt, watching Drew turn redder and redder as he continued yelling. "Look at the play! Kate's totally pissed at first. We just have to go through *every aspect* of the plan. *That's* when we'll see results."

"Uh-huh." Amy still seemed skeptical, even though Drew had finally worn himself out and stopped shouting. He looked pretty red though. "Ooo, we totally had a moment earlier, though!" she squealed excitedly, her face brightening.

"Details, *por favor.*"

"Well," she said breathlessly, "he said, 'You probably have a highlighter,' and I said, 'Yes, of course,' and then I gave him my blue highlighter, and then he said, 'Yeah, I forgot to highlight this line,' and then I said, 'Yeah, I hate when that happens. It's the worst!'" She concluded triumphantly, "Pretty amaze, am I right?"

"Totally," I agreed, even though I couldn't see what was so *amaze* about it. But she looked so hopeful and happy, anything less than an enthusiastic response would have made me feel like I was kicking a puppy. I sighed as she skipped off to join Noah onstage. I had been so sure that Shakespeare couldn't steer us wrong, but the further we "tamed" the Drew, the less sure I felt of anything.

One thing I *did* feel sure about was that I couldn't wait to see Taylor again. I must have been doing okay at rehearsal because Nevin didn't give me many notes—or maybe he was just busy trying to keep Drew under control—but I felt like my whole being was vibrating, consumed by thoughts of

Taylor. In some ways it was a relief not to have cell service, so there was no point in constantly checking my phone—he had no way to get in touch with me. But on the other hand, why *hadn't* he gotten in touch with me? Didn't he want to see me again? Shouldn't we have made a concrete plan? Nevin yelled at me for biting my lip, and I snapped out of it. I was in Padua, not Vermont, and there were no skateboarders in Padua.

Declining to follow Amy and Heidi back to the house, the minute rehearsal ended I fled into the woods, Keds smacking the path as I raced back to the spot where I'd met up with Taylor. As I skidded to a halt in the clearing, I looked around wildly. Of course, there was no one there but me. And a squirrel. I sank into a seated position and blew an unruly curl that had escaped from my ponytail out of my eyes. What did I expect, that he would have just been waiting there? I was sure Taylor had better things to do than hang around in a field all day, waiting for sweaty redheads.

Sighing, I flopped on my back into the warm grass and stretched my arms over my head, watching the sun dapple through the leaves above me. The minutes ticked by as I watched the progression of a ladybug across a twig. The birds chirped a chorus that sounded remarkably like "stupid, stupid, stupid."

"You're right, birds!" I called back at them. Because, seriously, I was *beyond* stupid. Waiting in a random field for some boy who might or might not show up?

The crackle of breaking underbrush interrupted my stream of self-loathing.

"Taylor?" I asked as I popped up. Nope. I sighed as Drew appeared at the edge of the clearing and covered his eyes.

"Please tell me I'm not interrupting anything," Drew called from across the field, peeking through his fingers.

"Not a damn thing. Put your hands down—you look stupid." I flopped dramatically back down into the grass.

"*I* look stupid? I'm not the one rolling around in the mud."

"It's not even muddy. Go away." I covered my face with my arm, hoping that if I couldn't see him, he would simply cease to exist.

"Nope. Because as impossible as it sounds, you could actually be useful right now. Get up." He prodded my leg with his toe.

I bolted upright and aimed my best soccer kick directly at his left shin.

"Ow!" he shrieked, grabbing his shin as he hopped away, the baseball bag on his shoulder swinging wildly. Look at that. Maybe I should have stuck with soccer after all.

"You kicked me first!" I retorted as I pushed myself up to standing, brushing the dirt off my butt.

"That wasn't a *real* kick, that was—ow, are you wearing steel-toed boots?" He shot me a wounded look as he rubbed his shin.

"If they made steel-toed Keds, I'd be first in line."

"Of that I have no doubt," he muttered. "Come on, follow me. Assuming I'm not crippled for life."

I rolled my eyes but followed him deeper into the woods. I certainly wasn't going to hang around and wait for Taylor any longer than I already had. I'd veered dangerously far into pathetic girl territory.

"Do you have your walkie-talkie, Ranger Rick?" I asked, breaking the silence. "Just want to make sure we're practicing wilderness safety."

"Of course."

Apparently he had missed my sarcasm. Drew unceremoniously dropped his baseball bag into the center of the next clearing, a more densely shaded space than the one we'd previously been in, with shorter, trampled-down grass.

He crouched down to unzip the bag as I looked around, still unsure of what exactly we were doing here.

"Catch," he said calmly, before a heavy metal object started hurtling its way toward me. My brain briefly registered it as a sword before going into panic mode. Miraculously, I managed to grab onto the non-pointy end and kept myself from getting impaled.

"You threw a sword at my face!" I squawked.

"You caught it." He shrugged nonchalantly as if he hadn't just flung several feet of steely death at my vulnerable parts. "Have you ever used one of these before?"

"What? A sword? No. Why do you have this?" I asked incredulously.

"You've never used a sword before? Really?" Drew tossed his sword up and caught it, and then did something that looked like it should have been called a thrust or a parry. "No stage combat? Not in class? In camp? A weekend seminar?"

"I can do a mean forward roll," I said defensively. "A great slap. A pretty good punch. But not so much with the swords, no. That wasn't covered in the stage combat unit in drama club."

Drew looked surprisingly natural with a sword in his hands. Kind of like a sexy pirate. I swatted that thought out of my brain the minute it popped up. Where did that come from? I must have been losing it.

"Why are you blushing?" he asked curiously.

"It's hot!" I barked. "The sun. I'm very susceptible to sun poisoning. Redheads produce less melanin."

"Okay," he said equably. "We'll go in the shade. Want to be my sparring partner?"

"Wait a minute." I followed him into the shade. "You're seriously going to teach me to sword fight?"

"Seriously." He got into some kind of ready position. "If you're interested."

"Totally interested," I answered more enthusiastically than I'd meant to let on, but I couldn't help it. I'd always wanted to learn but had never gotten into weapons combat in any of the shows I'd done in high school. Like when I was Beatrice opposite Jeff Butts and said, "Oh, God, that I were a man! I would eat his heart in the marketplace," I *meant it*. Not that I wanted to eat anyone's heart. Beatrice just meant that she wanted to be able to fight her enemies with a sword, and so did I. Jeff Butts was terrible at combat. I would have been way better.

"Just don't, like, come at me out of nowhere and make me defend myself like this is Zorro or something. I want to learn how to poke you before you attempt to decapitate me," I said.

"It's stage combat, not real combat. The whole point is *not* to decapitate you."

"Just checking. You've got a shifty look. Especially holding a sword."

"First of all, it's not a sword. It's a rapier."

"Isn't a rapier a type of sword?" I asked skeptically.

"Well . . . yes. Technically," he admitted as I grinned victoriously. "It's a slender sword used for more athletic fights and thrusting attacks. But just call it a rapier, to make sure you differentiate it from a broadsword. That's the accepted, accurate terminology."

"I'll call it whatever you want"—I swished my sword dramatically—"as long as I get to poke you."

"Again, no poking." He sighed heavily. "First, we warm up. And then I'm teaching you to parry. You're clearly not ready to thrust."

"I'm ready to thrust all day long," I said before I realized what it sounded like, then quickly clamped my mouth shut and prayed that Drew chose to ignore it. Thankfully, he did.

Drew led me through a series of warmups that consisted of jumping jacks, squats, stretches, and making tiny circles with my arm while holding the sword. After a couple minutes my arms were killing me! That sword, um, rapier, got so heavy so fast. My arms burned worse than when I went to one of Mom's Yogabooty classes.

"And we do this for how long?" I asked eventually.

"Till you can't take it anymore, which is clearly right about now." I exhaled with relief as I lowered the heavy sword. "It's important to build up the muscles in your sword arm."

"In case of roving bands of brigands?"

"Something like that." Drew grinned. "Now, for Harry, England, and St. George, let's do this."

"Now I know what you were doing with that warmup." I tried to copy Drew's ready position stance. "You were trying to drain all my resources so I couldn't put up a fight."

"Precisely. You plus unlimited energy plus a sword seemed like a deadly combination."

"Hardy har har," I laughed sarcastically. "Shut up and fight."

CHAPTER 14

Despite what he'd said earlier, Drew did teach me how to thrust first. So stage combat was basically broken into two parts: thrusts, when you attack your opponent, and parries, when you block an opponent's attack. Slowly, Drew showed me how to swing the sword in a safe, nonviolent way, first practicing making cuts toward the left and right legs, then the left and right shoulders, and finally, the most dangerous overhand swing, straight to the head. He expertly parried each thrust, blocking the flat of my sword with the flat of his, metal clanging throughout the clearing. Even though we were going about as slow as molasses, it was still impressive how gracefully he moved. And what a good teacher he was.

The hardest part was resisting the temptation to poke him with the sword. Because the ends were blunted I knew I couldn't hurt him, and I would never poke hard enough to do any kind of real damage. But it was fun to annoy him.

"No poking," he reprimanded me for the fifth time.

"I am determined to prove a villain!" I cried, quoting Richard III.

"I'd prefer it if Vermont didn't weep in streams of blood today," he quoted right back at me. Well, kind of—Richard III didn't rule Vermont. "Particularly not my blood."

"Oh, don't be such a baby. The end is blunted," I grumbled. "What, do you tremble? Are you all afraid? Alas, I blame you not, for I am excellent at poking."

"How do you know so much of *Richard III*?" he asked curiously. "Were you in it?"

"Yeah. I was Lady Anne at theater camp." I tried to execute a cool spinning maneuver with my sword that probably didn't look very cool. "I'm kind of weirdly obsessed with it."

"You'd be weird if you *weren't* obsessed with it. It might be my favorite. I was Richard senior year."

"Perfect type-casting, you defused infection of a man," I said with a laugh.

"Alright, that's it—come at me."

I brought the rapier down with a satisfying clang and returned to aiming for the center of his sword like a good little stage combat pupil.

After several hours of thrusting and then learning to parry, I was beyond sweaty and gross. My arms were killing me, practically throbbing with pain, but I felt exhilarated. Eventually my sword arm pretty much gave out, and I tossed the rapier back to Drew.

"That was awesome!" I shouted as Drew started wiping down the swords with a white cloth and some mysterious liquid. "That was so, so cool. I *loved* it. I wish people still had swords so I could fight all the time! Or at least in shows. I wish we could put a sword fight in *our* show. Are there any Shakespeare heroines who fight?" I tried to think of an example.

"Traditionally? Not so much. Well, Viola in *Twelfth Night* has that almost-kind-of duel with Sir Andrew."

"Pfft." I waved my hands dismissively. "That's a fake fight; it's supposed to be silly. I want to do some *damage*."

"I have no doubt that you could do some serious damage. But I saw a female Tybalt once in *Romeo and Juliet*." He carefully laid the swords back in the bag and zipped it up. "She kicked butt."

"A female Tybalt. Wow. That would be awesome," I marveled. "I would *love* to play Tybalt."

"It's a good role for you. You've got the constantly flaring temper and uncontrollable rage necessary for the part."

"Hey!" I punched him in the arm as he stood up, slinging the baseball bag over his shoulder.

"My point exactly." He gestured to his arm. "Uncontrollable rage. I think I can already see the bruise forming."

"Hmph," I sniffed. I couldn't see anything. Except for a slight bicep bulge. "No one would fleer and scorn at *my* solemnity," I muttered, quoting the part of *Romeo and Juliet* where Tybalt is super pissed that Romeo crashed his family's party.

"They wouldn't dare." Drew laughed as we started along the path back to the house. "They'd be afraid for their lives. *No one* would mess with your solemnity."

"Damn straight."

"Seriously, though, it would be a good role for you. You're a natural with a rapier. You picked everything up really quickly. I'm surprised no one's ever put a sword in your hands before."

"Thanks." I blushed at his praise, then cursed myself for blushing. Why did I care what Drew thought? Even if being a natural with a sword was an objectively awesome quality.

"It's also a good, healthy outlet for your unbridled rage," he said, grinning.

"I don't have rage!" I balled up my fists to prevent myself from giving him the pummeling he so justly deserved and proving his point.

Drew threw back his head and roared with laughter. With his heavy beard and suntanned skin, he looked like some kind of devil-may-care pirate. Or like Richard Burton in the movie version of *The Taming of the Shrew*. I wondered idly what he would look like without the beard. Even though he was wearing a normal, modern T-shirt, the beard made him look so old-fashioned, like he should be leading the charge at Agincourt or thundering across the countryside on horseback. He looked like a real Shakespeare hero. Not someone wimpy like Romeo or whiny like Hamlet, but someone tough, like Henry V—someone brave and rakish.

"What are you thinking about?" Drew asked as we made our way back into what passed for a town center on the shores of Lake Dunmore. "Usually you can't stand to be quiet for more than forty-five seconds."

"What? Me? Oh, hmm, nothing," I answered quickly. I certainly wasn't about to answer "thinking you look like a sexy pirate or a Plantagenet prince." I'm not *that* stupid. "Um, bacon?"

"You were thinking about bacon?" he repeated.

"What? I'm hungry," I snapped, grateful it was now dark enough that there was no way he could tell my cheeks were flaming with embarrassment. Bacon? Yikes. Not my finest example of thinking on my feet.

"Milady needs a snack," Drew declared before shoving the sword bag into my arms and jogging off toward the Bait 'n' Bite.

"Hey!" I called out as he disappeared, staggering slightly under the weight of the swords. Clearly, medieval weaponry was no proof of chivalry. Grumbling, I soldiered on after him. By the time I made it to the Bait 'n' Bite, Drew was on his way out the door.

"Would the lady like Twizzlers or M&Ms?" Drew held out the two giant bags of candy. "I wasn't sure if you were a candy or a chocolate kind of girl."

"Both," I answered honestly, tearing into the M&M bag. "The key to a perfect snack is in the balance."

"You want it all, huh? I'm not surprised." He laughed, but there was nothing mean-spirited about it.

"Have a Twizzler," I offered generously. After all, it was really nice that he'd bought all that candy for me. Us. It was weird to think of us as an "us," even if "us" only meant two humans in the same vicinity sharing two enormous bags of candy. Whatever. Still, it was nice. Almost *too* nice. I sniffed the M&Ms for traces of poison. Oh, who was I kidding? Most likely, the only person here who would be that diabolical was me. And I didn't know what poison smelled like anyway.

"A Twizzler from the bag I bought?" Drew raised an eyebrow. "How benevolent of you. Unfortunately, they're not gluten free. Hand me the M&Ms." He shoveled a giant handful into his mouth. "I'm starving. I can't believe that mouse ate all my food. I still don't get it. It just doesn't make any sense! Why would a mouse only eat *my* food? How is that even possible?"

Rather than respond to that, I stuck a long red vine in my mouth and chewed it contemplatively, like a farmer with a piece of straw, trying to look my most nonchalant. I pushed all the guilty feelings out of my mind and tried to focus on the twigs crunching beneath our feet and the hoots and chirps of birds in the woods.

"Why do you have swords?" I blurted out. Not my *most* suave change of subject, but certainly better than "um, bacon."

"In general, or why do I have them here?"

"Either. Both, really."

"Ah. Well, Lola asked me to bring them. I have no idea why, since there isn't a sword fight in *The Taming of the Shrew*, but I complied. That's why they're here."

"She's a weird one."

"No kidding. I thought she'd be checking in on us periodically, but I haven't seen her since that insane climb-a-mountain exercise. That was an epic waste of time." He snorted derisively. "What do you think she does all day?"

"I have no idea. Gives bongo lessons?" I guessed. "Maybe she's setting up for the rest of the season?"

"Maybe. Still, it's strange that we haven't seen her since. Home sweet home," Drew announced as we arrived at the boathouse. The moon seemed enormous, glowing as brightly in the lake's reflection as it did in the sky.

"And why do you *own* swords?"

"They're for stage combat. Obviously."

"How'd you get into that?" I asked. I certainly didn't want to prolong our time together, but I *was* curious.

"Well, for me, Shakespeare and swords have always been synonymous. You remember that production of *Henry V* I told you about?" I nodded. "Well, the minute I was old enough to take a combat class, I did. Then workshops, camp, pretty much anything I possibly could. I recently got certified."

"That's awesome."

"My turn for a question." He turned to face me, and there was something I couldn't quite name sparkling in his hazel eyes. "Have you ever been skinny-dipping?"

"What?" I asked, shocked. That was the last thing I expected to come out of his mouth. "No, of course not!"

He laughed. "I had a feeling you weren't quite the badass you make yourself out to be."

"I don't think I'm a badass—"

"Hey"—he held up his hands defensively—"nothing wrong with being afraid of skinny-dipping. Totally normal."

"I am most certainly not afraid," I protested.

"Prove it."

This time I instantly recognized what was in his eyes: a challenge. And if there was anything I hated more than raisins, it was backing down from a challenge. I swallowed uncomfortably, and it sounded ridiculously loud.

Just like Marty McFly in *Back to the Future*, I needed to learn how to deal with someone calling me chicken. Or, you know, telling me to "prove it." Because now I was trapped. If I just went back into the house, like a normal, sane person, Drew would have full right to mock me for being a chicken for the rest of the summer. And that I could not handle.

So, really, I had only one option. I peeled off my sweaty T-shirt.

"No way." He laughed in disbelief. Then the laugh turned to a kind of strangled, uncomfortably choking noise as he realized my bra was about a foot below his eye level. Good lord, I knew my boobs weren't much to look at, but they weren't so terrifying they deserved a weird choking noise. "You're really gonna do it?"

"Watch me," I said levelly as I kicked off my shorts. "Well, no, don't *watch* me. Turn around!" At this point I was about as covered up as I would be at a beach, thanks to the excellent coverage of my Target undies, but I certainly didn't want to stand there as I went any farther. *If* I went any farther. Oh, why was I doing this?

"Modest all of a sudden." He turned, and tapped his foot impatiently. "I'm waiting, milady. Always time to chicken out."

"Never," I said determinedly. I would *not* chicken out. Certainly not in front of Drew, of all people.

Before I could think about what I was doing, I whipped off my underwear and bra, and hurled myself full-speed off the end of the dock, breaking the stillness of the lake with a satisfying splash as Drew whooped and cheered.

"Holy shit!" I spluttered as I rose to the surface. "It's cold!"

It wasn't freezing, but it was cold enough that every hair on my body must have been standing straight up. If hair could do that underwater.

"I can't believe you did it!" Drew ran to the end of the dock to peer into the water.

"Told you I was going to!" I splashed triumphantly. "Who's the chicken now? Buk-buk-bakaw! Buk-buk-bakaw!"

"Is that supposed to be a chicken?" he asked critically. "That is a terrible chicken."

"Shut up!" I tried to splash him, but it fell a few feet short. "That was an inspired chicken! I really *felt* that chicken!" He chuckled as I did a sort of casual backstroke around, making sure to keep any and all lady parts under the dark cover of the water. "Are you coming in or what, chicken?"

"Am I coming in . . ." He contemplated the question. "Should I? Probably not. What I *should* do is steal all your clothes and run back into the house."

"You wouldn't." My heart stopped. I was paralyzed with fear that I'd be stranded, naked, in Lake Dunmore.

"You're right." He nodded, before pulling his T-shirt over his head. "I wouldn't."

I was not prepared for what was under that shirt. Stunned, I stopped moving and started sinking to the bottom of the lake like a stone, until I regained my composure and started madly treading water once more.

"No peeking!" Drew called.

"As *if*," I said snottily as I paddled myself around to face the opposite shore of the lake. I had to admit I'd been caught off guard by the surprisingly muscular chest I'd glimpsed. Body by stage combat. Who'd have thought? Well, Amy would be pleased to hear that he had at least one inarguably not-at-all-horrible trait.

There was a loud splash, and a giant tsunami wave splashed over me.

"Bleargh!" I burbled, coughing up lake water. Drew popped up to the surface of the lake, hair slicked back and beard matted down like a furry otter boy. "How did you displace so much water?"

"Cannonball!" he cheered, lifting his arms up in victory as his legs churned below the water. I sank down a little deeper, trying to make extra sure nothing below my neck was visible. Suddenly, I was all too aware of the fact that I was completely naked and mere feet away from another completely naked human being. At least, I assumed he was naked. Quickly, I glanced over to the dock. I spotted a pair of plaid boxers on top of a pile of clothes. Totally naked. This was the first time I'd been this close to another naked human being since my mom made me take baths with other babies when I was little.

"Oh, Cass." Drew chuckled. "It doesn't matter how far you sink down in the water. You're so pale that you're glowing like a fluorescent light bulb."

"Are you serious?" I shrieked, trying to find a more full-coverage area of water. If such a thing even existed.

"Redheads." He chuckled again. "Don't worry, I promise I won't look," he added kindly. "Too much."

"Hmph." I doggie-paddled away, trying to put a little distance between us. Because everything was just feeling too naked and too close.

"It's beautiful, isn't it?" he asked, swimming gracefully beside me.

"Um, hello, a little skinny-dipping etiquette, please?" I yelped as I tried to paddle a little farther away. "Do they not have personal space in Rye?"

"Sorry, sorry," he apologized, and floated a few feet away.

"But you're right," I said softly. "It is beautiful."

The water was so bright it almost felt like we were swimming in the moon. I could see Drew as clearly as if it were daylight. He cocked his head, like he was considering me. I felt this weird moment of anticipation, a happy buzz of energy, just like I always feel right before the curtain goes up and I walk on stage. Except there was obviously no play here, and I couldn't understand why I felt that feeling—that pre-show feeling that makes me happier than anything else, that heartbeat before something truly amazing begins.

"Finally!" a female voice cried jubilantly. Whatever was going on between us was broken, and we both turned to face the dock.

Heidi ran out of the house completely buck naked, long limbs flashing white in the moonlight. She executed a graceful dive, barely making a splash, and resurfaced near us. "I've been waiting *forever* for someone to jump in! I just didn't want to be first!"

Drew and I both laughed. Of *course* Heidi was a skinny-dipping aficionado.

Noah and Amy came out a few minutes later, clad in their underwear. I noticed Drew's appreciative glance at Amy's matching pink bra and panties set with annoyance. I mean, not that I cared, good for her, since she was in love with him or whatever. But it seemed completely against the code of skinny-dipping to ogle your fellow participants. I turned away from the splash as Noah and Amy jumped into the water.

"Hey." Amy popped up out of the lake near me, smiling brightly. Maybe a little too brightly. "This is unusual."

"Is it?" I asked. "Summer night, big lake—seemed like a logical turn of events."

"Nothing about you and Drew voluntarily hanging out seems all that logical to me." She was still smiling, but there was something in her eyes that made me feel like I had done something wrong. "You guys are friends now? Naked friends?"

"What? No! I mean, yes, we are naked, but we are not friends." Somehow that didn't make it sound better. "We are separately naked. In the same space. No, it's still weird. I'm sorry," I apologized. "He just dared me, and I jumped off the dock, and . . . yeah. Here we are."

"God, Cass, it's not a big deal." Amy laughed, slicking her wet hair back. "I was just curious, that's all."

She disappeared under the water, resurfacing near Drew. I heard her laugh ring out across the water, and although she hadn't sounded mad, I still felt bad, like I'd done something wrong. At the time, it had seemed totally normal to jump naked into a lake with Drew, but now, looking at it through Amy's eyes, I wasn't so sure.

"I brought towels you crazy mofos!" Rhys arrived in a leopard print bathrobe, carrying a stack of towels and a mug. "But the cocoa's only for me. You lazy bastards can make your own." He perched at the edge of the dock, dangling his feet in the water, watching the moon and sipping his hot chocolate contentedly, while the rest of us splashed and dove in the lake.

"Best summer ever!" Amy cried much later, as we all hauled ourselves out of the lake and onto the dock. I executed a particularly crafty towel maneuver to keep myself from being exposed. "Oh, my God, that was so fun. This is the best summer *ever.*"

Amy leaned her head on Drew's shoulder, and while he seemed surprised to see a small blond head resting against him, he didn't move away. They looked sickeningly cute in their stupid matching striped towels. Nauseatingly cute, like a marshmallow peep wedding. I knotted my own striped towel more forcefully around myself.

"You kids are crazy." Rhys sauntered back toward the house.

"Come in next time!" Heidi encouraged him, dancing through the grass, still naked. I had never seen anyone so comfortable with being naked before.

"Please. We have *no* idea what's in that water." Rhys shuddered. "Leeches? Eels? Water moccasins? Loons?" He stopped, bending down to pick up a piece of notebook paper that was folded in half, waiting on the doormat. "My, my, my, what is this?"

"Ooo, a secret note!" Amy squealed. "Read it!"

And so Rhys did:

Red—
Missed you today. Didja check out the script? Same place as before? Meet me their.

"'Their'?" Drew read over Rhys's shoulder, then threw back his head and laughed. "Oh, that's just precious. Tell me, has your *boyfriend* completed fifth grade yet, Cass?"

"Oh, shove it," I snapped, and snatched the note out of Rhys's hands. "Reading someone else's mail is a federal offense."

"I don't think that applies to hand-delivered love notes. Good God, is that written in crayon?" Drew asked in disbelief.

"No!" I sneaked a peek. It was totally written in crayon. "Oh, just shut up! All of you!"

I crumpled the note into a ball and stomped angrily into the house.

Stupid, stupid Cass. Why had I wasted a whole evening with that moron? Just when I thought he might have a few redeeming qualities, he reverted right back to his natural, troll-like self. I definitely should *not* have gone skinny-dipping with him. That was an activity best reserved only for people whose company you actually enjoy, not condescending jerks with swords.

It was time for the next phase of the plan—and we would see who was laughing then.

CHAPTER 15

Despite a renewed interest in tormenting Drew, I was feeling a little nervous about the next phase of our plan. It was Heidi, surprisingly, who was super gung-ho about it.

"They're just material possessions, Cass," she reminded me for the millionth time, shaking her head like I was being silly for worrying about the destruction of Drew's personal property. Or maybe I was just particularly attuned to the perils of destruction of personal property at the moment, thanks to a certain parent's recent incarceration. "When you think about it, we're actually doing him a favor. We're liberating him from the chains of commodity. Maybe we should liberate everyone!" she added brightly.

"Let's just stick to ruining *Drew's* clothes," I said. Although "Shakespeare in the Nude" did have a certain ring to it. I knew Heidi would be on board.

"Please count me out for clothing liberation." Amy shook her head. "I would *die* if all my clothes were ruined—"

"In a totally accidental, freak laundry machine incident, for which absolutely no one was responsible," I finished for her, grinning wickedly. "Ready to go?"

"All set!" Amy proudly displayed the bright red thong draped around her index finger, then twirled it a few times for good measure. "I've got a feeling, Cass. This is totally gonna do it. This is our Act Four moment—the big event before everything is resolved in Act Five. I wouldn't be surprised if he dropped down to one knee in the laundry room and asked to put his hand beneath my foot, Kate-style."

What was wrong with me? Heidi and Amy were so optimistic, and I was just plagued by little nagging worries. I had to get it together. I'd come up with this plan in the first place. I couldn't be the weak link now.

"You're sure the colors will run?" I whispered urgently as we tiptoed down the stairs.

"I got this out of a bargain bin at the Rainbow in the mall for two dollars ninety-nine cents. Look, the color's already coming off on my hands." Amy rolled her eyes. "Ridiculous. That's what I get for buying bargain bin underwear."

"Out out damn spot," Heidi giggled, pointing at Amy's Lady Macbeth-esque hands.

"Will all the perfumes of Macy's sweeten this little hand?" Amy wailed dramatically.

It felt good to laugh—and to be en route to messing with Drew. Crayon love note aside, Taylor hadn't shown up after rehearsal today, either. I waited for ten minutes, then ran home to cause mayhem with Heidi and Amy. To be perfectly honest, I was a little relieved Taylor hadn't shown up.

I'd finished the script he'd given me, and, well . . . to put it nicely . . . it wasn't good. I knew I couldn't avoid him forever—nor did I want to—but I just needed a little time to think about how to put my most diplomatic foot forward. Which wasn't exactly my strong suit.

"Should we do this?" Amy asked as we arrived at the laundry room. Laundry room was perhaps too generous a term— an Eisenhower-era washer and dryer were crammed into a kitchen closet. So, technically, it was a laundry closet.

"If it were done when 'tis done, then 'twere well it were done quickly," Heidi proclaimed solemnly.

"Go for it." I nodded. Drew had gotten the house's only laundry basket back from Rhys a couple minutes ago, which meant our window of opportunity would be closing soon. Amy darted into the laundry closet while Heidi and I stood guard. Moments later she reappeared.

"Done?"

"It's jammed so far back there he'll *never* see it," Amy said confidently. "Good thing the laundry room is dark."

"Then let's go!" I hustled us all back up the stairs. The plan depended on Drew never knowing we were anywhere *near* the laundry room. We tumbled up the stairs and I shut the bedroom door behind us. "One wash cycle from now, Drew will be the proud owner of an all-pink wardrobe."

"You're kind of an evil genius," Amy marveled.

"Me? Hardly," I scoffed. "All credit goes to Shakespeare. He's the real evil genius here. I'm just the vessel."

Thanks to the thin walls in just a couple minutes we heard the washing machine thumping away. Drew must have started his laundry. Heidi crept downstairs to turn it to its hottest possible setting—because a tiny pink wardrobe was even better than just a pink wardrobe.

Exactly thirty-two minutes later, a roar of outrage shook the walls of the boathouse. Honestly, it felt like we were in the first fifteen minutes of *The Wizard of Oz* or something.

"It's go time." I rubbed my hands together as I scampered down the stairs, Heidi and Amy behind me.

Drew's roaring seemed to have brought everyone into the laundry closet. Not that I was particularly surprised—he'd reached the approximate decibel of an air raid siren. Plus, it's not like there were a lot of places to go in our rehearsal-free time.

I pushed past a still sweaty post-run Noah and a bathrobe-clad Rhys to get a good look at Drew, who was staring into the belly of the laundry machine like it was an empty pit of despair.

"Pink," Drew spat. "It's pink. It's . . . all . . . pink."

"And tiny." Rhys reached around Drew to pull a minuscule, splotchy pink T-shirt out of the laundry machine. He held it far away from his body between two fingers, like he was afraid it would contaminate him.

"I'm sure you've got other stuff to wear." Noah clapped a comforting hand on Drew's shoulder.

"Nope," Drew said tensely. "That was it. All of it. I put off doing my laundry too long, and now all my clothes are pink. Or splotchy. Or pink and splotchy."

"This looks okay." Rhys pulled out a black T-shirt and held it against Drew's chest. It was now so small I doubted he could even fit an arm into it. "Or not." Rhys dropped the shirt to the floor.

"I just don't understand how this happened," Drew muttered as he started pulling his ruined clothes out of the laundry machine, flinging them behind him distractedly. Rhys narrowly dodged a pair of newly pink boxers. "I don't *own* anything that's pink. What the hell could have done this?"

And then, finally, he reached the back of the machine and found what he didn't even know he was looking for. Drew stood and turned to face us, holding the blotchy reddish remains of Amy's formerly crimson thong. As I watched his face grow pale and his lips compress into a thin line, for the first time I understood the expression "white-hot rage." I felt a totally inappropriate, horrifying urge to giggle hysterically. I couldn't even tell if they were funny giggles or fear giggles, but either way, I tamped them down like my life depended on it. Now was not the time to poke the bear.

"Don't even point that cheap underwear in my direction." Rhys backed away out of the laundry closet and into the kitchen.

"Whose is this?" Drew growled, doing a fairly passable impression of an angry bear. Amy darted a quick, frightened look at me, like a rabbit backed into a corner. I knew immediately what that look meant: if Drew thought Amy had ruined his clothes, even accidentally, he was going to be super pissed. Which would put a serious stumbling block into their romance. Guess it wasn't time for that Act Five reconciliation Amy had been hoping for after all. "WHOSE IS THIS?" Drew repeated, even louder.

"Mine," I answered quickly. "It's mine." So what if Drew hated me a little bit more? I certainly wasn't going to lose any sleep over it. And the thong couldn't have come from nowhere. Better I take the fall than try to deflect attention onto some implausible mystery thong bandit. Amy exhaled loudly in relief. Luckily, Drew didn't seem to notice.

"This is yours?" Drew asked skeptically.

"Yes. Yes it is. I am a super sexy lady who is careless with my super sexy lingerie," I babbled, reaching for the thong. "Sorry 'bout that."

"This is certainly a change of pace from what you were wearing at the lake the other night."

"You weren't supposed to be looking!" I snatched the thong away, cheeks flaming. "What about the sacred bond of skinny-dipping trust?"

"I'm a guy." He shrugged. I looked over at Amy. She rolled her eyes and grinned at me, but there was something brittle about it. I shifted uncomfortably. "This is really your underwear?"

Why was he being so suspicious?

"Yes, it's mine!" Sheesh. What was with the third degree? "I clearly didn't know it was in there, and now my favorite underwear is ruined, too. You're not the only victim here!"

"Oh, for the love of . . ." Drew groused. "You know what? Forget it. Just forget it. You're insane, and you can't reason with an insane person. You're out one pair of underwear, and I'll be stuck wearing sweatpants and a Rye Country Day School T-shirt all summer. Seems very fair."

"I'm sure the Bait 'n' Bite has a lovely selection of Lake Dunmore souvenir tees," I suggested sweetly.

"Don't worry, man, we'll hook you up," Noah promised. "Right, Rhys?"

"We'll see." Rhys narrowed his eyes. He seemed about as enthused about sharing his wardrobe with Drew as I would have been.

"Why does all this . . . this . . . this *shit* keep happening to me?" Drew bellowed, like he hadn't heard anything Noah said. "I'm allergic to this house, a mouse eats all my food, and now I have no clothes! What the hell is going on?" By the end of his tirade, Drew sounded more confused than angry. He looked at each of us, shaking his head in bewilderment. "I don't understand why this is happening to me."

"The wheel spins for us all in time," Heidi said consolingly. "Fortunes rise and fall. That's how the universe works. I brought my tarot if you'd like some further clarification."

I was shocked that the look Drew shot her didn't incinerate her on the spot.

The next morning, the fruits of our prank proved sweeter than I ever could have imagined. Drew had never looked so ridiculous. He was wearing a Dallas Cowboys jersey that must have been Noah's and a pair of batik-printed lounge pants that were undoubtedly Heidi's. Jock on top, yogi on the bottom.

"Is Drew wearing your pants?" I whispered to Heidi, unable to believe my eyes.

"The other boys are too skinny, and they only had fitted pants. Jeans and stuff. And Drew refused to wear Noah's running shorts. Luckily those pants have a lot of room to breathe and flow."

"Very lucky," I agreed. Those pants were the highlight of my summer.

"We only have half a rehearsal today, so let's move it!" Nevin shouted. I'd been so distracted by the yoga pants I hadn't even noticed his arrival. He was sitting in his usual spot behind the folding table with Langley. "Top of Act One! Move it! Let's go, let's go, let's go!"

"Why do we only have half a rehearsal today?" I asked Amy as we hustled backstage, narrowly avoiding a collision with Rhys.

"Costume fittings. There was a schedule in the hand-book, you know."

"Of course there is. I knew that."

Nevin rushed us into rehearsal so quickly that he either didn't notice Drew's ensemble or didn't feel like it was worth commenting on. And, to give him some credit, Drew didn't let his clothing situation detract from his performance. The run of the show that morning went extremely smoothly. After lunch, Nevin handed us off to Langley for our costume fittings.

"So, where are the dressing rooms?" Amy asked.

Oh yeah. I hadn't thought of that. I'd never done a show outside before. I really hoped we weren't going to have to change in a field or something.

"Thataway." Langley pointed to the big red barn. I'd seen it every day during rehearsal, but I'd never really given much thought to what it was. Most likely it wasn't a ginormous super luxurious dressing room—although that would have been nice. Bypassing the huge barn doors at the front of the building, Langley walked around to the side and confidently pushed open a small door.

"What is this place?" I asked, curious, as we trooped in behind her.

"The town uses it for storage," Langley answered. That much was obvious. But I couldn't figure out what exactly they were storing. Inside the cavernous warehouse space, I saw an enormous fake Christmas tree, lots of American flag bunting, two full-sized parade floats, enough animals to outfit a taxidermy zoo, and a life-size cardboard cutout of Elvis.

"Look!" Rhys called from somewhere behind me. "This Coke bottle is as big as me!"

"Guys, don't touch the stuff," Langley reprimanded. That would be a challenge. The whole place was chockablock full of the most random assortment of crap I'd ever seen. Feathers and shiny things competed for my attention. But on the far side of the barn, I saw two racks of Elizabethan garb with a makeshift curtain strung up between them. That must have been for us.

"One mirror?" Amy tsked softly, warily eying the wobbly full-length mirror leaning against an easel. "That'll be a challenge."

Langley pointed the three of us towards the girls' rack. There were three dresses labeled clearly with our character's names. Mine was, of course, bright red. Redheads do not look good in red! Why was this theater so insistent on proving otherwise? Sighing, I took my fiery ensemble off the rack. Once

I'd flung off my clothes, the dress slipped easily over my head. It had a little corset-type bodice that laced up the front, which I pulled tight to make it fit right. It had long sleeves with little poofs at the shoulders, slashed with red and cream.

"I'm in love!" Amy had dressed at the speed of light and was now twirling around in front of the mirror. "Cass, couldn't you just die?"

I came to stand next to her. Her dress was almost identical to mine, except hers was a lovely rosy shade of light pink.

"It's silly, I know—but I just love wearing costumes," she sighed happily.

"It's not silly. It's fun. And it finally makes everything feel real. This is the moment the play comes to life. For me, anyway."

"It's nice, isn't it?" Amy leaned her head against my shoulder. "To lose yourself in someone else's life. Even for only a couple hours. It makes you feel so . . ."

"Invincible." My eyes met hers in the mirror.

"Exactly." She nodded. "It feels like nothing bad could ever happen to you. Or, you know, if bad things happen, it's because they were supposed to—so even if everything goes wrong, you always know what to do. All the steps are laid out in front of you. It's right there in the script. You're safe, because you're not *you* anymore."

It was hard to imagine Amy not wanting to be Amy. From the outside, at least, it seemed like her life would be so easy. Whenever I'd seen all the beautiful people sitting at the popular table back in the cafeteria, it seemed like they were always having the time of their lives. But maybe there was a kind of pressure in that, too. Maybe it was hard, to have people only consider what you looked like on the outside.

A golden glow appeared in the mirror behind us, breaking the moment—it turned out to be Heidi. She was just taller than the mirror, so I couldn't see her face.

"Heidi, those sleeves are not messing around." I eyed them askance. They were seriously long—they reached all the way down to the floor.

"No one messes with these sleeves," she agreed, starting to flap her huge fabric wings. "I think I could take flight."

"What a precious little family," Langley said behind us. Was she making fun of us? I could never tell. "Okay, everything fits fine. Wear your ballet flats tomorrow. Change and get out of my hair."

Once we'd changed, we came around in front of the curtain. The boys were all lounging in various states of Elizabethan dress. Drew wore deep burgundy breeches and a white, open-necked blousy shirt. Burgundy. Why couldn't *I* wear burgundy? That would have been much better than bright red. I watched him as he shrugged on a leather vest-type thing that I knew from previous shows was called a jerkin. Rhys was busy trying out different angles for his crushed velvet cap with a feather on the side.

"Listen up," Langley announced. "Girls, you'll be doing your own hair and makeup tomorrow." Amy looked thrilled. I could only hope they weren't expecting something particularly complex. "Guys, stay behind for haircuts and beard trimming."

"Who's cutting our hair?" Drew asked suspiciously.

"You're looking at her," Langley answered calmly.

"*You?*" Drew's eyebrows rose up to his hairline. "Can I see your qualifications?"

"Nope." She pulled a pair of scissors and an electric razor from somewhere deep within the cargo pockets of her shorts. "And just for that, you're first."

Drew blanched. A giggle escaped before I could stop it.

"No audience!" Langley barked. "Out, girls, out!"

To avoid further incurring the wrath of Langley, we quickly made our way through the storage barn and back out into the sunlight.

"Hey, Cass!" I looked up. Taylor Griffith was running toward me. I walked slowly toward him, ready to meet him a third of the way, but no more than that. Glancing over my shoulder, I saw Amy dragging Heidi in the direction of the boathouse. "Where were you yesterday?"

"What do you mean?"

"Well, didn't you get my note?"

"I got it." I adjusted my bag on my shoulder, trying to project nothing but cool nonchalance. Extremely cool nonchalance. With all the nonchalance I'd been practicing around Drew post-pranks, I was practically a nonchalant expert at this point.

"Then why didn't you come?"

"I came. You weren't there. I waited for ten minutes, then left."

"Ten minutes? That's all I'm worth to you? Ten minutes?" Taylor placed his hands on his heart and started staggering around. A smile involuntarily tugged at the corners of my lips. "Dag, that's cold."

"I'm a busy girl, Taylor. I can't spend all day waiting around for you."

"Lady, you have cut me to the quick," he declaimed. "Boom! Shakespeared!"

"I don't think that was Shakespeare—"

"Come on, forget yesterday. Let's just get out of here, aight?"

"Aight," I agreed. The jumble of vowels felt weird in my mouth, like talking through a wad of jelly beans.

He started walking assuredly away from the stage, and I followed.

CHAPTER 16

W/here are we going?" I asked. We definitely weren't heading back to the clearing. This was the totally opposite direction.

"Shangri-La," Taylor answered.

"Is that, um, far?" I had no idea what he was talking about.

"Much closer than you might think."

Taylor led me across the street and through the gates of Camp Dunmore. Instead of going deeper into the woods, to where I knew the skaters' cabin was, he led me around the periphery of the camp, past some tennis courts, a basketball hoop, and a bunch of archery targets, until we finally reached what I knew was our final destination.

"So, this is a skate park." It looked like an empty swimming pool with a bunch of different levels. There were railings and benches and wooden ramps dotted randomly about the cement structure. The other skaters were down there, flying around the track. Or whatever you called it.

"Welcome to Shangri-La, Red." Taylor grinned happily. I watched, mesmerized, as the skaters whizzed back and forth. "Cop a squat, Betty." I turned. Taylor was sitting on top of a picnic table behind me. He patted the space next to him. I hopped up to join him and took a deep breath. I knew what I had to do next.

"So . . . the script." I pulled it out of my tote bag. For once, my laziness about cleaning out my bag had proved useful. A more organized person would have put that script away days ago.

"Oh yeah!" Taylor's eyes lit up with surprise. "Shit, I totally forgot about that."

He forgot? If someone offered me the lead role in a major motion picture, I sure as hell wouldn't forget.

"Well, here's the thing," I began.

"It's crap, isn't it?" he asked flatly, interrupting me.

"Well—I, um, I—well," I hemmed and hawed, unsure of how to begin. It didn't matter anyway, because what I thought was clearly written plain across my face.

"I knew it!" he snapped his fingers. "I knew it! I so totally knew it, man. And that's why I asked you to read it. Because I knew you wouldn't bullshit me. Thank you." He grabbed my face and deposited a big, smacking kiss on my forehead. "The only honest person left in America, ladies and gentlemen!" He held a pretend glass aloft and toasted an imaginary crowd. "I knew I could trust you."

"We can talk about it more—"

"Talk? Why bother." He took the script from me. "If it's crap, it's crap. Talking's not gonna change that."

That was it? We were done? I was kind of surprised he didn't want to talk about it more. But then he stood up and flung the script as far into the woods as he could. Guess we really were done.

"Forget that noise. Words, man. Who needs 'em. Ammiright?"

"Well, I don't know, I think words are kind of necessary—"

"Don't be so literal, mama!" Taylor laughed. "I'm supposed to *skate*. That's what I'm here for. And everything else is just noise. Yeah?"

"Sure."

"Nah-uh." He shook his head. "You're not getting it. That's cuz you've got to *feel* it. Watch me, Red."

Seamlessly, he leapt off the picnic table, hopped onto his board, and slid down the sloping swimming pool side of the skate park. The other skaters whooped and hollered at him as he joined them in the middle of the park. There was, of course, more of that "bow-ow-ow" howl as they cleared out of the way to watch from the sidelines. Something about the hush that settled over the place as the howls died down made me think that there was something special about the way Taylor skated—there was something almost reverent about that sudden silence. He propelled himself back up a ramp that had a railing next to it, like a staircase with no stairs. On the way down, he somehow leapt up into the air and rode down the rail, his board flying down the metal railing.

"This is grinding, Red!" he shouted, flying off the rail and landing smoothly as he rolled across the asphalt. He propelled himself back up the ramp, then gained speed as he flew off it. "Three-sixty flip!" he called, the board leaving his feet as it spun in a complete circle beneath him. Somehow he found his way and landed neatly at the bottom as the other skaters cheered. It was unbelievable. I'd never seen anything like it. Again and again he flew down the railing or off the ramp, grabbing his board or flipping and spinning it. It was like skater ballet or something. Every move was completely smooth, totally seamless. He made it all look effortless.

One last time, he rolled his way back up the edge of the swimming pool space—it almost looked like he was defying gravity. The skate park erupted in howls and chants of "Bowser! Bowser! Bowser!" He silenced them like a conductor, and one by one they hopped back on their boards and rolled down into the cement expanse.

"Wow."

"Your turn." He grinned.

"What?" I shook my head. "No way. This whole thing defies physics. I don't trust it. It's crazy."

"You think this is crazy? You should see the vert skaters."

"What's vert?"

"Skaters on a half-pipe. We're street skaters. Totally different thing."

"Right."

This must have been what Jane Goodall felt like among the apes. This was a totally different culture, with its own language and everything. And I felt like I hardly understood any of it.

"Come on. Let's go."

"Taylor, I don't know—"

"C'mon, we'll just stay on the flat part up here," he wheedled. "Nothing scary. Don't be a chicken."

"I'm not a chicken," I protested, jumping off the picnic table.

"Then prove it."

He rolled his skateboard toward me. I stopped it with the heel of my sneaker.

"Prove it or do it, Red."

I sighed, contemplating the board beneath my foot. "You guys say that a lot."

"Yeah. Cuz it's, like, my mantra."

"What does that even mean? Prove it or do it makes absolutely no sense."

"It makes all the sense," Taylor said seriously. "It's a challenge, aight? Like, if you're claiming, you have to either prove it or do it. That way you can, like, back your shit up. So you prove you're not a pusher."

"Right . . . but don't *prove it* and *do it* mean exactly the same thing? I don't understand what the two different options are."

Taylor stared at me for a long time. I appeared to have stumped him.

"Quit stalling and get on the deck, Red," he said eventually. And so *prove it or do it* would remain a completely nonsensical mystery for another day.

"Fine. I'm in. What do I do?"

"Put your right foot back here, by the tail." I scooted my foot back, perpendicular to the board, right above the wheel part, grateful that Taylor was holding on to me so I wouldn't fall. "Left foot in front. No goofy-foot bidness up in here."

"My feet are totally serious right now!"

"Goofy-foot is when you lead with your right foot."

"Hmph. Sorry, I don't know the secret language."

"Relax, Red, relax!" he admonished. "You'll never be a skater if you keep taking yourself all serious and shit. Now scoot that right foot all the way back to the end of the tail. Keep the left in the middle of the deck."

"Whoa!" I shifted around, wheels rolling back and forth. "This feels wobbly." I couldn't imagine doing anything on this unstable plank of wood, let alone flying into the air off a ramp.

"You've got this. Now take your back foot, and push off."

"Like off the ground?"

"Yeah, like off the ground. They're not just for standing on, genius."

"Hey!" I protested.

"C'mon, chicken." He tickled my sides. I swatted him away. "Push off!"

Gingerly, I took my foot off the back of the board and pushed. The board started rolling. I immediately leapt off.

"Hey, you bailed!" Taylor jogged after the board and scooped it up. "There's no bailing on the Gangsta Raw Pro Skate Team. That kind of wussy behavior doesn't win medals."

"But—but it moved! And it was all wobbly!"

Being on a skateboard was extremely unsettling. I hated the way I felt like I couldn't control it, like nothing was stable or sturdy. I couldn't ever imagine being as confident on that board as Taylor clearly was.

"Cass." He looked right at me, and the way his blue eyes sparkled in the sunlight, I felt like my heart was doing a 360-kickflip mctwist or whatever. "You have got this. Let's try it one more time."

So once again, I arranged my feet, put my back foot down, and pushed off. Only this time, I quickly placed my right foot back up on the tail end of the board.

"I'm doing it!" I cried. "Well, kind of." I was rolling down the sidewalk at the approximate pace of a snail. "How do I stop this thing?"

"Just put your back foot on the tail and lean back."

"What?" I tried leaning. "It's not doing anything!"

"Lean back, Red!"

"I'm leaning, I'm leaning!" I tried to lean for all I was worth. "It's not stopping!"

I simply kept rolling along. What would happen when I ran out of asphalt? I could see the grass getting closer and closer.

But I never found out. Taylor jogged up to meet me and caught me around the waist to bring me to a stop. I rolled right into his arms. Up on the board, we were almost exactly the same height. He kept his arms around my waist, and I knew the unsteady feeling now had nothing to do with the skateboard.

"Maybe stopping will be our next lesson."

"Maybe. If you think you can get me back up on this thing."

"It wasn't a bad first effort, Red. You should be stoked."

"I should most definitely not be stoked. That was a heinous first effort. I rolled four feet and was unable to come to a complete stop."

"Gotta start somewhere." He laughed, and, God, he was just so cute, and here he was with *me*. With his arms around my waist. There was still a part of me that couldn't quite believe it. "Are you *blushing*?" he asked curiously.

"Not blushing," I muttered. Lying.

"You make me blush, too, Red."

And then he closed the space between us and kissed me. I could hear the other skaters hooting and whistling, but I could have cared less. The sun was shining, birds were chirping, and Taylor Griffith was kissing me. All was right with the world. But then, at the worst possible moment in the history of moments, my stomach growled. Loudly. Like *really* loudly. Like space-shuttle-launch loudly.

"Dag, Red, was that your stomach?" He sounded impressed, not horrified, so at least that was something.

"Um. Yes. Yes it was." Stupid corset messing up my appetite! "Can we go get some ice cream or something?"

"Sounds like I'm gonna have to buy out the whole Bait 'n' Bite." I elbowed him in the ribs. "I'm just teasing! Chillax, chillax."

Hmm. He told me to relax a lot. I was starting to think I just wasn't a very relaxed person.

"Stay up on that board. You're gonna skate there. Gotta practice, Red."

"You want me to travel an actual distance on this thing? We won't get there for weeks."

"I'll tow you there. Just stay steady, and I'll do all the work."

"You can tow someone on a skateboard?" I asked as he grabbed my hand and started pulling me along. I wobbled once, then centered myself. We were holding hands! Well, sort of. We *were* holding hands, but I wasn't sure if that was because he wanted to hold my hand or because it was integral to the whole towing process. Well, who said it couldn't be both?

"Hell yeah, you can. You can car tow—"

"Like skateboard behind a car?" I asked, aghast. That sounded suicidal.

"Yeah. Hook up a cable to a car and go. Hella dangerous. Mad fun, though. You can do it on bikes and dogs and stuff, too."

"Dogs?"

"Big dogs. Not like a Chihuahua. Like sled-dogging but on a skateboard."

"Crazy."

We chatted companionably about skateboards and ice cream flavors as we rolled slowly toward the Bait 'n' Bite. I enjoyed skateboarding a lot more when I wasn't responsible for actually making myself move.

Of all the rotten timing, just as we reached the Bait 'n' Bite, the door swung open to reveal . . . Drew. Of course. I knew there weren't a lot of places to go in Lake Dunmore, but this was ridiculous. It was like he was everywhere I went!

He was still wearing his football jersey and yoga pants ensemble, but there was something different about him. I couldn't quite put my finger on it, though.

"Nice outfit, bra," Taylor sniggered as Drew made his way down the stairs. "Cool pants."

"My pants are about as ludicrous as yours are," Drew countered. "I can see your boxers, Marky Mark."

"I don't even know who that is, so burn on you."

"I think that makes the burn on *you*, actually."

Wow, that got surprisingly combative faster than I'd expected. I hopped off the skateboard, eager to diffuse the tension and just get rid of Drew so I could get my ice cream. Beard! His beard. *That* was what looked different.

"What happened to your beard?" I asked.

"This is my Petruchio facial hair." He rubbed his jaw self-consciously. "Looks weird, doesn't it?"

"No, it doesn't, actually, it looks . . ." Good. It looked really good. Underneath all that lumberjack beard Drew was actually handsome. He now bore a striking resemblance to Ben Affleck's character in *Shakespeare in Love*. Not that I would ever tell him that. "Fine." I settled on. "It's fine. It's not so hideous it'll throw me off or anything."

"Oh, great," he said sarcastically. "Because that's what I was really worried about. How my face made *you* feel. Never mind the fact that it's, you know, *my* face."

"What's with the baseball bag, bra?" Taylor interrupted us. "Trying to play a little game? That's cute, dude. Totally cute."

"That's an interesting attitude, coming from someone whose 'career'"—he air-quoted—"consists of doing tricks on a child's toy."

I winced. Things were about to get awkward. Oh, who was I kidding? They were already awkward.

"Child's toy, huh?" Taylor growled. This was the most heated I'd ever heard him get—a stark departure from his normally chill vibe. "If it's so easy then let's see you play, playa."

Taylor slid the skateboard across the sidewalk. It rolled in a perfectly straight line until coming to a stop at Drew's feet.

"This is stupid."

"Stupid easy, right?" Taylor challenged. "Then prove it or do it, son."

"Fine," Drew said tersely. "Whatever." Carefully, he set his baseball bag full of swords on the stairs to the Bait 'n' Bite, leaning them against the railing. Drew tentatively placed a foot on the board, but somehow the thing flew out from underneath him and he landed flat on his back, like a turtle.

"Yikes." I cringed. That sounded like it hurt. At least I didn't hear anything crack. Wincing, Drew slowly started making his way back up to standing.

"Classic!" Taylor cried, resting his hands on his knees, bent over double he was laughing so hard. "Classic, man." He mimed wiping tears from his eyes. "That was beautiful, son. Way to prove it."

"Taylor," I warned, "come on." I had thought that I would have loved nothing more than to see Drew fall flat on his back. But this wasn't even remotely satisfying. I just felt bad for him. He looked mortified.

"What's the problem, Cass?" Taylor seemed confused that I wasn't laughing. "The pusher schralped his ass like he deserved. Justice is served."

"I don't know. He's just . . . he's trying," I finished lamely. Drew was back up on his feet and, a look of grim determination fixed to his face, he stepped onto the skateboard. Tentatively, he pushed off and started rolling down the sidewalk, wobbling madly, but staying upright.

"You call that trying? My grandma skates better than that!" Taylor called. "Even Cass does!"

"Where does that put me on the suckage scale? Above or below your grandma?" I said, feeling a little offended.

"What? Stop trippin', Red. I'm just playin'. Just a little talky talk."

Drew stuck his arms out like a giant bird, fighting for balance. Taylor only laughed harder. Something twinged within me.

"Listen, I have to—I have to go," I blurted out.

"What do you mean, 'go'?" Taylor's brow furrowed. "What about ice cream?"

"I have sparring practice. With Drew." Drew's back was to me, but he was more than close enough to hear what I said. He rolled to a halt. "We need to practice our stage combat."

"With this chode?"

"I am not a—"

"Yes." I grabbed Drew's arm and pulled him off the skateboard. "Sorry, Taylor. We have to go rehearse."

THE TAMING OF THE DREW

"Now? Seriously?"

"Seriously now." I reached down and grabbed the bag of swords. "Bye, Taylor. I'll see you soon. Promise."

"I've heard of playing hard to get, Red, but this is some seriously gnarly shit!"

"Soon, Taylor!" I called over my shoulder. "Soon. Promise!"

I looked back, once. By that point Taylor was just a blondish blur in a black T-shirt leaning against the railing of the Bait 'n' Bite.

"You know, I didn't need you to rescue me from your boyfriend," Drew said as we power-walked into the woods. "I was handling myself just fine."

"Sure you were."

"Then what is this about? Finally had enough of that scintillating conversation?"

"No, I just—I just wanted to practice combat, okay?" To tell the truth, *I* wasn't even sure why I had left Taylor. It was just like a strange impulse or something. Seeing Drew flopping around like a fish out of water while Taylor cackled had unearthed some deeply buried ember of empathy I hadn't even known was lurking within me.

"You really like it that much?" Drew seemed surprised.

"Yeah, I do, okay?" I snapped. That much was true, at least. "And you said I was good. Remember?"

"You are good. You're crazy, but you're good."

"I'd like to see you say that when I've got a sword in my hands," I mock-threatened him.

"That's true. You are a poking menace."

"Maybe that should be my superhero name. The Poking Menace!" I declaimed grandly as we made our way back to the combat clearing in the woods.

"Sounds more like a supervillain."

"Good point. Ah, who am I kidding? With unlimited power, I'd go evil. Absolutely."

"You're more self-aware than I'd given you credit for."

"That's about as close to a compliment as I'll ever get from you. So, thank you."

"Not a compliment, but take it as you will." Drew set the bag down and pulled out a slender rapier. "Milady."

"Thanks." I got into combat stance and thrust back and forth. The sword swished satisfyingly through the air. I leapt forward, stabbing and slashing at imaginary villains.

"Hey!" I exclaimed, coming to a stop. "I just realized you've never seen my award-winning forward roll."

"They do not give out awards for forward rolls."

"I'm sure they do," I protested. "At like, gymnastics camps. Or Gymborees or preschools or something. I just don't technically happen to have one. But I should. That's how good this forward roll is."

"Uh-huh."

"Stand back and watch, smartass."

"What about the sword?" he asked. "Please don't impale yourself while executing a mediocre somersault. That would be too embarrassing to explain to the EMT."

"Mediocre!" I swished the sword through the air with a flourish. "I'd challenge you to a duel, sirrah, if I wasn't busy preparing to knock your socks off with my *exemplary* somersault."

"You can't just duel free-form in stage combat. Everything has to be choreographed. That's kind of the whole point."

"Sheesh, Captain Safety, calm down!" I admonished. "Do you want to see this forward roll or not?"

"Not really."

"Well, too bad!" I stuck my tongue out at him. "This is how I roll, suckaa. One arm!"

Holding my sword aloft, I flung myself forward onto my left forearm, rolling and flipping over until I arrived triumphantly back on my feet.

"Yaah-haah!" I cried, sword aloft. I felt like a lady Zorro or a pirate queen or something. I wished I could carry a sword all the time.

"That was pretty impressive," Drew chuckled, slow-clapping as he walked toward me. "It was the 'yaah-haah' that really sold it."

"Vocals are fundamental to selling stage combat, Drew."

He laughed again, softly this time.

"Hey. Wait a minute. You've got something . . ." He gestured toward my face. I started patting myself. Oh, God, was there a bug on me? "Hold still."

Drew stepped in closer, and now we were really close. Like acting-for-the-camera close. He lifted his hand to my hair and ran it through a few red curls before it came to rest on my cheek. I shivered as he stroked the side of my face. He cupped my chin and tilted it toward him and . . .

"What are you doing?" I asked suddenly. What *was* he doing? Was he trying to . . . *kiss* me? No. It couldn't be. Not possible. And yet . . .

"Nothing!" he barked, jerking back from me. "There was a leaf in your hair."

"Sure there was."

"Exhibit A!" He held up a small green leaf with a flourish, thrusting it millimeters from my nose.

"Get that thing out of my face." I swatted the leaf away with my non-sword hand, and it floated gently to the ground. "You sure took your sweet time getting that leaf out."

"I was being thorough!"

"Were you trying to . . . *kiss* me?" I knew I shouldn't have asked it. I regretted it almost the minute it popped out of my mouth.

"No!" he bellowed so loudly a few birds took flight. "Absolutely not! Are you *deranged*? Why would I try to kiss you? I don't even *like* you!"

"I can assure you, the feeling is mutual," I shot back.

"A person would have to be *mentally unstable* to like you!"

"Hey!" That stung more than I would have liked to admit. "You're not exactly a picnic either!"

"Compared to you?" he snorted. "I'm a *gourmet* picnic. With champagne and strawberries and white linen napkins."

"Your picnic would give people food poisoning!" I retorted. "And this picnic metaphor is stupid, and I refuse to participate in it anymore. Just keep your face away from my face and your lips away from my lips."

"Fine!" he shouted. "No problem!"

"Great!" I shouted back. "In fact, not kissing you will be a true pleasure."

"The pleasure, you harpy, is all mine."

By this point we were standing inches away from each other's faces. Drew was bright red and breathing heavily. But then he started to lean down toward me like he was going to . . .

"Dammit!" he roared, then leapt backward like I was in danger of scalding him, raking his hands through his hair until it was standing up in exaggerated peaks. "Satan, avoid! I charge thee, tempt me not!"

"Don't quote Shakespeare at me!" I roared right back at him. "Don't you dare! Avaunt, thou dreadful minister of hell!"

"You're doing it, too!"

"You started it! So blush, blush, thou lump of foul deformity!"

"Lady, you know no rules of charity—"

"Villain, thou know'st no law of God nor man nor—oh, I'm not going to sit here and do *Richard III* with you! This is ridiculous. I wish I'd never even seen your stupid sword." At that, I immediately started blushing. Stupid, stupid Cass. "Oh, forget it!" And with that I threw my sword to the ground and stomped through the woods, leaving him alone in the clearing. Thankfully he didn't follow me.

What the hell had just happened? Clearly there was something much more dangerous than swords in that corner of the woods.

CHAPTER 17

Since whatever-it-was had happened—or almost had happened—in the woods, I'd been preoccupied with thoughts of Drew. And Taylor. Taylor! I had to see Taylor again. He was the only guy in Lake Dunmore I *wanted* to kiss. Hopefully he wasn't super pissed at me. I had to get this summer back on track. I vowed to make things up to Taylor and to apply myself to making Drew miserable with renewed vigor. The only emotion of mine Drew deserved was disdain. Sitting cross-legged on the floor of our room with Heidi and Amy, I realized exactly what the next phase in our plan would be.

"Drew's sleeping too well," I announced suddenly. "Like, way too well."

"Don't you *dare* touch his eyes again," Heidi warned me.

"Oh, ick, please don't. That was *gro-o-oss*," Amy agreed.

"What? No!" I scoffed. "I'm not crazy. I promised not to inflict any more physical harm. There's more than one way to keep a shrew from sleeping, you know."

"You're so right. We *need* to keep him up or this'll never work. Petruchio plays a trumpet to keep Kate awake in the play. Do you have a trumpet?" Amy asked.

"Um, no."

"Don't tell me you're going to steal Nevin's trumpet?" Heidi said.

"Heidi, come on! Of course not! Besides, a trumpet would probably wake *everyone* up. I have no interest in missing out on any sleep myself. And if we did that, Drew would for sure know it was us." I chewed my lip meditatively. "We need something smaller, that we can hide. And something that will only keep Drew awake."

"Like a baby monitor?" Amy suggested. "You know, put one in Drew's room, put one somewhere else. Where would we get a baby monitor, though?"

Inspiration struck. "Who needs a baby monitor when we've got walkie-talkies?" The same ancient walkie-talkies Drew was always carting around were currently sitting on one of the kitchen counters, waiting for his next excursion into the woods.

"How is a walkie-talkie going to keep Drew from sleeping?" Heidi asked.

"We put one in Drew's room, some place he'll have a hard time finding it. Like, um, in the ceiling or a floorboard or something." Heidi looked skeptical. But this boathouse seemed pretty structurally flimsy—I was sure I could pry something open in order to stash the walkie-talkie. "Then we put the other walkie-talkie next to an iPod with speakers or something and we play an annoying playlist. We hide *that* walkie-talkie somewhere within range but far enough away that we can't hear it. That's good, right?"

Not to brag, but I was pretty impressed with myself. Not bad for a plan I'd just come up with on the fly.

"Not just good, Cass, that's *great*. Ooo! I have iPod speakers!" Amy cheered, leaping up to get them from her dresser. "What do we want to play? Like One Direction or something?"

"Hmmm . . . maybe something that doesn't sound like music?"

"What, like animal calls?" Amy asked. "Or cars honking?"

"Yeah! That way he might not assume it was coming from *inside* the room."

"Crafty." Amy nodded in approval.

"What about my Viva la Vuvuzela playlist?" Heidi suggested. "It's music, but it's not quite, um, traditional music. In a Western sense."

"Vuvu-what-now?"

"Oh, you remember. Vuvuzelas. Those super annoying South Africa horn things from the World Cup like forever ago," Amy reminded me.

"Oh, yeah. Why do you have that?"

"I think they're interesting!" Heidi said defensively.

"Well, it's perfect for this, so thank you." I didn't want her to get upset and rescind her iPod loan, but I was still confused about who would buy a Vuvuzela song. Or record one, for that matter.

"But what if Drew just turns the walkie-talkie off?" Amy asked. "This has to work. It's the final phase in the Petruchio-shrewing-Kate plan. This'll be the exact push he needs."

"It'll work," I said with more confidence than I felt. "We'll just have to make sure the walkie-talkie is really, really well-hidden."

"Drew's leaving," Heidi announced from her perch on the windowsill. "Like, right now. He's walking toward the Bait 'n' Bite."

"We've got to act now," I barked. "It'll take him fifteen minutes to get there and back, tops. We've got to get that thing hidden."

"Right," Amy agreed. "Okay, I'll guard the door. Heidi, you stay on alert at the window."

"What do I do if I see him coming back?" Heidi asked. "Make a bird call? Ca-caw! Ca-caw!"

"There's no way we'll hear that from Drew's room." Amy shook her head.

"We'll just be super speedy," I said decisively. "Come on. Let's go."

Luckily, the house appeared to be deserted. After a quick trip down to the kitchen to steal the walkie-talkies, I snuck easily into Drew's room, saluting Amy as she closed the door behind me.

His room was messier than I would have imagined. For someone who had lost most of his wardrobe in a freak washing machine incident, Drew's floor was covered in an awful lot of crap. Sweatshirts and T-shirts and what looked like a fleece blanket were flung all over the place. Each corner of the room had its own haphazard stack of books and DVDs. Curious, I bent down to examine the top book on the stack closest to Drew's bed. Hemingway. Typical.

Speaking of Drew's bed, it definitely *was* a rollaway cot. He hadn't been lying about that. The whole room had the cramped, awkward appearance of a closet that had been hastily converted into sleeping quarters. There was, I noticed, no real closet or dresser—maybe that's why his clothes were all over the floor. Besides the cot, the only furniture in there was a straight-backed wooden chair. Very Harry Potter at the Dursleys'.

Now, where to hide the walkie-talkie? I kicked some stuff out of the way as I dragged the chair against the wall closest to Drew's bed. The sloping ceiling was comprised of aging wooden planks. With any luck, I'd be able to wiggle or pop one of them up. I felt around, pushing and prodding the ceiling. Stretching to the side, I finally reached a plank that was as wiggly as a loose tooth. It creaked and groaned as I pushed it up, but I was able to get enough space to chuck the walkie-talkie into the ceiling above Drew's bed. We probably should have tested this whole setup first, but I guess I'd just have to keep my fingers crossed that he'd be able to hear the Vuvuzelas. I carefully dragged the chair back to where I'd found it. Mission accomplished.

On my slog out the door, my toe connected with something solid in the fabric mass. I bent down to pick it up.

I pulled one of those old school journals with the black and white marbling out from underneath the fleece blanket. *Taming of the Shrew*: SAD *Summer* was written on the front cover. I figured it probably wasn't a personal journal, or anything, but I probably shouldn't have looked at it. I just couldn't resist taking a quick peek. I'd basically been pulling amateur backwoods Jack Bauer business on Drew all summer. In comparison, a little diary snooping was nothing.

Inside the journal, he'd taped printed copies of each of his monologues. Every single line was scanned and analyzed; key words were highlighted, margins littered with notes, references, allusions, and definitions. It was incredible. I didn't think I'd ever seen someone approach a role with so much care and dedication. He had enough research in there to probably write a scholarly article about Petruchio. He may have been a jackass, but he was a prepared jackass.

I flipped to the next page, where he'd made some character notes in an untidy, miniature, nearly illegible scrawl. Typical boy writing.

There at the top was a list titled, "Why do I Marry Her?" It read: "Money, Winning, a Challenge." I skipped the rest of the list.

Skimming farther down the page, a paragraph entitled "Why do I love her?" caught my eye. I read on:

Well, she's hot. No, more than hot. She's beautiful. But the messed up thing is, she's the most beautiful when she's angry. Sometimes I feel like I'm living just to piss her off, to watch her cheeks flush bright red and her blue eyes turn stormy. I love that she never takes shit from anybody. I love that she never backs down. Even when she's wrong, which she usually is. I love that she'll defend what she thinks is right, no matter what. Jesus . . . I'm supposed to be writing about Kate, not Cass. I'm having a hard time telling the difference.

Ho. Ly. Shit. I immediately dropped the journal like it had burned my fingers.

"Cass?" Amy knocked softly at the door. "Are you done yet? Hurry up. I'm getting nervous."

"Yeah. I'm coming," I stuttered as I hastily buried the journal under a pile of sweatshirts, scrambled to my feet, and got out of Drew's room as quickly as possible.

"Did it go okay?" Amy whispered as she shut the door and quickly dragged me down the hall and into our room.

"Yup, yup, totally fine," I answered quickly. I could barely hear myself over the sound of my heart beating. It was like reverberating through my ears.

"Hold up. Are *you* okay?" Amy grabbed my arm and pulled me to a halt.

"What do you mean?"

"You look like you're having a stroke."

"Guess I'm not as cut out for a life of crime as I thought. Ha-ha." I let out a strangled laugh.

"Don't tell me you're going soft on me."

"Never!" Man, I *had* to get it together. But how could I un-see what I had just seen? I could see *I'm supposed to be writing about Kate, not Cass* stamped on my eyeballs in that tiny, cramped, serial killer handwriting. It was impossible. And yet, I had seen it. In Bic pen black and white.

"God, I hope this works," Amy sighed as she flopped onto her bed. "Like, personality-wise, he still hasn't really turned it around."

"We always knew this would take time. Just like in the play." Good. This was great. Perfect. We should keep talking about the plan. Because that way I could forget what I'd seen in that notebook. "I'm sure by opening night it will have totally worked."

"We should probably stop messing with him when the show opens." Heidi chewed her lip worriedly. "I don't want to do anything that will affect his performance."

"We've got, what, a couple days till the show opens? Jeez, is that it?" I marveled at how short our rehearsal period had been. How could the show be about to open if Lola hadn't even seen it? I had a sudden panicky thought that she'd show up at dress rehearsal, hate it, and insist everything had to change. "He'll have a couple nights of restless sleep, then we'll stop it all. Promise."

Amy masterminded the setup of the other walkie-talkie, and whatever she'd done, it must have worked like a charm, because for the next few mornings Drew showed up to rehearsal in a progressively worsening mood. He'd also taken to nodding off between scenes. Despite Heidi's worries, however, it didn't seem to negatively affect his acting ability at all. He was turning in an excellent performance run after run. Playing against his Petruchio, I could actually understand why Kate would fall for him. Drew's Petruchio was everything Drew was not—while Drew was insufferably arrogant, Petruchio was charmingly cocky. That's what Drew was missing. A modicum of charm.

CHAPTER 18

The morning of dress rehearsal, faced with a spectacularly grumpy Drew, I just couldn't resist saying something. "Wow, someone woke up on the wrong side of the bed this morning."

"The phrase 'woke up' implies that I actually slept," Drew snapped.

"I'm sorry your luxurious single room hasn't been providing you with the dreamless slumber you so richly deserve." I pulled my red fireball of an ensemble off the costume rack. Drew grabbed his leather jerkin.

"Has anyone else heard some kind of a weird honking noise?" Next to me, Amy stiffened, arm frozen as she reached for her pink dress. "Like a bird or a horn or something?"

"Sorry, man, I haven't," Noah shrugged.

"It's been driving me crazy," Drew griped. "Seriously? No one's heard anything?"

Silence. Everyone I could see was shaking their heads. Amy's shake looked a little too manic to be totally natural, but Drew was too preoccupied to notice.

"How is that even possible?" Drew continued. "Why would I be able to hear it, but no one else? That house is so small it doesn't make any sense. Maybe it's a bird that's nesting right outside my window or something?"

"A bird, huh? Does it sound kind of like 'cuckoo, cuckoo'?" Rhys asked innocently, positioning his velvet feathered cap atop his head.

Drew glared and stalked behind the curtain to the boys' half of our makeshift dressing room.

"We'll stop playing the music, tonight, though. Promise?" Heidi whispered, once we were on our own side of the curtain. "I don't want to mess him up before the show opens."

"Yes," I hissed, "and shhh. That's just a piece of cloth. So . . ." I mimed locking my lips and throwing away the key. She did the same.

Heidi, Amy, and I helped each other into our corsets and costumes, then applied makeup and tried to approximate some kind of Renaissance-suggestive hairstyle. Amy, of course, came up with an elaborate braided half-up half-down thing that looked absolutely flawless. Heidi pulled her hair into a low bun and tucked it into the golden snood that had appeared pinned to her costume. I pulled two small sections of hair back, bobby-pinned them so they'd stay away from my face, and decided to hope for the best. When all was said and done, I had to say, we looked pretty good. Amy, especially, looked like a princess—like Rapunzel from *Tangled*.

I still pretty much looked like a splatter-painted fireball, but not a totally heinous fireball.

By the time we were dressed, the boys were already on-stage. It looked like their costume boots had turned out to be much more slippery than they had anticipated. They were skating around the stage, trying to gain traction.

Once they had a few more minutes of boot practice under their belts, we started running through the show. It wasn't our best work, not by any stretch of the imagination. Every-one seemed uncomfortable in their clothing, trying to navi-gate massive skirts and jumbo sleeves. And the boots were the biggest mystery factor of all. At one point Rhys slid four feet downstage and ended up in a split.

Finally, Noah pronounced the last line of the play: "'Tis a wonder, by your leave, she will be tamed so."

Silence. Then a half-hearted slow clap. Even from back-stage, I could tell that Nevin wasn't pleased with our run. We straggled slowly onstage, the collective dread at Nevin's reaction palpable.

"Actors." Nevin stroked his goatee pensively, clutching a clipboard to his chest with his other hand. "I know we're all feeling a little stiff in our new costumes, but let's try to bring this to life, shall we?" Nope. Nevin was not pleased. "Drew, Cass, where is the heat?" As he posed this question to the heavens, I wasn't sure if it was rhetorical or not. To be on the safe side, I decided not to answer. "I feel the heat when you're fighting, but I need to feel it while you're *loving*." Someone—I think it was Rhys—giggled. Nevin pressed on, undeterred. "Bring me the passion! The romanza! Make it *fiery*!"

Fiery. Shocking that it looked easy to hate Drew, but not to love him. I could have told Nevin that on day one. But for the sake of the play, I vowed to dredge up whatever romanza lurked deep in my cynical soul. Not that I had any hopes that Drew would do the same. Except . . . *I'm supposed to be writing about Kate, not Cass* danced across my brain. No! I needed to forget what I'd seen in that notebook. I wanted to go back to a world where I was one hundred percent confident that the only thing Drew felt for me was hatred. After a few more notes, Nevin dismissed us for lunch. We changed out of our costumes quickly—heaven forbid we get so much as a crumb anywhere on our brocade-tastic ensembles.

"I can't believe we've only got one more run before the show opens," Amy murmured, breaking the silence as the cast walked to the Bait 'n' Bite. "My parents have already started the drive up to see it. This has gone by so fast. It's crazy."

"Totally," I agreed. I couldn't believe we'd be doing this show in front of actual people tomorrow. I wondered how many would be there. I knew we were only the apprentice company, but all the pictures on the Shakespeare at Dunmore website boasted pretty full audiences. People who didn't know me or anyone in the cast would be coming out here, *paying* to see me act, for the first time ever. I wasn't in a school play anymore. This was real theater. Something flipped over in my stomach as the reality of it all hit me.

"We're in fine shape," Heidi said, putting a positive spin on things, as always. "That run was just a little . . ."

"Flat," Drew said. Flatly.

"It was fine," I retorted. It hadn't been our best run ever, but there was no reason to be all negative about it. That wouldn't help anything. "We just had a lot to adjust to."

"Costumes, boots, props," Noah listed.

"And now I have to stare at Seneca Crane all show. Talk about an adjustment," I added.

"I do *not* look like Seneca Crane!" Drew protested, rubbing his jaw with concern.

Drew's facial hair looked fine—much better than when he'd been a crazy lumberjack, actually—but he didn't need to know that. I flounced into the Bait 'n' Bite to get a sandwich.

The less-than-perfect run that morning had left everyone a little subdued. After a hurried lunch, we grimly laced each other back into our corsets and costumes, like warriors preparing for battle.

"Drew, it's time," Nevin announced once we'd arrived at the stage. "Get out the swords."

"Swords!" Rhys squawked. "The run wasn't *that* bad."

"Now? You want them *now?*" Drew's voice dripped with incredulity.

"Yes, now," Nevin commanded. "The moment has come."

"When Lola asked me to bring the swords, this was not what I anticipated. Why do you want them the *day* before we open? It doesn't make any sense. It's not—"

"SWORDS!"

Heaving an almighty sigh, Drew retreated to the back of the field where all our bags were jumbled in a pile.

"Drew has swords?" Heidi raised an eyebrow as we watched Drew march back with his baseball bag slung over his shoulder.

"It's a stage combat thing," I said.

"Huh." Amy wrinkled her nose, staring at Drew like she'd never seen him before. "That's . . . interesting."

Carefully, Drew lay the bag at the edge of the stage.

"Act 2, scene 1," Nevin barked. "But with swords."

"What do you mean, 'with swords'?" I asked.

"I mean, hit him on each line."

"Okay!" I agreed readily.

"That's not safe," Drew interjected. Probably because he was afraid of my expert poking skills. "You can't have a fight onstage that's not choreographed. Even just as part of an exercise. It's not safe."

"I don't want you to be choreographed, I want you to *feel*! Stop making the safe choice!"

Nevin seemed on the verge of a full nervous breakdown. I looked nervously over at Drew.

"Directors," he muttered under his breath. "Lola's even more insane than I thought for leaving our entire production in the hands of that lunatic. Come on, let's go." He grabbed the back of my bodice and started pulling me onto the stage.

"I'm not a kitten!" I protested, disentangling myself as I hopped up on the platform. "You can't drag me around by the scruff of my neck."

"True. Kittens are way too cute and fuzzy."

"Say that again once I've got a rapier in my hands."

"I'm not letting you attack me, you maniac." Drew turned to face me.

"But Nevin—"

"But Nevin nothing. You remember enough of the moves to commit to a routine?"

I nodded. The rest of the cast was watching us curiously from the grass. Drew spoke low and fast into my ear, careful not to let them overhear. I jumped as he leaned in, suddenly self-conscious about standing so close to him.

"Attack three, parry five, bind down to the ground. Then you parry three, attack five, bind down to the ground other side. Slash at my abdomen and I'll jump back. Attack one, parry two, and I'll croise. Then parry one, attack two, and you'll croise. Then slash at my head, and I'll duck. Make sure you signal that head slash with your elbow and make it *obvious*. Got that?"

"Got it." I wasn't quite as confident as I sounded. My mind was racing, trying to remember all the different positions. Three was by the bicep, five over the head, two by the hip. I could do this. I could totally do this.

"If you put one foot out of line," Drew glowered, "so help me—"

"I said I got it, okay?" I interrupted. "Stop yapping and start fighting."

"I'm not kidding about that obvious elbow." Drew tossed me a rapier. I caught it nimbly by the handle. "If you decapitate me the day before opening night I will be seriously pissed."

"I might prefer to act opposite a headless corpse, actually." I swished my rapier through the air. "It would certainly improve the kissing scenes."

"You'll pay for that." Drew settled into ready position. "En garde!"

I assumed a ready position of my own: wide stance, knees bent, sword arm out at the ready. Hopefully my skirts wouldn't get too tangled.

"I should be hearing Shakespeare's words, not Drew's and Cass's!" Nevin reminded us.

Drew rolled his eyes and adjusted his stance.

"Ready?"

"Born ready," I replied.

"Good morrow, Kate," he began, swishing his sword with a flourish, "for that's your name, I hear."

Show time. I took a deep breath.

"Well have you heard, but something hard of hearing." *Clang*! I brought my rapier down in attack on position 3 then before I knew it I was parrying and by the time Drew said, "You lie, in faith," the bind had successfully landed on the ground.

We went through the routine twice to make it last the length of the scene and, shockingly, I didn't step one toe out of line. I even made sure to include the world's most obvious elbow signal to avoid any errant decapitation. The whole thing flowed seamlessly like we'd been rehearsing it for weeks. I only wished we could always have swords in this scene, as opposed to one measly hand slap.

"Never make denial," Drew panted, as we stood blade's length away from each other. I struggled for breath, forced to take shallow gasps in my stupid corset. "I must and will have Katharina to my wife."

"YES!" Nevin roared as the rest of the cast cheered. "There's the heat I was looking for! The fire! The *passion*! That's what I'm talking about!"

"Can we run the show now?" Abruptly, Drew broke eye contact and the loss was so startling I staggered back a few feet. I'd been so used to keeping my eyes locked on his during the fight scene it felt out of place to look away. Although most likely I was just lightheaded from forced aerobic exercise in that stupid corset.

"Of course, of course!" Nevin chortled, suddenly all benevolence. "Drew, sheath your weapons. Actors, to the stage!"

"Um, when did you learn how to sword fight?" Amy asked, looping her arm through mine as we headed backstage.

"Oh. Uh, drama club." It felt wrong lying to Amy, but it would have felt much worse explaining where I'd *really* learned how to sword fight. I knew I hadn't done anything bad by fighting in the woods with Drew. I just couldn't figure out a way to explain it that didn't sound kind of . . . sketchy. Which, of course, only made me feel sketchier.

"Amazing. You were such a badass up there!" she squealed. Luckily, Amy didn't seem to notice the squirmy somersaults of sketchiness my stomach was performing. "I can't believe you didn't get tangled up in your skirts. I totally would have face-planted."

"I think the not-face-planting thing was mostly luck." I picked the length of rope off the prop table and started binding her hands together for our first entrance.

"And ohh emm geee, could someone have looked sexier with a sword?" she whispered. "Seriously, I was, like, dying. At first, I thought the whole sword fighting thing was going to be kind of nerdy and lame, but it was *so* not. It was like ridonkulous sexy fairy tale prince. He makes that guy in *Once Upon a Time* look like a total reject. I totally wouldn't mind unsheathing his sword, if you know what I mean. Ouch!"

"Sorry!" I apologized. "Didn't mean to tie that so tight."

"Yeesh, Cass. Careful." She maneuvered her hands, trying to rub her wrists. "I've only got a scene to get out of this."

"Sorry, sorry," I muttered. I had no idea what had come over me. Overzealous knot tying wasn't usually a problem I had.

"No biggie." Amy shrugged cheerfully. "Show time!"

Thankfully, after our earlier attempt, the final dress rehearsal went much smoother. Everyone was giving it their all, and the play flew by. Maybe the sword fight really had helped, or maybe everyone had been scared by the earlier bad run. Probably it was just one of those unknowable mysteries of theater. Whatever it was, before I knew it, we had made it to the final scene. I took center stage to give my "women are so simple" speech, and much to my surprise, I actually enjoyed it. Imbuing each word with the most over-the-top sarcasm I could muster certainly made it enjoyable—for me, at least. I ended my final line in an elaborate curtsy at Drew's—er, Petruchio's—feet, my red brocade skirts fanned out in a perfect circle around me.

"Why there's a wench!" Drew cheered, extending a hand to pull me up to my feet. We stood as face-to-face as it was possible while still keeping most of our faces toward the audience. I couldn't help but smile at the way his eyes twinkled, like he knew some wonderful secret. I was pretty sure the secret was that he just really enjoyed calling me a wench. "Come on, and kiss me, Kate."

A stage kiss is about as romantic as a fist bump. It's just that you're touching lips instead of knuckles. By this point in my life I'd been kissed onstage by at least a dozen more people than I'd been kissed by offstage. Just another day at the office, as it were. Come to think of it, since we'd been up here, I'd probably kissed Drew like twenty times, and it was so asexual I didn't even register revulsion. It felt like just another piece of blocking. But this time, something was different.

I leaned in for our perfunctory lip bump, but Drew encircled my waist with his arm and pulled me up against his chest, extinguishing the space between us. His other hand wound its way through the hair at the nape of my neck, pulling my head back as he leaned down and his lips met mine. I melted into him, my arms snaking involuntarily around his neck as our mouths opened, deepening the kiss. It was like the world melted away, and there was nothing but me, and Drew, and this kiss. My knees turned to jelly, and I was positive I would have collapsed if it wasn't for Drew's strong arms keeping me together. Kissing Taylor had been fun, but this . . . this was a revelation.

"But a harsh hearing when women are forward!"

We sprang apart as Noah shouted his line. My heart was hammering in my chest. I felt like it was about to shoot straight out of my corset.

"Sorry, y'all," Noah apologized sotto voce. "Didn't mean to burst your eardrums. But I'd said my line three times."

He had? I hadn't heard anything. A fighter jet could have taken off next to me and I probably would have missed it.

"Right." Drew cleared his throat. "Right, right." Drew coughed again, turning red. "Come, Kate, we'll to bed!" he boomed out at full volume, blushing redder still. "We three are married, but you two are sped."

Drew grabbed my arm, as he was directed to, and power-walked me offstage. As soon as I was deposited safely behind the curtain he sped away from me, never once meeting my eyes.

"Cass!" Amy squealed, squeezing my arm. I jumped—I hadn't noticed her backstage. "Oh, my God. Cass. Oh, my *God.* That was incredible! We are going to crush opening night. This play is, like, *seriously* good."

"Seriously good," I repeated dumbly, bringing my free hand to touch my lips. It felt like they were still buzzing.

"It's amazing. You'd never be able to tell how much you two hate each other offstage. The chemistry is bananas. It looks really real. So weird, right?"

"So weird," I agreed fervently. What the hell had just happened? I'd been stage kissed enough times to know *that* was no stage kiss. That was a real kiss that had just happened to take place on a stage. Or maybe Drew was just a really good actor. Like a totally Daniel Day Lewis method acting phenomenon. Putting Nevin's notes into practice, trying to make it all passionate and stuff. Except . . . no. Not possible.

I couldn't have been the only one who felt that. That had felt real. Disturbingly so.

"'Tis a wonder, by your leave, she will be tamed so." And with that, Noah finished our final dress rehearsal.

"Brava!" Nevin cheered from the audience. I could hear him and Langley clapping, an enthusiastic, if paltry, audience of two. Dress rehearsal was finished, and Lola hadn't shown up once the entire rehearsal process. She must have had a lot of faith in Nevin. And us. "Actors to stage!"

Amy and I walked back onstage, as the rest of the cast ambled up to center stage. "That was exactly what I was looking for! Except next time, Drew, please pick up your cue."

"Right. Of course," Drew mumbled.

I was thrilled that the show was in good shape and excited to open tomorrow night, but it was hard to focus on Nevin's notes. I had to keep reminding myself not to stare at Drew. Not that it mattered, as he was studiously ignoring me. It was like I was boring holes in the back of his head with my gaze. That kiss had been real. I knew it. Onstage or off, I'd *never* been kissed like that before.

Amy squeezed my arm at something Nevin had said that I'd missed. Amy! Crap, what was I doing? I'd kissed the guy she liked. That violated every tenet of girl code—everything I stood for! I hoped there was some kind of stage kissing exception clause. I hadn't kissed Drew, I'd kissed Petruchio. But then why did I feel so shitty?

Besides, I liked *Taylor*. Taylor, who was a perfect combination of blindingly hot and unbelievably cool, and who had, for some reason, chosen me. Sure, the female population of

Dunmore, Vermont, was somewhat limited, but that didn't make me feel any less special. Taylor was perfect for me. We could have an awesome summer fling with no messy attachments or entanglements or any kind of feelings where someone might get hurt. And that was all I really wanted . . . wasn't it?

After numerous exhortations to relax and get lots of rest before the show opened tomorrow, Nevin dismissed us. Everyone chattered excitedly as we walked home, but I couldn't think of anything to say. Drew was also uncharacteristically silent.

"Love note!" Amy squeaked as the boathouse came into view and ran full force to the door. I was shocked she could see anything from that distance. Maybe she had extra special love note powers. She pulled a small white square of paper off the screen door. "Ohhhh emmmmmmm geeeeeeeee," she sighed, eyes rapidly scanning the note, as the rest of us caught up with her.

"What does it say?" Drew asked. "Please regale us with the further misadventures in spelling of Cass's illiterate lothario."

I glared at him. Not that it mattered, because he still wouldn't look at me.

"Nope. Girl business." Amy folded the note closed and tucked it safely down her shirt into her bra. "Ladies, to the girl cave."

Amy started sprinting inside and up the stairs, Heidi and I following as close behind her as humanly possible.

"What the hell does that note say?" I demanded the minute we got to our room, slamming the door behind us. The bunk bed rattled in response.

"Voila!" Amy unfolded the note, and we leaned over her shoulder to read:

Red! Party 2nite. Then later . . .
U + me
Special nite <3

I exhaled a breath I didn't even know I was holding. Clearly, Taylor wasn't mad at me if he'd sent me a note! He wanted to see me. Tonight.

"Tonight? Nope. Not going to happen," Heidi said decisively. "He'll just have to wait."

"But Heidi, it's a *special* night. You know what that means." Amy waggled her eyebrows suggestively, then burst out laughing. "Cass knows what I mean. She just turned tomato red."

"Did not!" I protested.

"You look like you're about to spontaneously combust. Thinking some *special* thoughts?" Amy teased.

"Shut up, shut up, shut up!"

"Doesn't matter if she's a tomato or a cucumber or a carrot or a full-on salad bar. Nothing, special or not, is happening tonight," Heidi said firmly.

"But he drew a little heart! It's so cute!" Amy pleaded. Jeez, it seemed like she wanted this to happen as much as I did.

"Not cute enough." Heidi shook her head.

"Oh, where's your sense of romance?" Amy scolded, clutching the note to her heart. "Cass, you like him, don't you?" she prompted.

"Of course I do." And I did. That's why that kiss with Drew hadn't meant anything. Because I had Taylor. Who I liked. A lot.

"See, Heidi, she likes him! And that's why she deserves an extra *special* night." She pinched my cheek. "Ah, she's still red! It's so cute."

If Taylor meant what Amy clearly thought he meant, I couldn't help but blush. It wasn't like I was some *Twilight* vampire waiting for marriage or anything, I'd just never met anyone who seemed like a worthwhile candidate. Most of the boys I knew I barely wanted to have touch me, let alone, you know, *touch* me. But if anyone had worthwhile candidate stamped on his impeccable shirtless self, it was Taylor Griffith. After all, wasn't this what summer was for? First loves and bold moves and adventure. Besides, it's not like I *had* to hook up with him once I got to the party. I just had a semisuggestive note written in crayon, not a legally binding contract. There was certainly nothing wrong with simply going over there to see what was up. Either way, Taylor was totally awesome and unbelievably hot. And he was *nothing* like Drew. Not that it mattered. Obviously.

"No. This is the worst idea I've ever heard. Sneaking out of the house the night before the show opens to sally forth once more into that den of non-recycling iniquity? Come on, Cass." I squirmed under the full force of Heidi's open, trusting gaze. "Our actions have consequences. That's not just physics, it's karma. We act and the universe reacts. That's why I know you wouldn't do that to the show. To us. To yourself." She tapped me gently in the general direction of my heart. "Listen. Here. You know what's right. I know you do. Now, if you'll excuse me, I'm in desperate need of some aromatherapy."

"Well, she's right about one thing," Amy muttered as Heidi gathered up her body wash and towel. "You should listen to your heart. Not your head. Not to misquote a thousand song lyrics, but we are young. And alive. And free. And we should set the world on fire! Just *do* it like life's a mother-eff-ing Nike commercial and you're wearing rhinestone sneakers. You know?"

I nodded, staring at Amy in wonder. She was so fired up, eyes sparkling like Joan of Arc or something. I thought back to the first day I'd met her, when she was sitting on the bed awash in tears. It was almost like she was a different person.

"Cass," Amy said softly, checking over her shoulder. Heidi was safely ensconced in the bathroom. "You can't live your whole life onstage, because that's not really living. Your greatest adventures should be *yours*. Not Shakespeare's. Live your life. Don't just perform someone else's."

I mean, I'm totally on board with seizing the day, but I didn't want to do anything that would put the show in jeopardy. And when whatever ancient Roman had first said *carpe diem*, I don't think he'd been talking about maybe hooking up with a pro skater. But who was to say that my meeting up with Taylor would mess up the show, anyway? We'd snuck out of the boathouse before without anyone noticing. No harm, no foul. I could have my perfect summer fling, then make it back in plenty of time to kick butt on opening night.

STEPHANIE KATE STROHM

Heidi started singing in the shower. As the sweet refrain of "Look to the Rainbow" floated into my ears, tiny pinpricks of guilt stabbed at my conscience. Her warning about consequences echoed in my mind, like some kind of ominous, sonorous refrain. Amy was still staring at me, perfectly tweezed blond eyebrows arched meaningfully. What would Shakespeare do?

I knew, of course. The man who had written "Boldness, be my friend! Arm me, audacity, from head to foot!" would have been out the door ten minutes ago.

Boldness, be my friend, indeed.

CHAPTER 19

JJ flung the door to the skaters' cabin wide open.

"Betty!" he cheered. "Just one Betty?" He looked behind me, squinting into the darkness beyond the porch. "Where's tallie and smallie?"

"Just me tonight. Sorry to disappoint."

"You could never disappoint, Red Betty! Entrez!"

As JJ mangled some French, he turned to let me into the cabin. This time his back was adorned with a strange drawing in Sharpie. Was that a slab of ham with angel wings? I squeezed inside and closed the cabin door behind me.

It wasn't nearly as crowded as it had been at the last party, and no music was playing. There was just a small group of guys clustered around a keg, talking in a low murmur. The cabin, however, was even messier than the last time I'd seen it. Crushed Monster Energy Drink cans and empty Doritos bags littered the floor. I shook a particularly stubborn Cool Ranch bag off my sneaker.

"Red!"

I looked up. Taylor was pushing his way through the small group toward me, holding a red Solo cup aloft. He clinged and clanged as he walked, covered mysteriously in large sparkling pendants and platinum chains. He looked like a refugee from Island Def Jam. The only thing he was missing was a grill.

"What's with all the bling?" I asked, lifting up the diamond graffiti print GANGSTA RAW dangling at the end of a long chain around his tan neck.

"It's a special night, Red!" he crowed, pounding his fist against his chest. His blinged-out YOLO knuckle ring sparkled in the light. "We're having a party! And later on, it's gonna get extra special. Like extra choice special."

Wait. Did he just pinch my butt? I looked down. His hands were nowhere near my butt—one clutched a red Solo cup, and the other was flung casually around my waist. I must have imagined it.

"To the knives, gentleman!"

The crowd roared like he was Henry V leading the charge at Agincourt. I had no idea why we were going to get knives—maybe a cheese tasting was about to materialize—but regardless, I let Taylor steer me to a large kitchen table with mismatched wooden chairs.

Taylor sat at the head of the table, cocking the brim of his trucker hat until it perched on his sun-bleached hair at a rakish angle. I had the uncomfortable feeling I was sitting next to a stranger. Had he always looked like such a douchelord, or was this a recent development? Underneath the bling and the Ed Hardy I was sure he was just as mind-numbingly hot as always, but boy, it was hard to tell. He patted one knee for me to sit on it. Please. I looked pointedly at the knee, back up at Taylor, and then pulled out my own chair.

"Miss Independent," Taylor said fondly, barely waiting until my butt had touched the seat to scoot it as close to his as humanly possible. Maybe Heidi was right and coming here *had* been a mistake. I barely recognized the Sean John factory reject sitting beside me. But then he smiled a blessedly grill-free, devastating smile, and something shot right through me. Stay. I should stay. I leaned into the arm Taylor had flung around the back of my chair.

"What are we doing?" I asked. Taylor, Ragner, JJ, Skittles, Ferret, and some skinny guy with a soul patch I'd never seen before sat around the table. It looked like we were about to have birthday cake. Or play a board game.

"Tell us, Townie," Taylor commanded, gesturing grandly at the skinny soul patch guy at the other end of the table.

"Tonight, the sheep leads," Ferret giggled, stroking the omnipresent mammal circled around his neck. "Baa ram uu. Baa ram uuu." He giggled, then oinked like a pig, then dissolved back into giggles.

"Thanks." Taylor rolled his eyes. "Some people cannot handle their substances," he whispered to me.

"Is he okay?" I asked, concerned. Ferret was giggling into a red plastic cup, and the actual ferret somehow managed to maneuver around his human and dip his head in it. "Can ferrets have alcohol?"

"It's fine. It'll probs be hilarious later. Drunk rodents!" Taylor laughed. "The knives, Townie, the knives!"

Ferret looked like he was about to fall asleep. I turned my attention to the end of the table, where sure enough, there were three knives lined up in front of the Townie guy: a butter knife, a sharp serrated kitchen knife, and some kind of enormous deadly weapon.

"What the hell kind of knife is that?" I pointed at the mammoth scimitar.

"The biggest, baddest knife I could find in the state of Vermont," Townie said a little more lustily than I was comfortable with. He ran his hand carefully around the edge. "Sharp, too."

"Are you carving a turkey?"

"You're hilarious." Taylor squeezed my side. "Tell the girl the game, Townie!"

"The game of knives begins thusly," Townie began with great relish. "We start off with this little baby." He held up the butter knife. "We toss the knife around the circle, one to the other. Anyone can toss the knife to anyone else at any given time. If you miss the knife, or puss out, you drink. If you catch it, you don't drink. Once we establish a pattern, we move on to this beauty." He held up the serrated kitchen knife. "And, finally, Big Bertha." He gestured to the knife that looked, in my opinion, much more like a sword than a knife. They were seriously going to *throw* that thing at each other? While *drinking*? This had to be the worse idea I'd ever heard. "The game ends when our hands are too slippery with blood to successfully hold any knives."

"When *what*?" I shrieked.

"Shh, Red, it's cool," Taylor whispered.

"Cool? Really?" I whispered back. "This seems insane! Tell me you're not doing this."

"Hell naw. I'm not that dumb." Taylor squeezed my hand. "We'll just watch. And record it for posteriors."

"Posterity," I muttered under my breath.

"I just wanna watch theses dumbasses maim themselves." Taylor pulled out an iPhone.

"Your phone works here?" I asked, shocked. Of course, I should have been more shocked that a room full of sort-of-almost-adults was about to fling knives at each other, but I hadn't seen a working cell phone in who knows how long.

"Naw, Red. Just use it for the camera." He held it up, starting to frame a shot. "Throw, son, throw!"

The butter knife wasn't that big of a deal. They threw a few rounds with it, until they got bored or deemed themselves successful enough to move on—who knew which.

Thiago turned out to be some kind of deadly assassin knife-throwing genius.

He never missed a single throw, never caught it on the sharp end, and threw each knife with surgical precision. His knitted cap was pulled so low over his eyes I wasn't even sure how he was seeing anything, but he must have had the eyes of a hawk.

The others, however, weren't faring quite so well. Ferret and his ferret had fallen asleep and were curled up under the table, which was probably for the best. Big blond Ragner was getting increasingly frustrated with his poor catching skills, cursing in Norwegian until the roof shook. The more frustrated he got, the more he missed, and the more he drank. Each time JJ flung the knife with great velocity but little accuracy, I cringed, hoping my life wouldn't end in a hoarders-worthy cabin in rural Vermont. And Skittles—well, I had yet to hear him utter a word. He was just a giant splatter-paint hoodie with eyes.

By the time the biggest knife came out, everyone except Thiago was bleeding. They were all now drunk enough that their tosses were getting less accurate and their catches less frequent. Townie, however, was by far in the worst shape. Warm, wet rivers of blood dripped down his palms, puddling onto his Carhartts and staining the blade of the knife a bright Macbeth red.

"Taylor"—I tugged on his iPhone recording arm—"we have to stop this. Some of them are bleeding pretty, um, profusely."

"Everybody seems fine." He shrugged. "Look, they're laughing!"

Townie used his bloody hands to put two handprints on his T-shirt, like some kind of gruesome Little Mermaid seashell bra. Bile rose in my throat.

"Seriously, Taylor, I'm gonna be sick. We have to stop this. They're losing a lot of blood, and their throws are getting worse."

"Yeah, you're right," Taylor said disappointedly, clicking the camera app on his iPhone shut. "Their skills are not maintaining. Except for Thiago, you guys suck!" he shouted, and threw his empty cup at JJ. "Game over!"

"At least we played!" JJ said defensively. "Didn't puss out like you, knuckle-dragger. Not even sure you're the Bowser anymore, man."

"Dude. I *am* the Bowser. Always." Taylor fixed JJ with an icy stare, then broke into an easy grin as soon as JJ looked away. "Come on, man, I'd play if I could. Gotta keep my hands clean for later tonight."

Taylor help up his hands and wiggled his fingers, as the rest of the table looked at me and laughed. As they howled like dogs, that trademark "bow-ow-ow," I cringed and turned bright red, sinking lower in my seat. Blessedly, conversation soon turned to a lively debate over what the next game should be. No one, unfortunately, seemed in a hurry to look for Band-Aids.

"Sorry, Red," Taylor leaned in to whisper, his warm breath tickling my neck. "That was not my most couth."

"Ya think?" I shot back, as I tried to remember whether or not *couth* was a word. "I should probably just go."

"Don't go! Please. Cass. Please." Before I could even stand all the way up, Taylor grabbed my wrist and turned the full force of his hotness upon me. "I was just frontin'. Have to prove it with these guys, you know. Stay. Please."

"That was lame, Taylor." I glared at him.

"The lamest. I'll make it up to you. Promise."

He stroked my hand so tenderly, and his eyes looked so sincere, I melted like a Kit Kat in the sun. Had ever a girl been such a fool for lust? Ugh. I was making bad choices every which way, and yet I just couldn't bring myself to get up and walk out of the cabin.

"Spin the Shotgun!" JJ shouted suddenly. "I choose Spin the Shotgun!"

"If someone pulls out a gun, I'm leaving," I said flatly. There are limits to even *my* idiocy.

"No guns. Just this beauty." Townie brandished the giant knife again and slid it to the center of the table. Great. Just what this evening needed. More knives.

Weaving slightly, JJ tottered into the kitchen and returned with his arms full of beer cans. He triumphantly placed one in the center of the table. "Your highness." JJ bowed sarcastically to Ragner. "Worst goes first."

"Dra til helvete," Ragner rumbled, but he approached the knife anyway. He spun it, like we were beginning a deadly game of spin the bottle. The knife's tip stopped directly in front of Thiago, who leapt up onto his chair, grasped the knife by its handle, and plunged it into the heart of the beer can. As the foam exploded, splattering the room, Thiago placed his lips to the hole in the can and gulped the beer. The boys roared with appreciation as Thiago finished his beer and crushed the can, tossing it to the floor.

"Rule number one: no one leaves the table! The game ends when someone pukes, passes out, or pisses themselves!" Townie shouted.

"That's not a rule. That's torture! Taylor, this game is ridiculous. Everyone is still bleeding. How 'bout we play a game called Seeking Medical Attention?"

"Relax, Red. It's fine." He'd gotten his iPhone out again. "No one's gonna pass out. Just a little bit of on-the-road fun."

I bit my lip—I didn't want to seem lame, but I was getting progressively more uncomfortable. I had thought this night would be some kind of carefree fun adventure, like in a movie, but it felt more like a mash-up of *American Pie* and *Friday the 13th* than the summer lovin' I had envisioned. Olivia Newton-John would certainly never sing about any of this. At that moment I would have given anything to be tucked safely into my bunk bed, listening to Heidi's garbled Sanskrit dreams. I shouldn't have come. Or I should have left the minute the first knife came out.

Thiago spun the knife, and it stopped, pointing at Townie. He stabbed the can wildly. I shielded my face as foam exploded everywhere. He brought it to his lips, but he seemed to have trouble getting it down.

"Hurl alert!" JJ screamed. "He's hurling!"

"Oh, my God." I leapt away from the table, determined to put as much distance between myself and the vomiting man as possible.

"Dude, I think he pissed himself, too!" JJ cackled. "This is epic!"

Epically gross. The room started to spin, and my knees went all wobbly—and not in the good way. Heidi was right— our actions did have consequences. I had always thought that consequences just came from the outside, like getting in trouble with teachers or adults or whatever, but just being here felt like a punishment, and I had no one to blame but myself. If this was the universe telling me that sneaking out of the house was wrong, I heard it loud and clear. I was in way over my head. And I *had* let down Heidi and Amy and everyone in the show. Whether I got caught or not, my selfishness was betrayal enough. I never should have jeopardized the show by coming here.

"Dag, Red, you're turning green." Suddenly Taylor was beside me, and I felt myself sort of half collapsing into him. "Let's get you out of here," he said firmly, and whisked me straight up the stairs. Thank God. I had to get out of there. And sit. Sitting would be good. Everything was so spinny.

It was such a relief to be upstairs, away from that circus in the kitchen, that I could have cried. As Taylor ushered me into a lowly lit room and sat me down on the bed's pine cone–printed counterpane, I felt distressingly queasy.

"You gonna ralph on me, Red?"

"Potentially," I muttered, sticking my head between my knees.

"Hey," Taylor said softly, coming to sit next to me on the bed. After taking off his YOLO ring, he started rubbing my back gently. "You're okay. We're okay. It's all chill up here. Things just got a little out of hand."

"A little!" I popped up from between my knees. Whoops— too fast. I put my head back down.

"Yeah, out of hand." As he rubbed my back, Taylor kept taking off his bling one by one, resting each piece on the bedside table with his other hand. "But it's all good now. As long as you don't barf on me."

"I think I'm okay." Slowly, I raised my head to its normal, upright position. Not too bad. It was nice and cool in the bedroom, and everything smelled faintly of pine needles and Axe body spray.

"Solid." Taylor grinned, and placed two mercifully bling-free hands on either side of my face. "I'm feeling you, I think you're feeling me, so I think we should feel each other."

I stared at him in silence, open-mouthed. What did one even *say* to the worst line of all time? Never mind the fact that I was teetering on the brink of queasy and had just witnessed several grave incidents of bodily harm. It was so quiet I could hear crickets. And a roaring in my ears that sounded suspiciously like Drew laughing.

Drew. Why was he in my brain? I could hear him laughing in my mind so clearly, I could practically see him perched at the edge of the bed, like the ghost of Christmas Past or something. And Ghost Drew wasn't wrong. This whole situation was pretty ridiculous. I could not seriously be contemplating losing my virginity to a blinged-out pro skateboarder after having just witnessed a poorly choreographed knife fight. I should have been straight out the door. And yet . . . I was still here. Ghost Drew smirked. He thought it was hilarious, clearly.

"Hey, you." Taylor tapped my temple gently. "What's going on up there? You're like a million miles away."

"Oh, n-nothing." Nothing at all. Just having a mild hallucination involving my mortal enemy. Whom I had kissed passionately. Once. Accidentally.

"Sweet." He seemed satisfied with that non-response. "You just chillax right here, and I'll be back in uno momento."

He then mouthed something that might have been "el baño" as he sidled out of the room and into the hallway.

It was like that part in *Toy Story 3* where Buzz Lightyear turned Spanish. Maybe it was supposed to be extra suavamente, but it really just made me think about *Toy Story*. Okay. I would get myself together, and as soon as the room stopped spinning, I would head back to the boathouse. And if I didn't get caught, I vowed to the universe that I would be good forever and do whatever it took to repay my karmic debt.

Like a tiny bomb, Taylor's iPhone started beeping and vibrating. Startled by the din, I jumped about half a foot off the bed. The force of its vibrations were causing the phone to flop all over the nightstand like a fish, so I picked it up to stop it. I didn't mean to spy, I really didn't, but the words JESSA ANNIVERSARY! filled the screen.

Jessa Anniversary . . . that was weird. Maybe it was his sister's anniversary or something? I closed the calendar notification and the screen filled with Taylor's iPhone background: a picture of him with his arms around another girl.

She was beautiful, in a totally clichéd California girl way—giant sunglasses perched on top of her long golden-blond hair, deep tan, clear blue eyes, a few cute freckles sprinkled across her adorable nose. She was laughing, head thrown back, and grinning from ear to ear. The worst part of it was, she looked nice. I didn't even want to hate her. Taylor looked ridiculously happy, too. And was he giving her bunny ears?

"Hey, lady in red," Taylor said softly. I looked up. He was standing in the doorway, shirtless. But not even his impressive abdominal musculature—or the fact that I wasn't wearing red—could distract me from the Jessa conundrum. It was the first time a shirtless Taylor Griffith hadn't sent me into heart palpitations.

"So, who's the blonde in the bikini?" I asked as casually as humanly possible.

CHAPTER 20

W hat blonde in what bikini?" Taylor asked. He noticed the phone on the bed. "Who? Jessa?"

"As in 'Jessa Anniversary'?"

"Aw, shit, was that today?" He grabbed for the phone and started typing away at it, fingers flying.

"I'm guessing she's not your sister," I said flatly.

"What? No!" he said emphatically, looking up. "Gross! Jessa's my girlfriend."

"Your *what*?" I shrieked. I mean, I knew that's who she was. I wasn't an idiot. But I hadn't expected him to *admit* it.

"My girlfriend," he repeated.

"Yeah, obvious much! I got that! I can't believe you have a girlfriend!"

"Well, I do." He looked confused, like he was trying to do long division in his head.

"Why aren't you freaking out?" I demanded. "Aren't you pissed that I caught you in your lie?"

"I never lied to you." He shrugged. Damn him for being so calm! We could have been talking about Funyuns for all the emotion he was displaying.

"And you were about to *cheat on her* on your *anniversary!*" I steamrolled over him. Never lied to me. Ha! Exhibit A—mystery Jessa.

"The timing *is* mad regrettable, Red." He winced. "That's on me. That's my bad. But I wasn't going to cheat on her."

"What, you asked me over here to play Boggle?" I arched an eyebrow.

"I wasn't going to cheat on her," he continued, like I hadn't said anything, "because we have an open relationship when I'm on the road."

"Really." I folded my arms protectively across my chest. I didn't believe him for a second. That poor girl was probably innocently drinking her Kombucha on the beach right now without a care in the world, perfecting that perfect tan, no idea that her rindonkulously hot boyfriend was a philandering asshat. "That's awfully convenient."

"I'm not frontin', Red!" Taylor exclaimed, finally displaying something other than a megachill vibe. Thank goodness. There is nothing more aggravating than trying to fight with someone who is implacably calm. "It's totally legit. I travel too much, and long distance is a major bummer. While I'm on the road, I've got a girlfriend, but not in, like, any kind of traditional sense. Jessa's totally cool with it. She doesn't ask me about what went on in Tokyo, and I don't ask her what she gets up to in Hermosa while I'm gone. So it's all good, Red."

"Really, is it? Is it, Taylor? It's all good? Well, it's not all good for me!" I shouted. He winced again. I knew I was getting really loud, but I didn't care. "Did you ever think about that? Did you ever think about how *I* would feel? Because guess what? This feels shitty. This feel really, really shitty. I don't want to be some sloppy second backwoods consolation prize because your bikini model is in another state."

"She only did that one campaign for Roxy. It's no biggie. Nothing to be intimidated by."

She was an *actual* bikini model? "That's not even the point, Taylor. And I'm not intimidated, FYI." I shot him my fiercest glare, and he quailed in terror. "I want all or nothing." I realized once I'd said it how true it was. I didn't want to just sleep with Taylor Griffith, or anyone else for that matter, and then never see him again. I wanted more than that. "I don't want to be some story you tell your bros—about the time you banged a redhead one weekend in Vermont. I don't want to be a weekend. I want to be someone's every day. I want to be someone's Jessa. Except, you know, without the open relationship part. Because quite frankly that sounds like a disaster."

"Well, actually—"

"Shut it!" I hollered. "I wasn't asking for your opinion!"

"So . . . this is not happening, then?"

"Definitely not." I threw his shirt at him. "And put on some clothes."

And with that, I prepared to flounce out of the room, making my grand exit. Unfortunately, after I flung the bedroom door open, my grand exit was stymied by a most unexpected sight. The staircase was filled with furniture. It looked like every piece of furniture from downstairs—couches, tables, chairs—had been piled together, completely obscuring the stairs and reaching up to the ceiling.

"What the hell is this?" I shouted. I was facing an impenetrable, impassable barrier, and I started to feel panicked. Trapped.

"What the . . . oh, man." Taylor came to stand behind me. "That's whack."

"Beyond whack," I snarled.

"Easy, Red. It's no biggie. Just a joke or some shit. Why are you so mad?"

"Why am I so mad? Why am I so MAD?" Taylor flung his hands in front of his face protectively, like he was afraid I was going to throw something at him. If there had been something at hand, I probably would have. "I am *mad* because your idiot friends have barricaded me in a room with the last person in Vermont I want to be around right now!"

"They were just trying to be funny," he said meekly as he retreated to the bed.

"Funny? HA!" I barked sarcastically. "I'm not laughing. Are you?"

"Not laughing," he muttered. "This is some scary-ass psycho shit."

"You think *this* is psycho?" I laughed maniacally. "Trust me, we are nowhere near psycho. And you don't want to be around when I get there. So help me get all this stuff out of the way!"

I reached under the couch and pulled up with all my might. Nothing. I tried to pull the chair on top of the couch down, but it was wedged so neatly in between several other chairs and the ceiling that nothing moved. The whole thing was like a perfectly balanced, immobilized game of furniture Tetris.

"Give it up, Red," Taylor said lazily. "That shit's gonna be mad hard to move. Just wait 'til the morning, I'm sure the guys'll clear it out from downstairs. You can crash here. I won't try anything, promise."

"I can't 'crash' here." I air-quoted. "First of all, I have a curfew, and to avoid getting caught, I need to be back way before the sun rises. Second of all, I cannot spend another minute with you, let alone hours. And third of all, I have a show tomorrow. Oh God! I have a show tomorrow!" With all this Jessa business, I had forgotten. I could practically feel Shakespeare's ghost looking at me with baleful disappointment. Worst of all, Drew was right—Taylor *had* put the show in jeopardy. Well, *I'd* put the show in jeopardy. I'd never felt so stupid.

"Whatever, Red." Taylor flopped back on the bed. "Knock yourself out. But that shit's not going anywhere 'til the morning."

Some help he was! Not that I was expecting much from that corner, but he could have at least *tried*. He clearly didn't want to be trapped in a room with me, either; he was just too lazy to do anything about it. Lame. I gave the couch one more tug. Nothing. I kicked it as hard as I could, and it still didn't move. Ugh. The stairs were not an option. There had to be another way out of here. Think, Cass, think. I started pacing around the room, hoping a trap door would appear in the floor or something. Or maybe I should just jump out the window . . .

I strode purposefully over to the open window. Since it was only a cabin, I wasn't *that* high up. But then again, I was still on the second floor. I stuck my head outside. The night breeze would have been deliciously cool if I hadn't been contemplating jumping out of a window. Well, maybe I wouldn't have to jump, technically. Taylor's bedroom window looked out over the porch. I could easily climb out the window onto the porch roof, then shimmy down one of the supporting poles. That wouldn't be so bad. Sure, I'd never climbed out a window before, but I'd climbed a tree. It couldn't be all that different.

I stuck a leg out the window. Luckily it was wide enough that I was easily able to pass through it.

"What the hell are you doing?"

Oh, right. Taylor. I'd kind of forgotten about him. The porch roof was surprisingly flat and sturdy. It would have been a nice place to hang out on a sunny day.

"I'm leaving." I stuck my head back in the window. Taylor was watching me curiously from the bed.

"Dude, you can't jump out the window! That's insane."

"*You're* insane if you think I'm spending the night here."

"Whatever, man. I give up." Taylor suddenly appeared in front of me. "I can't deal with your psycho vibe anymore."

"*I'm* the psycho? I'm not the one who watched his friends throw *knives* at each other as they slowly bled to death!"

"No one's dead! And you were there, too!"

"You know what? You're right," I agreed, and he looked shocked. "Not getting up and leaving the minute the first knife showed up was completely psychotic. I never should have stayed. I never should have even come here in the first place!"

"Whatever. Have fun breaking your neck, psycho." And with that he shut the window closed. I stuck my tongue out at him from behind the glass.

I wasn't going to break my neck. Although now that the possibility had been mentioned, I felt less confident in my ability to clamber down the porch with ease.

Carefully I scooted along on my butt until I reached the edge of the porch roof. There. The easy part was done. Now for the hard part. I peered over the edge of the roof and saw nothing but black. Somehow the porch roof seemed much higher up from here than it had looked from inside. But now all I had to do was shimmy down a pole until I hit the porch railing. Totally doable.

My heart was in my throat as I reached a leg out into the inky darkness. I felt around until my foot connected with the supporting pole. Fortunately, it felt reassuringly solid. Oak? Maple? I transferred my weight off the roof and onto the pole. I was clinging to that thing like a giant red koala. What if I wasn't able to move? What if I was just stuck here like I was back doing the rope climb in fourth grade? No. Failure was not an option. I took a deep breath and started to slide. It wasn't so bad, really. Just scooting along the pole. But then, about halfway down, I heard a loud crashing sound.

If Taylor thought the noise was me plummeting to my death, he didn't bother to look out the window for my corpse. Which was, frankly, kind of rude. The crashing continued. Arms still clinging to the pole, I craned my neck to peer around the side of the house. I squinted into the darkness, trying to make out what was crashing around the silver trash cans. And then my eyes connected with two large glistening black eyes . . .

Bear! I squeaked in distress and hugged the pole even tighter. Had the bear seen me? God, I hoped not. Why hadn't I paid attention to Amy's bear safety tips? What if bears really *did* hate Shakespeare? I was stuck up a pole with a ravenous, trash-eating, Shakespeare-hating bear prowling the grounds. Should I go back up to the roof? What was worse: being trapped inside with Taylor or outside with a bear? I tried to pull myself up, but it was like my arms had gone limp. I couldn't move. I was stuck on that pole like a big stupid barnacle.

Suddenly, two headlights flooded the darkness with light. I shut my eyes against the glare. As the battered Jeep rumbled over the gravel, my eyes adjusted just in time to see the bear lumbering away into the woods. Thank God. The last time I'd seen that Jeep it had been smack up against my fender—excuse me, bumper. Who could have guessed I'd ever be happy to see it again?

"Cass?" Drew climbed out of the driver's seat and made his way over to the pole. "What the hell are you doing up there?"

"Things got complicated."

"A little late for you to bust out the koala impression, don't you think?"

"Funny. It just *killed* at the last party I was at." Drew snorted in response. "What are you doing here, anyway?"

"I'm here to rescue you," he said, like it was the most natural thing in the world.

My heart did some kind of weird, traitorous flutter. If I hadn't been clinging to a pole for dear life I might have slapped myself.

"What kind of half-assed rescue is this?" I said snidely, trying to squash any and all traitorous flutters. "Shouldn't you have a cape? Where's your sword?"

"Sword's in the back of the car. I'll get it out, if that's really necessary. As for the cape—not gonna happen."

"Fine. A cape is unnecessary, since I don't need rescuing, anyway. I can rescue *myself*, thank you very much."

"I can see that. You've clearly got a great handle on the situation here." He chuckled.

"I can get down by myself," I insisted. And yet, my arms kept betraying me. Curses. I was 100 percent stuck.

"Clearly, you can't."

"Can, too," I retorted.

"It's okay to let other people help you, Cass," Drew said gently, and suddenly he was right behind me. "It doesn't make you weak. Now, let go of the pole."

"Never!" I cried.

"I'll pry you off of there if I have to."

"I'm not a barnacle."

"You are the most barnacle-like girl I have ever encoun-
tered." He placed his large, strong hands around my waist,
and without the corset between us, he felt all too warm and
near. "Please, for once in your contentious life, cooperate."

Drew easily peeled me off the pole and I sort of half fell into
his arms. I guess I hadn't been quite as high up as I'd thought.

There was a scene in the play where Drew hoisted me
over his shoulder so I knew he was strong enough to carry
me, but being carried in his arms like this felt about a billion
times more intimate. I really wanted him to put me down,
but my legs felt all wobbly.

"This is mortifying." I hid my face as Drew carried me to
the Jeep, but the only place to hide my face was in Drew's
neck. He smelled disturbingly good, like clean laundry and
Christmas. Like home. "I'm like a stupid cat stuck in a tree
or something."

"No scratch marks yet. Shocking."

"You don't have to do this," I muttered as he slid me into
the passenger seat. "I'm not a giant baby."

"I'm not so sure about that. You sure do throw a lot of
tantrums."

"Hey!"

He shut the door behind me and walked around to the
driver's side.

"Seriously, though. Why are you here?" I asked as he
leapt into the driver's seat.

"Heidi's 'intuition'"—he rolled his eyes—"woke her
up. She checked your bed, and you weren't there, and she
freaked out."

"My carefully constructed pillow person didn't fool her?"

"Cass. Please tell me you didn't stuff pillows under your blanket to make it look like you were still in there."

"Did. Got into bed fully dressed, waited until she fell asleep, built my pillow decoy, and headed out."

"This isn't a sitcom, you know." He rolled his eyes. "Anyway, I was in the lounge, reading . . . couldn't sleep . . . and she forced me into my car to go look for you. Well, after I refused to let *her* drive my car. I don't let *anyone* with such disregard for material possessions get behind the wheel. Anyway, she marched me downstairs and into the car, and here I am."

"I'm glad you are here," I said quietly, thankful he was driving so I didn't have to meet his eyes.

"Me, too," he said softly. After a small pause, he joked, "I guess it's a good thing I can't sleep anymore."

"I'm sorry."

"It's not your fault."

"Actually . . . " I swallowed noisily, my throat suddenly dry. "It kind of is."

"How could that possibly be your fault?" He laughed.

"I'm the reason you can't sleep," I confessed. "And why your eyes got all red and itchy. Why your room is full of strange noises."

"Cass, what are you talking about?"

"I decided to . . . shrew you."

"What do you mean, 'shrew me'?" he asked, his brow furrowed.

"Like . . . in the play. Like Petruchio does to Kate. Taming the shrew," I swallowed again, uncomfortable.

"Wait a minute." The tires squealed as Drew came to an abrupt stop, pulled over to the side of the road, put the car in park, and turned to face me. "So all the shitty stuff that's happened to me this summer, you're saying *you* did that? On purpose?"

"Um, yeah. Pretty much."

"The itchy eyes?"

"Me."

"The crazy crying baby horns?"

"That's a vuvuzela, and yeah, me."

"All my clothes turning pink and tiny?"

"Me."

"The mouse who ate my food?" His eyebrows marched further and further toward his hairline, rising with incredulity.

"Wasn't a mouse," I squeaked in a mouse-like voice. "That was me."

He stared at me with murderous intent, glowering with rage, for about a full minute, until suddenly, unexpectedly, he burst out laughing.

"You're not mad?" I asked apprehensively.

"I'm *furious*," he said, but he couldn't stop laughing. He bent over the steering wheel, shaking with mirth. "Furious," he giggled. "What the hell was that?" He sat up straight, wiping tears of laughter from his eyes. "Some kind of crazy meta-theater experiment?"

"Well . . . um . . . sort of." I squirmed uncomfortably. The actual road to shrewing Drew seemed even stranger and more implausible than an acting exercise.

"You absolute lunatic." He shook his head, still smiling. "You beautiful lunatic."

"You think I'm beautiful?" I breathed. I don't think a boy had ever called me beautiful before. I *had* been called a lunatic before, on several occasions, but that didn't seem nearly as important as being called beautiful.

"Unfortunately for me, I do."

He tried to pull me in for a kiss, but I placed my hands on his chest, stopping him.

"What do you mean, 'unfortunately'?"

He grinned.

"I have a feeling you're gonna spend the rest of your life driving me crazy. And for some reason, I'm looking forward to it."

"The rest of my life?" Shakespeare's characters constantly spoke in terms of always and forever, but real teenage boys, in my admittedly limited experience, did not. But the way Drew said it, so casually and confidently, sent this swoop of joy right through me as a huge grin broke out on my face. I couldn't think of anything I'd rather do than drive him crazy for as long as humanly possible. "If we keep spending time together, that probably won't be very long. I assume we'll end up killing each other."

"It'd be worth it," he said simply. "I'd rather have a scene with you than five acts with anyone else."

"Cheesy," I teased. I didn't *really* think it was cheesy. It was so nice I had a sudden urge to write it down so I'd never forget. But it was like my mouth refused to agree with my melting, mushy feelings and continued to soldier on sarcastically without me.

"That was an extremely well-constructed theatrical metaphor, and your objection is, quite frankly, offensive. Come on, Cass." The way Drew said my name it sounded almost like a caress. "Cheesy can be nice. It can't be all banter, all the time."

"Banter is underrated."

"God." He ran his thumb along the side of my jaw, sending a tingly shiver straight up my spine. "I really must be crazy."

"I've said it from the beginning. You're insane."

"Peace," he said firmly. "I will stop your mouth."

He pulled me in to kiss him, and this time, I didn't resist.

CHAPTER 21

$\mathcal{E}$ ventually we had to drive back to the boathouse. We were now mere hours away from the sun rising and the show opening. So much for Nevin's exhortations to get lots of sleep. I leaned my head contentedly against the window of the car, watching Drew's cute frown of concentration as he drove. I knew there was a big, stupid, goofy smile on my face, and I didn't even care.

"Crap," he muttered, frown deepening. "I think someone's up."

"Are you serious?" I sat bolt upright, straining against my seatbelt as I peered into the darkness, trying to discern whatever—or whomever—Drew had seen in the gloomy darkness.

"Yeah. There's someone there. I can see who through the screen door.

"Oh, shit."

"Oh, shit is right. If that's Langley we are seriously screwed."

"You really think she'd kick us out? Right before the show?" My voice was getting all high and panicky. I knew I deserved nothing less for how recklessly I'd acted, but I really, really didn't want to ruin the show. And now I'd taken the leading man down with me. Please have it not be Langley, I prayed silently. Please not Langley. Hopefully it was just a raccoon or something. I wasn't sure why a raccoon would be clinging to our screen door, but this was Vermont. Practically the wilderness. Stranger things had happened.

"Why not? She'd have every reason to. We're in violation of about fifteen different rules right now." Drew pulled the car into the driveway and parked. "Well, if we're going down, there's no one I'd rather go down with."

I smiled. "We'll always have Vermont."

He tilted my chin up with his hand. "Here's looking at you, kid." He kissed me once—quickly, fiercely—and then we prepared to meet our doom.

But as I got out of the car, I saw that the face in the screen door wasn't Langley's. It was worse, a thousand times worse. That bright blond hair was easily distinguishable, even in the unlit stairwell. Amy. Oh, Amy. What had I done?

Drew tried to grab my hand, but I ran ahead of him to push open the door. Amy stepped back to let me in.

"Amy!" I whispered urgently. Drew walked in behind me and carefully closed the door, minimizing any creaking sounds. "What are you doing up?"

"I heard a car start. It woke me up." Drew and I exchanged glances. Could that have woken Langley, too? Our window happened to overlook the parking lot, but the walls in the

272

boathouse were awfully thin. "Heidi was awake, and you were gone. I decided to stay up because I was worried about you. Clearly, I shouldn't have been," she said coldly, her eyes flicking back and forth between me and Drew.

"This is not what it looks like. At all."

"Really? Because it looks like you were kissing."

"Okay, well, that part is what it looks like. But—"

"I'm sorry, is it a problem that we were kissing?" Drew interrupted. "I'm confused."

"How long has this been going on?" Amy demanded.

"All summer, really," Drew answered.

"All *summer*?" she gasped.

"No!" I shouted. "No," I repeated more quietly, conscious of waking up the house. "This only happened this one time. Just once. And it was an accident!"

"An accident?" Drew sounded like he'd been punched in the stomach.

"It was like some kind of post-traumatic stress reflex," I said desperately. "There were knives! Knives flying everywhere! And blood. So much blood. And a bear!"

"What, were you held captive in an Elizabethan circus?" Amy asked sarcastically. If anything she looked more hurt than before. "At least respect me enough to come up with a convincing lie."

I'd seen Amy cry before, but this stiff coldness was infinitely more awful than tears could ever be.

"I'm not lying! And I never meant for anything to happen. It was a mistake. A terrible, terrible mistake," I said desperately.

"I would really appreciate it if you stayed out of our room tonight." She flicked her eyes back over to Drew. "I'm sure you've got somewhere else to stay."

And with that she turned, shoulders perfectly straight, and walked back up the stairs. I dropped my head into my hands. Amy hated me. And I couldn't even blame her. I'd completely betrayed her, in the worst way possible.

"A mistake," Drew said softly. "A terrible, terrible mistake."

Oh, God. What had I said? I turned to face Drew. The hurt swimming in his eyes was almost more than I could bear.

"Drew!" I cried softly. "That's not what I meant, I—"

"I think you've said more than enough."

"I was wrong." I grabbed his hand. "Please, I—"

"No. You were right." He shook me off. "This was absolutely a mistake."

Just as Amy had, Drew turned and walked stiffly up the stairs.

I sank down, collapsing onto the bottom stair. In a span of mere minutes I'd ruined everything. I'd betrayed Amy, hurt Drew, and annihilated my relationships with both of them.

CHAPTER 22

Respecting Amy's wishes, I spent the few remaining hours left in the night in the actor lounge, on the sagging floral couch, redolent with the ghosts of a thousand ramen noodle cups. There was one couch spring in particular that kept stabbing me right in the area of my liver. Needless to say, I wasn't in the best of moods as I made my way to the theater before the show opened. I was exhausted, and I felt horrible. Probably because I was a horrible person who deserved to be stabbed by a sagging floral couch.

I should have been excited about the show, but I dreaded facing Amy and Drew. They had every right to hate me, but that didn't mean I wanted them to. I wished more than anything that I could just go back in time and erase parts of last night. Even though there was nothing about kissing Drew I wanted to erase. As I made my way, alone, through the field to the dressing room, I sighed. I'd really screwed things up this time.

"Cassiopeia!"

I cringed at the sound of my completely ridiculous full name, then realized there was only one person who would call me that. There was only one person who *ever* called me that.

I turned and saw my mom waving, burnished metal bangles jangling on her arms. Her hair was still just as red as mine, and even though it may have had a bit of help from Garnier, I would never tell. She was wearing a classic Mom ensemble, something strange and flowing topped off with a paisley scarf and giant earrings. She might have been kind of weird, but she was my mom, and I had never been happier to see her.

"Mom!" I cried as I dove into her arms, and she hugged me tightly. The smell of the ylang-ylang perfume she blended herself enveloped me.

"Glad to see you're alive after all these weeks," she said wryly, patting my back.

"Sorry." I reddened, grateful my face was hidden. "About the lack of communication. That wasn't my best work."

"None of the current or former Mackays have been at their best recently." She held me at arm's length to look at me, searching in my eyes. "So you're not mad at me anymore?"

"No," I mumbled. "Not mad."

"I am sorry, Cass. Which you would know, if you'd bothered to answer my calls or read any of my emails." Her mouth quirked into a funny kind of half smile. "We shouldn't have put you in the middle of everything."

"It's okay. Really. Love makes you crazy."

It was such a simple, common phrase, but I'd never really *gotten* it before. Beyoncé may have figured it out back in 2008, but I was no Beyoncé. Hell, Shakespeare had gotten it right back in 1600 when he wrote that "love is merely a madness." Love was for sure madness — but there was nothing *merely* about it. Look at me. I had acted like a certifiable nutball all summer. I guess, in this case, the apple didn't fall far from the staple-gunning tree.

"Love makes you crazy, *hmmm*?" I did not like the tone of that hmmm. "Is there a special boy I should meet? Or girl," she added quickly. "No judgment."

"Mo-om!" I rolled my eyes. "Let's just drop that, shall we? Before you being here turns from good surprise into bad surprise."

"Surprise? Why wouldn't I be here?" She actually looked shocked, her brow furrowing in confusion. But I hadn't talked to her in forever. If she hadn't shown up, I wouldn't have blamed her. I hadn't exactly been ideal daughter material recently. "Don't be silly. There's no way I would have missed this."

"I'm just really glad you're here." And then, to my horror, a sniffle escaped.

"Cassiopeia?" Now she seemed really surprised. I wasn't normally a sniffler. "Are you okay?"

"Not really." I sniffled. Again.

"What happened?"

"I messed up. Big time."

"How big time are we talking here?"

"Really super big time. Mega big time."

"Is anyone dead?"

"What? No, Mom! Of course not!" I scoffed. "Please. Give me a little credit here."

"And unlike some of us, you managed to stay out of jail."

"I learned a thing or two about resisting arrest this spring."

"No dead bodies, no jail time?" She shook her head. "Hardly qualifies as a problem. It's fixable." She smiled. "Whatever it is that went wrong."

"It might take a miracle."

"You want proof of miracles?" she chuckled, tucking a piece of hair behind her ears. "Guess who's here."

"Dad?"

"Your father brought the Energizer bunny." Mom sighed. Usually she preferred to refer to Heather by nickname. This, at least, was one of the more polite ones. "But he came."

She pointed and sure enough, standing under a tree at the edge of stage left, there was Dad, barking into his omnipresent cell phone. Of course, Dad would be the only person in Vermont to have cell service. I wouldn't put it past him to have invested in some kind of portable cell tower or something. Heather, clad head-to-toe in Lululemon, bounced around, blond ponytail flying as she yammered away at him. I still wasn't sure I wanted to talk to him—but he was here, and that was something. In the crowd of people setting up their lawn chairs—wow, there were more people here than I'd expected—my eyes drifted over to a gaggle of blonds who must have been Amy's family and an extremely tall couple who were undoubtedly Heidi's parents. I wondered if Drew's dad had come.

"And look at this! We're in the same space, being totally civil. No staple guns in sight. See? Miracles happen." Mom squeezed my shoulder. "You can make it right, Cassiopeia. It's okay to admit you were wrong. It's not fun, trust me." She sighed. "But it's okay."

"Easier said than done," I muttered.

"Good thing you're so brave." She smiled warmly. I hugged her tightly, one last time. "Now, go break a leg, and kick some butt."

"I will. Promise."

CHAPTER 23

Resolved to make things right, I ran off toward the big red barn. By the time I got to the dressing/storage room, it was deserted. I must have been running late. I hastily shimmied into my costume, slathered on some makeup, and ran a brush through my hair a few times. Well, it would do. No one ever said Kate was a fashion plate.

I sprinted backstage, trying to avoid the audience as I crossed the field. There were even more people out there than before. Families lounged on picnic blankets while older couples set up folding camp chairs. I immediately spotted Amy peeking through one of the curtains. I approached her cautiously.

"Amy." She stiffened. "Please listen. Just for five minutes." She didn't say anything, but she didn't walk away, either. That was something. "I am so, so sorry about what happened with me and Drew. I swear to you, I never intended for anything to happen. I certainly never *wanted* anything to happen. It just, well, did. But just that one night. I swear. And if you'll be my friend again, I promise I'll never even talk to him again. Or look at him. Offstage, I mean. I can't re-block the show."

"It's too late for that."

"It is?" My heart sank. I had so hoped we could rebuild things.

"I mean it's too late for you to start ignoring Drew or whatever. It wouldn't change anything. I see the way he looks at you."

"Looks at me?"

"Yes, looks at you. He's been staring at you since you got here. He's staring at you right now, as a matter of fact. Like he can't decide if he wants to kiss you or kill you."

"Sounds about right," I muttered.

"That's kind of the way he's looked at you all summer. And he's never looked at me like that. The best I've gotten is a slightly pleased indifference. Come to think of it, no one's ever looked at me like that," she added wistfully.

"You *want* someone to look at you with murderous intent?"

"You know what I mean, Cass," she said softly. "That passion. There's something between you two. Something undeniable."

"I think so, too," I said in a small voice. Like barely audible small.

"I'm not gonna lie," she said a bit more sharply. "It hurt, of course."

"Of course."

"Rejection sucks. It was like bombing an audition, but way more personal and painful."

"I know." I winced. I still hated myself for hurting her.

"I think I always knew there was something between the two of you. I could feel it. That's why I wanted you to get together with Taylor so bad."

"I wanted something to work with Taylor. I did, I seriously did," I said fervently. "I just didn't—"

"Love him," Amy finished for me. "See? I knew I'd convert you into a romantic."

Good God, did I *love* Drew? I hadn't really considered that, but now that Amy said it . . . I'd fallen in love without even realizing it. And then completely insulted and alienated the object of my affections.

"Anyway, Cass, look." She swished the heavy brocade curtain open just an inch. "The Prince of Norway is in the audience." I looked out. I spotted Ragner, Ferret, and Thiago on the picnic table, but blessedly, Taylor Griffith was nowhere to be seen. "The hope for romance springs eternal. There might still be time for a final plot twist in act five." She smiled wickedly.

"So this means we're okay?"

"We're okay," she confirmed. "But if I catch you kissing the Prince of Norway, I'm going to pull a full shrew on *you*. Sleep deprivation, food deprivation, ruining all your clothes, the works."

"Fair enough." I held out my hand for her to shake. Instead, she pulled me into a tight hug. Boy, this was the most hugging I'd done in a long time. Being vulnerable really takes it out of a girl.

"Friends again!" I heard Heidi cry delightedly as she stretched her long arms around the two of us.

"Heidi!" Amy choked. "Your sleeve is strangling me!"

"Ooo, sorry!" Heidi hastily pulled away, and we all disentangled ourselves.

"Now, Heidi," Amy said, "don't you think it's time that Little Miss Cynical gets her happy ending?"

"This seems like more of a happy beginning to me." Heidi smiled. I could only hope she was right.

Drew stood alone, all the way at the edge of the stage left entrance. If he'd really been staring at me all morning, there was no way to tell now. His back looked like a solid, impenetrable wall. I walked over to him, praying that Shakespeare would inspire me. I had no idea what to say. I figured I should probably steal someone else's work. I tugged on Drew's sleeve, and he turned. The look on his face was not encouraging.

"Say that he frown," I began timidly, "I'll say he looks as clear as morning roses newly wash'd with dew."

He didn't say anything. But that actually worked kind of perfectly with the next bit I uttered.

"Say he be mute, and will not speak a word." Something that looked like it might possibly have been the beginning of a smile tugged at the corner of Drew's lips. "Then I'll commend his volubility and say he uttereth piercing eloquence."

"Pack," he murmured.

"If he do bid me pack"—I grinned—"I'll give him thanks, as though he bid me stay by him a week."

"Those are my lines."

"I know. I just thought Shakespeare might be able to help a girl out." He looked willing to listen, at least. I took a deep breath. "Since coming to Shakespeare at Dunmore, I've made a lot of mistakes. Probably about a thousand. Ruining your clothes. Stealing your pillow. Trashing your food. Sneaking out of the house. Putting the whole show in jeopardy. Just to name a few. Pretty much just an endless series of idiotic behavior. But there are some things I did right, too. Things I don't regret, not for a second. Things that weren't mistakes at all. Like picking up a sword. And jumping into the lake naked with you. Every minute we've spent together, actually. And kissing you. That was about as opposite from a mistake as you could get. That was . . ."

"Perfect."

"It *was* perfect." I brightened. "I'm so sorry I said those awful things. I didn't mean it, honestly. There were just other — factors — involved and . . . and friendships," I struggled to explain without telling Drew about Amy's crush. He might have figured it out on his own, but I didn't want to embarrass her — even if she seemed over it.

Something in his face told me he might have understood what I was not saying. "I was so busy trying to protect someone else's feelings that I trampled all over yours. And you are the *last* person whose feelings I want to trample. Initially, of course, I just wanted to trample *you*. Not just your feelings. Like trample you physically." Now he looked confused. "I just mean we didn't get off on the best foot. Which is my fault, really. I make awful snap judgments, and I have a terrible temper, and I think I'm right about everything and

I'm usually wrong, and then I stomp all around being all wrong and bossy. Well, you know all that already. You've always called me on my bullshit. Oh, God, I've gotten way off track." I took another deep breath, trying to collect myself. "Basically, I'm sorry. I wish I could take back what I said. The worst mistake I made this summer was hurting you."

"I love her ten times more than e'er I did," he murmured, his face softening.

"I'm sorry, what was that?" My heart sped up until it was rapidly outpacing a hummingbird's pulse.

"I thought you knew all my lines." He smirked.

"No, I know that one. I mean, um . . . I know it," I finished lamely, still unsure if that was a declaration of real feelings or just a line reading.

"I love you, Cass."

That was definitely not in the script.

"What?" I knew that was not the appropriate response, but I was just too shocked. At best, I had hoped he would accept my apology. I never, ever expected "I love you." Drew tried to clasp me around my shoulders, but instead got two big fistfuls of red puffy sleeve.

"What is *in* these?" he marveled, patting my shoulders in wonder. "Are these stuffed with something? Bubble wrap? Oh, never mind. Your sleeves are not important right now." Swiftly he moved his hands from my sleeves to circle my waist, and despite the heavy brocade and the stiff corset, I could feel the heat from his touch. "I've been falling in love with you onstage and off since we got here. And I can't wait until the curtain goes up so I can fall in love with you all over again."

"You . . . love me?"

"Unfortunately for me"—he grinned—"looks like it."

"I'd really prefer it if you stopped using the word 'unfortunate' when describing your feelings for me." Feelings. Could he really mean what he'd just said? "Can you even fall in love with someone in two weeks?" I whispered.

"Before this summer, I would have said no. But now . . ." He looked down at me, and I was struck by the question Lola St. Clair asked us on our first day—"Where does his love lie?" I could see it now, clear as day, shining in his hazel eyes. Warmth shot through me. "Well, Romeo and Juliet fell in love in a day."

"That worked out really well for them."

"Good God, woman!" he bellowed. "I'm pouring my heart out to you, and you're just giving me shit!"

"Get used to it." I smiled. "Because I think I might sort of kind of love you, too."

"That's an awful lot of qualifiers . . ." He rubbed his jaw contemplatively, acting like he was weighing his options. "But I'll take it."

I smiled so wide my cheeks ached. For the first time, I really understood what Shakespeare had written all his sonnets about. Drew would have crushed any darling buds of May—he was more of a rough wind than anything temperate—but to me, he was the best of any summer's day. He was the warmth of a sunny field, the refreshing coolness of the lake, and even the sweet stickiness of a s'more. Amy had been right that night that felt like a million years ago, when we all went skinny-dipping in the lake. This *was* the best summer ever. And so much of that was because of Drew. He leaned down to kiss me, and I clung to him tightly. I would never let him go.

"Save it!" someone shrieked. Rhys. He was standing right behind us. We sprang apart, but Drew held fast to my hand, keeping it in his.

"What, art thou ashamed of me?" Drew whispered. "Trying to leap away?"

"No, sir, God forbid!" I protested. "But ashamed to kiss. In front of Rhys."

"That last part's *definitely* not in the script, bonny Kate."

"Save it for the stage, you animals!" Rhys scolded us. "Don't waste all your chemistry back here! We've got paying customers! More importantly, my entire family is here *including* Great-Aunt Mona and I expect this show to *deliver*! Great-Aunt Mona is a beast! A positively terrifying *beast*!"

"Circle up!" I did a double take—I almost hadn't recognized Langley as she made her way backstage. Her hair was now a soft, subdued brown. It may have been more Shakespearean, but I found I missed the electric blue. "We've got a pretty full house out there. Five minutes to curtain."

Drew led me by the hand to the patch of grass backstage where everyone was congregating. Smiling, Amy took my other hand. Heidi fought valiantly through her sleeves, but eventually got her hands free enough to clasp Amy's and Noah's. We formed a circle, holding hands, all of our poofy brocade sleeves rubbing together.

Nevin appeared backstage, accompanied by the mysterious Lola St. Clair. Well, well, well. Look who'd finally decided to show up. It seemed like years had passed since the last time I'd seen her. Nevin and Lola took their places in the circle.

"My young friends," Lola began, looking around the circle, making eye contact with each of us in turn. For once, Drew didn't roll his eyes. Neither did I. "So much has happened since last I saw you, at the beginning of your journey. Strangers turned to friends. Hatred turned to love. Risks were taken, and rules were broken." Amy squeezed my hand. "I speak, of course, of your time onstage." The twinkle in Lola's eye made me think she knew more than she let on. "Throw caution to the wind once more, my friends. Infuse each word with passion, each movement with life. Laugh at your fears and revel in your triumphs."

Nevin cleared his throat. "I have only one thing to say: put it all out there." He looked at us intensely. It was more of a glare than a look. "Leave it all behind up on that stage. All of it. Every last drop of what you've got. Return to me, in five acts' time, a husk of a human."

A husk of a human? I got what he was saying, but that wasn't exactly inspirational.

"Let's say 'bold moves' on three," Amy suggested, exchanging glances with me and Heidi.

"An excellent suggestion, fair Bianca," Lola approved. "One . . . two . . . three . . ."

"Bold moves!" the cast cheered quietly, careful not to disturb the audience.

"Places, everyone!" Langley announced. Immediately, backstage buzzed with excited energy as everyone moved toward their entrances, straightening skirts and smoothing jackets.

"Ready to fall in love with me?" Drew caught my wrist and spun me to face him.

"I'm ready to hate you," I purred into his ear. "As for love . . . we'll just see how act two goes."

Drew threw back his head and laughed. I loved his laugh, the way it was more like a roar than any laugh I'd ever heard, the way his hazel eyes danced mischievously. How could I ever have hated someone who laughed so wholeheartedly?

"Challenge accepted, sweet shrew." He kissed me quickly. "Bring me your worst."

"Nothing but the best of my worst for you, sirrah." I kissed him again.

"Did you not hear 'places'?" Langley reminded us. Loudly.

"Sorry!" I picked up my skirts, grabbed the rope off the prop table, and ran to join Amy stage right. I waved at Drew as he walked stage left.

"It's happening," Amy whispered, squeezing my hand with excitement as best she could as I tied her wrists together. "It's wonderful, isn't it? This moment right before."

"It's the best feeling in the world," I agreed. Well, maybe second to kissing Drew. The audience chatter gradually died down, and then, after a moment of perfect silence and stillness, the play began.

The show had never been better. The dialogue was alive, crackling in the warm summer air. The audience laughed in all the right places, more than I'd ever expected they would. Magically, none of the boys slid around in their slippery boots, and Heidi navigated her sleeves with panache. I railed at Drew, shouting and scolding, but by the time act five rolled around, Petruchio had won Kate over, just as surely as Drew had won me.

"Come on and kiss me, Cass," Drew coaxed, in the full, rich timbre of his stage voice, drawing me into his arms, the love in his voice palpable. I heard a soft but audible thump as, out of the corner of my eye, I saw Nevin fall off his chair.

"They call me Katherine that do speak of me," I whispered, conscious of the eyes of the audience. "You said the wrong name."

"I know what I said," he whispered. "Kiss me, Cass."

And so I did.

ACKNOWLEDGMENTS

Thank you to my amazing agent Molly Ker Hawn and everyone at the Bent Agency. Molly, I could write a whole second book just full of acknowledgments about how awesome you are.

Thank you to expert editor Julie Matysik and the whole team at Sky Pony Press. Your thoughtful edits have made this book what it is. Thank you to all the Skyponies at Team Rogue YA for your social media support and awesome ARCs!

Thank you to Max, for reading Drew's lines out loud when necessary, for your many thoughtful reads, and for always celebrating my successes. I love you.

Thank you to Dad and Mom, for everything but especially for answering the phone every time I walk the dog. Thanks to Ali for your constant efforts to grow my KIPP readership.

Thank you to Caitlin, a best friend and a wonderful editor, and to Evie and Lauren for your first reads and helpful notes.

A huge thank-you to all the wonderful friends I met doing three seasons of outdoor summer Shakespeare. Thank you for the s'mores, the stolen firewood, and the songs on the guitar—even "The Good Ol' Hockey Game." We know that everything that *really* happened is way too unbelievable to be included in a book.

Finally, thanks to the good people of Jugtown for the many, many peanut butter squares.

ABOUT THE AUTHOR

Stephanie Kate Strohm lives in Chicago with her boyfriend and a small white dog named Lorelei Lee. A former Connecticut Yankee, she is a proud alumna of Middlebury College in Vermont. She is also the author of *Pilgrims Don't Wear Pink* and *Confederates Don't Wear Couture*. Visit her online at www.stephaniekatestrohm.com.